GEORGINA JEFFERY

The Jack Hansard Series

Season One

Coblyn Press

For my daughter

Contents

Preface

The Jack Hansard Series began several years ago as a personal experiment in playing around with episodic storytelling. I rather liked the idea of a television-esque reading experience that told a story in bite-sized, standalone chunks - episodes instead of chapters - which would also build into a plot arc spanning a whole series.

I released the original drafts for *Season One* on my website and on the reading platform *Wattpad*, and was overwhelmed by the positive response it received. I owe a lot to those early readers.

This book is a much-revised edition of the original online version, with exclusive additional content including an all new episode.

Going forward, beta episodes of *Season Two* will also be available free online so you can read the first draft of the series as it comes out.

This is an evolving experiment, and I invite you to be a part of it with me.

Georgina

Episode 1: An Inspired Mess

I t's a strange sensation, being dangled upside-down over the side of a bridge in the middle of the night.

You might say that it brings about a contemplative state of mind.

Look at the way the light shimmers over the surface of the Thames, your brain tells you. *Probably big, sharp rocks under there*, it points out helpfully. *My, the rope around your ankles feels rather thin, doesn't it? Sure hope it's strong enough to continue holding a full-grown man . . .*

These were my unfortunate thoughts as I swung helplessly in the breeze. I was especially concerned about my coat, where it was slipping slowly down my arms towards the swirling waters below. I'm rather attached to that coat. It's a proper trench coat with lots of spacious pockets – I've no end of elixirs and doodads and curios stuffed away inside it.

There is a tendency to typecast men in trench coats as crooked characters, shady figures who lurk on the fringe of the crowd, generally with a range of dubious watches on offer for the discerning patron. This is totally untrue.

I don't sell watches.

'How are we doing, Mr Hansard? Have you reconsidered my offer?'

This was the slick voice of Mr Scallet from high above. It was at his leisure that I was currently being, ah, held.

1

'I think I could be persuaded,' I called up to him. I was quite proud that my voice barely squeaked.

I probably deserved this, I thought. I'd been going through a period of peace and quiet lately: not one of my sales had backfired in the past month, and no one had tried to kill me. This was quite an achievement, considering my usual run of luck was about as long as a one-inch length of string on fire.

'Haul him up. Let's see if he'll be more co-operative this time.'

This is the sort of thing you come to expect, when you're a dealer on the Black Market.

'You want we should rough him up some more, boss?'

The *real* Black Market, that is. Not the mundane one, with its tedious smugglers of sex and drugs and other humdrum illegalities. There aren't any laws that cover the goods you'll find on *my* Black Market, the one where abstract concepts can be purchased in neat little boxes. Mine is the one where success is sold in the form of an edible powder and fame can be hung round your neck on a piece of cotton thread. In need of a little luck? Heck, I know a guy in Blackfriars who can sell you it in a bottle.

I'm a here and there man, myself. I specialise in everything, if you know what I mean.

When Scallet had found me, I was specialising in inspiration.

'Mind his knees, boys. Wouldn't want him bent out of shape now, would we?'

Inspiration is a funny thing. Some people are naturally lucky, and stumble blindly over stray lumps of inspiration while going about their everyday business. Then they wake up in the morning with the next cultural innovation bouncing around inside their skulls. But for those of us not as blessed, inspiration is a bugger to get hold of. I should know. A bit of inspiration nearly took my arm off once. It has a tendency to bite.

But it's worth the effort (and risk of maiming) because there are many people out there – writers, musicians, talented *artistes* – who will pay through the nose for just a sniff of the stuff.

Mr Scallet had been in need of a bit of inspiration.

That was a month ago. He had stuck out in the crowd with his sharp Savile Row suit and equally sharp, well-groomed features. He'd approached my pitch, which, at the time, had been in the centre of the bustling Camden Stables Market. In the midst of the alternative scene, I offer the most alternative goods you could ever hope to find.

He flashed me a bleached white smile and asked for my best wares of 'speciality' interest, with that haughty tone of the wealthy and entitled. Instantly I took him for a naïve, rich fob looking for a novelty to waste his cash on. Perfect.

He listened to my spiel, and then dropped a grand on a purchase of nearly-rotten inspiration. I'm an artist myself, in my own way.

Except, it turns out he wasn't as ignorant as I thought.

'Steady there, don't lose your footing.' As I was yanked upright, Scallet made a show of brushing off my lapels. 'Now that you are with us again, Mr Hansard, perhaps we can discuss this matter like gentlemen.'

'Over a glass of wine and a cigar?' I said.

'Funny. You're a funny man, Mr Hansard. I enjoy your jokes. I find it especially amusing that a man in your position would take his own life so lightly.'

One of his thugs prodded me hard in the chest. I teetered dangerously on the ledge for a second and my stomach lurched. Vertigo. I vaguely remembered selling a package of vertigo recently.

'Of course, I'd be happy to offer you recompense,' I said hurriedly. 'This is all a misunderstanding. I never like to see a dissatisfied customer.'

'Ah, another joke.' Scallet pulled a handkerchief from his sleeve and

3

dabbed at his temples. 'Is that the reason you disappear the instant after you've sold something, Mr Hansard? You're a tricky man to find.'

'I see you had no trouble,' I said weakly. The back of my mind was ticking over how much I could sell a vertigo cure for.

'You leave a certain trail of, what did you say? *Dissatisfied customers.*' Scallet genteelly folded the handkerchief back into a square. It looked greasy, and his face still shone with sweat. 'Let's be clear, Hansard. The inspiration you sold me was stale. You've ruined a multi-million pound project and rendered an eminent engineer woefully worthless. Your life is not worth the profits I've lost.'

Ah, yes. The engineer. Perhaps the only innocent victim in this case, though I'd argue he was guilty by association. Anyone who associates with a man like Scallet must have *something* coming to them.

I cleared my throat. 'It seems to me,' I said, shifting my weight away from the chasm behind me, 'It seems to me, if I've understood your predicament correctly, that what you've really got here is a problem of *audience.* That is to say, a lack of one for the product you're selling, rather than a problem with the product itself vis-à-vis improperly applied inspiration, to wit–'

'Shut him up.'

Fist to the face. No messing about, these boys. They're professional goons. My head swam.

I suppose you could say I was starting to regret dealing with Scallet back in Camden. But how was I to know he was head bod of some engineering company that designed cars so expensive you'd have to be a millionaire just to purchase a brochure? How was I to know he'd give that faulty inspiration to his lead designer, expecting the next great Lamborghini to come rolling out the doors? You can hardly blame *me* for his poor life choices.

Besides, no one can say it didn't work. The inspiration performed like a charm. (I happen to sell charms as well, if you're interested.)

Scallet was speedily presented with the plans for five revolutionary new cars that were perfect in form and function. So what's the problem?

The form: bulky, lumbering, utterly unsexy people-carriers designed with single mothers in mind. The function: boot space and large crumple zones. Nothing like the sleek and stylish sports cars coveted by Scallet's rich and insecure customers.

Apparently, that's not the result he wanted.

Scallet tucked his sodden handkerchief away. 'We seem to be suffering a communication problem, Mr Hansard. You don't seem to understand just how much I want to throw you off this bridge. The only reason you are still alive is that you have a debt to pay.'

'I'm good at those,' I mumbled through the ache in my jaw.

Scallet frowned. 'Let me be clear. I want something more than just money out of you, Hansard. I want something to truly justify the continuation of your miserable life. A man of your unique . . . profession . . . must be able to offer *something* valuable enough to buy it back. If your life can be said to have any worth at all.'

'You're not wrong,' I said with what I hoped was a disarming smile. It was probably spoiled by the blooming black eye. 'Trust me, my life is the most valuable thing in the world to me, and I can happily offer you a fair trade. It's rather fortuitous that on this evening I do happen to have about my person an item that is widely considered to be the key to ultimate success.'

'I see it hasn't done you any good so far.'

'On the contrary, I appear to still be alive.'

'Appearances can be deceiving.'

'Hear me out. You won't regret it.'

Scallet pursed his lips. 'I feel I've heard that before. But very well, let's hear what you have to offer.'

Though his gaze was hard and sceptical, there was the faintest touch of intrigue in his voice. I know his type. I was wrong to misjudge Scallet the first time, I shouldn't have taken him for a complete mug. I wouldn't make the same mistake again. He might not be just a dumb tourist, but he's not from my world, either. Just because he knows all the cool slang and walks the walk, it doesn't make him one of us. You can tell by the way he wears his suit, his shiny shoes, the stiffness in his oily face. And by the shifty way he watches the shadows, because he doesn't really know what's in them.

He's still green. He's had a taste of my world and thinks just because his tongue's been scratched it makes him some kind of expert. He's the guy in the restaurant who makes like he knows all about authentic Asian cuisine because he once spent a business trip in Vietnam. But his fork never touched the bottom of the bowl, and underneath it all he's still just itching to find out what other dishes are on the menu.

Let's see how this one tastes.

'The key to ultimate success,' I said, affecting an air of calm, 'lies in a rare and mystical elixir from the Amazon which, when drunk, will grant the individual a charmed life of fame, fortune, and superior sexual attraction. It's a closely guarded secret, worth millions. It's in the left inside pocket of my trench coat,' I added nonchalantly.

With a nod of permission, one of the thugs plucked the glass vial from my pocket and proffered it to Scallet for inspection. He rubbed his chin thoughtfully.

'You just drink it, do you?' he asked.

'No. Well, yes. It must be consumed on a moonlit night at the strike of eleven in a meadow of thyme. Ideally with a virgin nearby. Tastes of strawberries. So I'm told.'

'Strange that you haven't tried it yourself.'

'I wouldn't have any wares to sell if I went around sampling them all the time.'

Scallet's eyes flashed. 'Do you really consider me so stupid, Mr

Hansard?' Rough hands closed around my arms and shoulders. 'Why don't you have a taste.'

It wasn't a question. My head was forcefully tipped back, and the liquid rammed down my throat. I spluttered and choked, but managed to swallow, all the same.

'Now let's see what your little trick really meant to accomplish,' he said triumphantly. 'Poison, perhaps?'

I grimaced theatrically. 'Not my style.'

'What is your style, Mr Hansard?'

'Not as greasy as yours.'

Scallet's lip curled. 'I'd have thought you could come up with something more *inspired*. Cut the rope.'

I closed my eyes again. I heard the *thunk* of a blade going through thick nylon. The boot planted in my chest was sudden but expected.

I tumbled backwards, air streaming past and the sound of blood rushing in my ears. I braced myself for the sting of water . . .

. . . and was pleasantly surprised to encounter a soft, rather slippery landing. A very ripe smell invaded my nose.

''Ere, Gary! Some bloke's fallen in the fish!' an astonished voice yelled. I grinned.

In the distance high above, I thought I could hear the faint sound of a car engine roaring into the wind.

One by one, the confused faces of the barge crew popped into my vision.

'Any chance of a ride?' I said.

They were kind enough – and puzzled enough – to drop me off at the next pier, and I stumbled up the ramp to the familiar wet, murky streets of London. I navigated by the light of yellow streetlamps and glittering tarmac. Eventually I found my car, in the same dark spot where Scallet's men had jumped me earlier.

I watched from the shadows for a while, checking for movement, voices. Nothing. I suppose Scallet didn't think I'd come straight back to it. Hey, with a little luck, he might have missed my miraculous escape altogether.

I'd have to give my mate in Blackfriars something to refund his loss. I was meant to deliver that bottle, not drink it.

I stepped back and surveyed my assets. One elderly Ford Escort: a pile of worn and slightly moth-eaten clothes on the back seat; a half-finished jam sandwich on the dashboard; a smattering of business cards for *Jack Hansard, Purveyor of the finest Occult Goods* – that's me, by the way – a map of London holding the remains of yesterday's chips; parking tickets scattered about like confetti . . . and a trunk full of second-hand, second-rate inspiration waiting to be offloaded.

I smiled. Time to move on.

Episode 2: Sandman

Dreams. People are full of them. They permeate us, define us, and reinvent us.

But dreams are just lies, when you think about it. Regardless of whether you're misremembering the past, speculating about the future, or making up stories about the present: people are constantly dreaming up new versions of the world around them. An active imagination could be better described as an internal network of self-deception.

So if everyone is already quite happy lying to themselves – dreaming to themselves – on a daily basis, then surely there's no harm throwing a few lies of my own into the mix? I mean, I'm just trying to further the cause of self-delusion.

Is it really my fault if a customer believes some tatty, broken piece of pot is actually a priceless relic of a bygone age? It's not like I outright *lie* about it. I just help them believe what they already want to believe.

I mean, who's to say that little piece of pottery *didn't* once belong to Pharaoh Whatsit of the Thingummy Dynasty? I can't know the entire history of every artefact I sell, can I? If anything, I'd be lying if I told you I was certain it *wasn't* of royal Egyptian descent. In that sense, I am a very truthful salesman.

And just what am I, Jack Hansard, a salesman of?

Well.

I sell dreams, my friend. Interested?

At least, dreams are what I'm selling this week.

Good dreams, bad dreams, fantasies, nightmares. I've got 'em all for sale, here in the boot of my car.

I suppose I should have mentioned, I'm not your regular 'it-came-off-the-back-of-a-lorry-guv' street vendor. I'm a *purveyor of Black Goods*: that is, I sell goods hot off the real Black Market. The one where you can buy anything from luck to revenge in a bottle, and cursed newts' eyeballs count as legal tender.

The Black Market isn't so much a place as it is a concept. Sure, there are some locations you can visit year-round to browse a limited array of specialist goods, but for the most part the Black Market is made up of many seasoned traders, like myself, who travel up and down the country, taking our wares where they will be most appreciated. It's a skill all its own, working out how to be in the right place at the right time.

You see, it's all about matching your stock to your audience. I once got hold of a crate of deliciously vindictive little voodoo curses and, as luck would have it, happened upon a divorcee speed-dating convention at the same time. I have never before made so much money in my life.

Lately, I've heard that dreams are very profitable if you're willing to put the work in. And if you can catch them.

Dreams are like wild creatures, see. They zip in and out of reality – and in and out of our heads – like flies flitting between dustbins. The garbage in our heads is the ideal nesting ground.

If you're in the business of selling, then first you must capture one of these wild dreams. Unless you're a fool, you leave that part to the professionals. I once met a man who'd lost his whole lower torso wrestling with the vicious dream of a six year old. Tore him clean in half. 'Legs,' he was called.

It was a boot that woke me. That, and a sharp voice commanding me to sit up. My eyelids lifted, dazedly, and then snapped wide to stare at the person looming over me. At least, I could only assume it was a person.

It wore heavy brown leathers with what looked like many layers of thick padding underneath. The face was obscured by a sturdy veil very similar to a beekeeper's.

'Uh,' I said, most eloquently. My eyes fixed on the weapon it held in one hand: a spear with a curved hook adjoined to the blade. I could feel my senses seeping back into a state of alertness. If anything is going to wake a dull mind, a sharp and pointy object will definitely do the trick.

One gloved hand grasped me firmly by the arm and hauled me upright.

'What are you doing out here, then?' said a man's voice from behind the veil.

'Not sure. You're a Sandman, aren't you?' I said blearily. At his waist a thick, heavy net hung from his belt. Looks like he was out hunting for produce.

'Aye.'

'Where am I?'

'Some town. Don't know it meself. You from here?'

'I thought I was in a desert . . .' I looked about me and saw he was right. It looked just like the same stretch of Worcester I'd seen on the way in. A flashing fluorescent sign told me that **P ZZA** could be procured from the decrepit takeaway across the street. Had I sleepwalked here?

'That was the Dreamscape you were in. Land o' dreams an' all that.' The veil seemed to be regarding me sceptically.

Thoughts rushed back into the empty spaces in my head. I've only heard tales of the Dreamscape. They say it's a vast ethereal plane that

17

exists inside all our minds, but only Sandmen can traverse it at will; unwary travellers are swallowed by the sand. I self-consciously patted my limbs, checking I was all there.

'Thanks for the wake-up call. I hope I'm awake, anyway.' I shook my head as if that would shake the cobwebs out of it. 'You were in the Dreamscape on a . . . hunting expedition, I take it? Glad you happened by me. Hansard. Jack Hansard,' I said, extending a hand. There had been a point in my life where I decided introducing myself with my last name was the epitome of cool, and it stuck. Too many Bond films as a kid.

The Sandman waved my hand away.

'I don't care what your name is. I *do* want to know where you're keeping the unlicensed dreams.'

'Can't say I know what you're talking about, friend.'

He leaned in and grinned toothily. His features were vague behind the veil, but his hook-spear glinted menacing orange under the street-light.

'I'd bet my own licence you've got a stash of 'em somewhere nearby, and I don't need to bet anything to know you ain't no Sandman. So why don't you let me take a look-see, and maybe I'll take 'em off your hands, proper like. No questions asked. What d'you say, *friend?*'

I hesitated. Technically, this was exactly what I had wanted. I could offload the dreams and scarper. But there was just one other thing.

'For a price, of course,' I said.

'Of course.' The Sandman grinned again. 'I'm a fair man, Mr Hansard.'

I sighed inwardly. That was a resounding *no chance* if ever I heard one. But the man had a spear-hook, so what can you do?

'This way, I think.' I tried to get my bearings. I remembered the nearby takeaway across the road – I'd bought chips for dinner – so the car park wasn't far away. I wondered how far I would have sleepwalked if the Sandman hadn't found me. Maybe I'd have walked right out of town. Or maybe I'd have stayed on the bench and fallen asleep forever.

The thought disturbed me. Clearly, being in the business of dreams was a lot more hazardous than I'd thought. I didn't even know what I'd done wrong and it was too late before I ever knew about it.

A chill ran through me as we crossed a road, passing a white and yellow traffic bollard.

'I think I was nearly run over,' I murmured.

'If the mind goes wanderin' the body will do its best to follow,' said my leather clad companion with a smirk. 'The trick is to make the body follow all the way so none of it's left behind.'

'That's what you Sandmen do, is it? How?'

'Tricks o' the trade.'

'Can you do it anywhere? You just cross into the Dreamscape whenever you like?'

We turned a corner and Shrub Hill came into sight.

'Don't you know anything, mister? What are you doing messing around with dreams if you don't know how to handle 'em, eh? Looking for a new kind of buzz, ah?'

'I don't sample my own wares. I'm selling them.'

This was met with guffaws.

'Do you even know how to mix dream-sand, little man? 'Tis an art, take my word. Mix the wrong consistency and you can sleep a man to death. That's why we have a Guild for this sort of thing. Gotta be licensed. Guild don't take kindly to freelancers like yourself. That your car?'

It was indeed my car, right where I'd left it, with the boot still open. As we approached, I could see the nightmare still snarling away in its own cage, but the other cage seemed empty of all but the oddly fluffy, big-eyed dream. Where had the others disappeared to? I tried to mask my surprise, but I don't think the Sandman noticed anyway.

He cast a critical eye over the two remaining dream-creatures and tutted loudly.

'No binding on the cages or anything,' he muttered. 'Christ, they ain't even iron. What good is steel? Don't you know they can leak out if they ain't in pure iron? Dumb question. I know you don't.'

I bottled my indignation. The steel cages really were an oversight on my part. I'd plumped for the cheap option.

'Forget the cages,' I said. 'They're good quality specimens. What's your offer?'

'My silence. And everlasting gratitude.'

'I thought you said you were a fair man.'

'I am. Seems to me you'd be better off if the Guild never hears your name. If they catch you selling without a licence, well, let's say you'll have a real *nightmare* of a time. So I'll take these 'quality specimens' and be out of your hair with nary a word. Seems mighty fair to me.'

I crossed my arms. 'No sale.'

Although he hadn't removed the veil, there was a sense that his expression had turned very black. Suddenly the spear-hook was more prominent than before.

'Seems to me you don't have a choice,' he growled.

I smiled brightly. 'There's always a choice.'

I side-stepped, reached out, and flipped the catch on the nightmare's cage.

And watched in mute astonishment as the fluffy fuzzball leapt out. *Wrong damn cage.*

But the Sandman kept a cautious distance, attention completely focused on the fuzzball now sniffing the ground. I darted forward again and fumbled open the lock on the nightmare's cage.

The nightmare shot forward, teeth gnashing and little pincer claws whirring. It avoided a deft swipe from the Sandman and pivoted to face its fluffy dream counterpart. I groaned as I saw it ready to swipe.

And then the fuzzball, this cute, saucer-eyed little creature made entirely of candyfloss fluff, unhinged its jaw and revealed a mouth – no, a *maw* – as large as itself, devoid of teeth but somehow all the worse for the frilly red gums flapping in their place. It leaned forward and swallowed the nightmare whole.

Suddenly I knew why the other captive dreams had been so frightened. And why they were all gone.

'*Move*, you idiot!'

The Sandman lunged. The hook caught the creature around the neck, pinning it briefly to the ground. But it seemed to be made of jelly and easily slipped free. Another sharp jab, this time with the spear tip, merely caught in the thick layer of fluff – the fuzzball pulled away, leapt up into the air and toward my throat.

I threw up my arm and the frilly red gums closed around it. I danced on the spot, flapping my arm to try and throw the beast off. The fluffball started to steam, and the world began to turn blue. Sand crunched under my feet.

'Get it off!' I screamed.

A blade sliced in front of my face, catching the dream square between its saucer eyes. It seemed to break apart and dissolve, and in seconds there was nothing there at all.

The world regained its usual colour. I looked up, and down, and stamped the tarmac beneath my feet.

'Did you kill it?' I said.

The Sandman gave a derisive snort. 'Of course not. Just shed its material form. Gone back to the Dreamscape. Nearly pulled you in with it, too.'

'It was so fluffy,' I said, still somewhat stupefied.

'*Never trust the fluffy ones.*'

We shared a gruff silence. There didn't seem much point exchanging threats with each other. The goods were gone, there was nothing left to bargain for, and I'd like to think there was a mutual, if grudging understanding that each of us were only trying to keep a livelihood.

The Sandman shrugged. He swung his spear-hook through the air like a scythe: the blade split open a shimmering tear in reality. He stepped through the translucent portal and returned to his hunt in the Dreamscape without a word.

I relaxed. No hard feelings. But I'd best steer clear of the dream trade for a while, and keep one eye open for any disgruntled Guild officials, just in case.

I hope that the Sandman stays in the Dreamscape a good long while. It's not a place I want to visit again. Unless there's a *really good* sales opportunity.

I wonder if there's such a thing as dream real estate?

more. Thee just look after your friends down the pit, an' make sure them nasty knockers dunna come knocking for them. Any road–'

'That's wonderful,' I managed to squeeze in. 'A great bit of local colour. I commend you to some busybody history society so that you may end your days drowning in nostalgia and tea. Do have a good day, madam.'

I gently pushed her away by the elbow and she relented, continuing down the street with a somewhat perplexed expression.

I'm sure the old bag could have talked for England and would have won the trophy for nonsense to boot. EGS, I call it – Everyone's Grandma Syndrome. Doesn't matter who you are, the afflicted will talk your ear off as if you were their long-lost grandchild, and if you're particularly unprepared they'll start showing you photos, too.

I rubbed my temples and reset my smile. Casting an eye over my table I selected a roughly cut stone and decided that today it would be a genuine piece of the original Iron Bridge foundations. Probably handled by the very same what's-his-face on the sign there. I mean, who am I to say that it wasn't?

I persevered against the disinterest of my audience while the air chilled and the sky clouded into the afternoon. After three hours I began to tire, and I had sold only one solitary ring. Perhaps bridge-enthusiasts are not my best market. But at least I could now afford one of the enticing pork pies from the shop across the road. Their beguiling smell had tortured me all morning.

The woman behind the counter wrinkled her nose when I entered. I don't always have that effect on women, I swear. But if I was honest with myself, I hadn't paused to wash since leaving London, and my crumpled suit and dishevelled hair weren't doing me any favours.

'One of your finest pork pies, dear lady,' I said, flashing a couple of pound coins to prove I wasn't some hobo.

She wrapped my prize in paper and handed it over with a begrudging expression. 'Have a good day,' she said. 'Weirdo.'

I decided to savour my pie on the Iron Bridge itself. Despite the grey sky it was a lovely view of the river. A dense thicket of trees framed the southern bank to my left, and a higgledy-piggledy forest of white and redbrick cottages rose to my right. This was as close as I had come to being a tourist in years.

It was as I was about to take my first bite that I heard it.

'. . . heave boys! . . . y'can rest when it's done . . . heave!'

It was a tinny sound, as if the voices were coming from a long way off. As I looked about in puzzlement, it continued.

'. . . ye are all a' igam ogam, get in line!'

It seemed as if the sound was coming from the other side of the bridge, but it was deserted. I turned in its direction, peering ahead towards an old toll house and empty road beyond.

'. . . put yer backs into it . . .'

And then it clicked. I knew what was going on.

People – that is, most people – think reality is straight forward. It's not.

Reality is fluid, and bulbous. Think of the way a length of cloth might contain the body of a voluptuous woman: the fabric bulges, stretches over the swell of her breast and the curve of her stomach, but creases and crumples under the arms, around the waist. And as she walks, the cloth crinkles further, the bulges shift with the bounce of her breasts. Her dress is full of curves and folds and hidden spaces.

From the perspective of Physics, that description is entirely wrong, but it keeps me warm on cold nights.

The point I'm trying to make is that within the folds of reality's dress you can find other bits of reality you didn't know were there. Worlds within worlds. Worlds *behind* worlds.

And bridges are one way of crossing over to them. The physical bricks and mortar bridges we build in our corner of reality are weak points. Places where the walls separating us from another fold of reality are particularly thin. It's why there are so many folk tales and superstitions about bridges (goats and trolls spring to mind) and why it always pays to be careful when crossing them.

Despite knowing this, I can't say I've ever heard voices floating across a bridge before.

'Not like that ye bastards . . . heave . . .'

Fascinated, I took a step forward.

Out of pure curiosity, I began to unfocus.

This is exactly what it sounds like. I exhaled, allowed the edges of myself to blur and fade into the background. In contrast, the world around me became sharper. This is how you travel between those weak spots – you weaken your own space in reality. Ironically, it takes a great deal of concentration to unfocus.

On the other side of the bridge the air shimmered and darkened, collapsing inwards and sucking the road into it. Tendrils of tell-tale fog snaked along the path, pulling my legs forward. I allowed myself to move into the mist and the darkness, colour slipping away behind me. The world blurred as I moved, and suddenly I was on the other side of the bridge.

For a heart-stopping second I thought I'd done it wrong, because the air was still filled with fog.

But as I took in my surroundings I realised it was in fact, more accurately, smog. Thick and yellow and sulphurous, it made my throat prickle.

'Heave! One more, ye scummy– eh? Who's this *mwnci*, then?'

As my eyes adjusted to the stinging air, I made out a gaggle of short shapes in front of me, between two and three feet tall. Hooked noses and pointed ears stuck out from under flat caps, while most else was covered up by grubby shirts and waistcoats and a thick layer of grime.

Them what knock in the dark.

29

I should have paid more attention to that old bat! Of course there would be knockers here, what with all the old mines. And that's what these little wretches so obviously were, though I thought they only lived down in Cornwall. But they fit the bill: short stature, grimy clothes, pointy ears and an accent so thick you could spread it on toast. I've done business with the little buggers from time to time, but all I really know about them is that they like their pastries.

One, the speaker, held a lantern. He prodded me in the shin.

'Ay, *twpsyn*. Get out o' the way. We're behind schedule as 'tis.'

They were clustered around a large lever dug into the earth at the base of the bridge. I looked back the way I had come, where this end of the Iron Bridge stretched into a cloud of fog. It still straddled a river, albeit a rather browner, sludgier one, but the most conspicuous difference was that the space where the northern bank and a jumble of redbrick houses should have been, there too, was merely fog.

My gaze swung back to the group of goblinesque figures and their massive lever. It looked, against all odds, like they were trying the pry the bridge out of the ground.

'What are you doing?' I asked.

'What business is it o' yourn?'

'I'm just curious. Perhaps I could be of assistance?'

The little hook-nosed creature chuckled croakily. 'What assistance could ye be? No miner nor quarryman – soft hands and a softer head. *Pen pigyn.* Go an' scratch.'

There was a ripple of cracked laughter. I smiled brightly. 'Maybe you need supplies? How about a hearty delivery of pies and pasties?'

Suddenly I had their rapt attention.

'Go on,' said their leader with the lantern.

'Oh, I can get you anything you want.' I brandished my uneaten pork pie for their inspection. Their eyes followed it like starved animals. 'Pork pies, steak pies, and definitely some Cornish pasties to remind

but to no avail.

I'm not afraid of the dark. How could I be, when I rely so heavily on it? Me and the dark are old friends, pals, buddies. But in all this time I'd never considered how my good friend is actually made up of patches of shadow. One doesn't move through real darkness, merely from one shadow to the next.

This was darkness. Real. Almost tangible. It sticks to your eyes like a goop. You get the feeling you could reach up and wipe the darkness off your face and come away with hands covered in tar.

'Ang?' I said weakly.

A small, blue-ish light flared to my left. Ang's lantern. 'Here, *gwas.*' There was a smirk in her voice. I bet she'd purposefully left the lantern unlit.

Small hands tugged at my coat and I was led down a narrow corridor, forced to stoop as the ceiling lowered. I groaned as the tunnel closed in further and I resorted to crawling on all-fours.

'Not good wi' tight spaces, *gwas?*'

'Keep going already.' I kept my eyes fixed on the pale blue light ahead. As we travelled further my stomach twisted itself into knots. 'Ugh, no, stop a minute.'

'Keep moving,' said the other coblyn, prodding my feet.

I gathered my wits and raised my head again, and noticed a *very* interesting sight to my left.

'Forward,' said the coblyn again, irritably.

'What's that room through there? I see blue light.'

Perhaps to spite her rude friend, Ang obligingly led me through to the glowing chamber. It wasn't a large space, but it didn't need to be, the things it stored were so small. In row and rows of shelves fitted to a semi-circular wall, glass jars full of dancing blue fire spilled their glow onto our faces.

'What are they?' I asked in hushed tones, inexplicably awed.

35

'Them's the bluecaps,' said Ang, matching my whisper. 'They work wi' us. Know where to find the richest seams and safest passages.'

'They're alive?'

'Of sorts. We treats 'em well and they do same fer us. Back we go now.' As Ang turned, I paid greater attention to the lantern she held. The source of the pale light it emitted was a flickering blue flame. It curled and twisted as if alive. Cogs spun in my head.

Further down the narrow tunnel we were eventually ejected into a cavernous room. I couldn't make out the full size of the dripping chamber but the feeling of open space around me was phenomenal. I stood up and stretched as if I had been confined for my entire life.

I was propelled forward with more insistent tugs. I began to gain a sense of the room, or hall, as it more accurately appeared. Lanterns of blue and yellow lined the walls, illuminating the black sheen of coal and duller shine of stone. The light also caught the beady eyes of many curious faces peering in from the edges of the room. At the far end on a raised dais sat a coblyn set apart from the others.

Must be the Gaffer. He (I hoped) was dressed differently. Where the others wore flat-caps or hoods, this one wore a yellow plastic hard-hat with a torch mounted on the front. The bulb wasn't lit.

No batteries, I thought.

In addition, it wore a neon orange vest with reflective strips and held a pickaxe in one hand, in the way a king might hold a sceptre.

Our rude escort bowed in front of him. Ang stayed by my side, studying me under the flickering light.

'Aye, Gaffer. This'un's the one yer wanted.'

The Gaffer squinted up at me with suspicious eyes. His voice was a croaky drawl.

'Rumours be running, you a merchant of pies, they say.'

'I'm a merchant of many things, pies among them,' I replied. 'Hansard's my name. I was hoping we could do business?'

'I saying if business be done. No saying by other coblynau.' He glared pointedly at Ang, who dropped her gaze to the floor. 'But pies we like, and pasties better. We trade you coal for pies, fair rate.'

'Coal's no good.'

The pickaxe thumped into the ground.

'Coal for pies,' said the Gaffer. 'Deal done.'

'*Coal for pies!*' went up the cry around us.

'*Juicy pork!*'

'*Squishy jelly!*'

'*Crusty pastry!*'

I had to fight to be heard above the excitement.

'Deal *not* done,' I stated vehemently. The silence returned, this time with hostility. 'I haven't any use for coal.'

'No good for coal? What world you living in?' said the Gaffer.

'The modern one. Look, people don't use coal any more. I won't be able to shift the stuff–'

'Care we don't, whether you can shift or not!'

'Well you *should* care. Because I'm your ticket to a lasting supply of pies. Maybe even pasties. Even, if I can get a hold of some, maybe even oggies.'

Amazing, the value these creatures placed on pastry. I made a mental note to find out exactly what an oggie was. I could tell I had the attention of the whole hall, and others were trying to squeeze in to hear.

'Listening,' said the Gaffer, after a moment's pause.

'What you need is a middle-man,' I said. 'Someone who can handle your transactions outside of this little world of yours. That's me, you see. I'm a big man out there. I travel all over the country to do business. I'm known at all of the big marketplaces – and trust me, they are *big* markets. I can help you trade what you have in exchange for pies, or whatever food you want. But to do that, we need something that will *sell.* Something with pizazz.'

The room erupted with animated whispers. Ang was watching me carefully.

'We have no 'pizazz,'' said the Gaffer as the noise died down. 'What would you have instead?'

I adopted an expression of deep thought, a practised furrow of the brow and pressing of the lips. After a while I said, 'It's difficult. There's not really much you have to offer. But I suppose, maybe those, whad'you call them? Those bluecaps of yours, they might be worth something.'

A different kind of hush fell over the crowd.

'Not bluecaps, mister middle-man,' said the Gaffer slowly.

'*Not bluecaps,*' echoed the coblynau in solemn whispers.

Not the reaction I had expected. I was baffled.

'It's worth it, for the pies and the pasties. And traditional oggies, just like mother used to make, right?' I tried.

The Gaffer shook his grizzled head. 'Good-bye, mister merchant. Wishing you safe travels.'

Disappointed, I was led back through the mine by Ang. I couldn't fathom it.

'What's the deal, Ang? Why's everyone so loathe to part with those bluecaps?' I said to the darkness ahead. Her lantern swung in and out of view, casting our elongated shadows on the walls.

'Leave it be, *gwas.*'

'Do you agree with the Gaffer, Ang?'

'Leave it *be.*'

'So that's a no, then.'

She spun round, temporarily blinding me with her bluecap's light.

'Gaffer knows what's best. We don't belong in the world no more. 'Tis foolish to trade wi' the likes of you.'

'Why? I don't mean you any harm.'

'Aye, maybe. But others do. Pies were a nice dream, *gwas*, but Gaffer knows best. Best we be forgotten, before others get lost in your world.'

'You don't sound like you mean that.' My knees and wrists were killing me. I folded myself into a sitting position, cross-legged on the damp rock. Then what she'd said really sunk in. 'Hang on, what do mean, 'before others get lost'? Some of your people nipped over the fence, did they?'

We stared at each other across the cramped passage. The coblyn's naturally wrinkled face creased further; I could tell she was fighting some inner battle. I waited.

'You really never heard of coblynau out there, *gwas?*' she said finally.

'Only ever met knockers before. You guys are completely new to me. Maybe I can get an award for discovery.'

'But ye be someone who would've met the likes of us, if we'd been out there, aye?'

'Well, you could say I'm a big man in my field. But I don't habitually deal in coal or dirt, so the chances of my doing business with your lot is rather slim.'

'Aye. But say there were coblynau out in the world. Makin' their way among men, as such. Ye would've heard tell of 'em . . . right?'

I leaned forward intently. 'Have some of your lot gone missing, Ang?'

Again she clammed up, staring me down as she decided what to say.

'Maybe some of your friends got curious?' I pressed. 'Maybe they were sick of mining for no reason, sick of fuelling fires just for the sake of burning? Maybe they went out into the world to look for some better purpose . . . and never came back. Something like that?'

She held my gaze a second longer, then turned and continued down the tunnel.

Over the damp sound of her footsteps I heard her mutter, 'Coblynau always send word home.'

39

I dragged myself up again and followed her. There was an in here, if I could figure out how to pry it open. Just needed to find the right leverage.

We passed the glowing bluecap chamber and I held down the urge to duck inside and fill my pockets. If I was caught and had to run, I would get nowhere in this underground labyrinth. This deep darkness was friend of the coblynau, enemy to me.

'You need help across the bridge, *gwas?*' said Ang when we reached the top.

I stepped out of the rickety lift and gratefully breathed in the smoggy air. 'No thanks. I'll see myself out.'

She hesitated, seemed to be mulling something over. There was a reluctance in her stance, as if she might be about to call me back.

I decided to try my luck once more. 'You're not happy the Gaffer isn't looking for your people, right?'

'Gaffer knows best,' she replied bluntly. 'Says they made their choice. Says they were foolish fer wantin' to leave, anyway.'

'You don't think so, though. I think you understand why they left. You're not really happy here either, are you?'

'S'not proper work,' she muttered. 'Not home.'

Then she caught my eye and bristled, like I'd seen something I shouldn't. 'Safe travels, *gwas.*' She gave me a businesslike nod, hoisted her lantern and set off across the cracked fields. I heard her calling in the distance. 'C'mon, boys! Back t'work wi' ye. This gorge ain't gonna close itself!'

I'd found their work humorous when I first arrived, but it failed to amuse me now. What sad little creatures. Desperately missing the world but determined to shut themselves off from it. Scared of change, maybe. Destined to fade to no more than a memory, just like countless curiosities before them.

I watched the big blast furnaces belching black smoke into the black

'He did bring pies, Gaffer.' That was Ang's voice. She was indistinct among the coblynau around us. 'Seems a good'un, I'd say. Not his fault ole' Cutty cut the ropes on him.'

'Why would he do such a thing?' I asked, all innocence.

Ang stepped forward and her sharp eyes found mine. 'Not a coblyn to be makin' deals with, is Cutty Soames. Likes cruel mischief.'

The Gaffer leaned in, breathing sour air into my face. His gimlet eyes gleamed. 'Coal for pies?'

I groaned inwardly, but nodded. 'Coal for pies,' I agreed.

'Coal for pies!' someone in the crowd shouted. The rest took up the call. Coblynau were already ferrying battered pastry out of the wrecked lift. 'Coal for pies! Coal for pies!'

'Coal for pies,' said the Gaffer with satisfaction. 'Deal done.'

* * *

I awoke in the dark. A familiar dark. The dark of my car, with the blankets all drawn up over the windows. Pale grey light filtered through some of the more moth-eaten ones.

I inspected myself: intact, if still somewhat dirty from crawling around in a hole in the ground. I should've known better than to trust that Cutty character, but I'd been desperate. It's been too long since I had anything to show for my troubles. This time my troubles had provided me with some new bruises, but thankfully nothing worse. I was grateful the coblynau had decided to send me home, no more questions asked. I hope they enjoy their pies.

They aren't creatures to neglect their end of a bargain (with that one rope-cutting exception), so I discovered that the boot of my car had been filled with coal. I looked it over in the dull morning light.

'Better than nothing, I suppose,' I said, scratching my head. I wondered if I could market it as a sort of ethnic item. 'Authentic

Coblynau Coal' or something like that.

'Pleased wi' y'haul, *gwas?*' said a voice by my knees.

'*Ang?* What are you doing out here? Come to make sure I leave this time?'

She smiled toothily. 'Of a sort. Thinking I'd be leaving wi' ye, in fact.'

'Are you asking for a lift? I don't take hitch-hikers.'

'Not a lift, ye daft *twpsyn*. Deal, eh? I purchase travel, I be paying.'

I laughed. 'I've got enough coal, thank you. Why do you want to leave, anyway? I thought you wanted to be all shut away at home, like the rest.'

A fleeting expression of sorrow passed across her face. 'That ain't home, *gwas.* 'Tis a poor reflection of times past. We mean nothing, holed up like that. Time to make new meaning.'

She dumped her bulky satchel and lifted a large tin box that had been sitting by her side. I noticed she had her lantern with her as well. When she opened the box, I know my face lit up like Christmas.

'You have yourself a ride, Ang,' I murmured.

She pulled the box away from me. 'One more thing I'm buyin', *gwas.*'

'And that is?'

'You help me find my missing kin,' she said. 'They be lost out here, somewhere.'

I weighed the value of the bluecaps in my head.

'Deal done,' I said.

She raised an eyebrow. 'And how's I to know ye won't make bad on our deal, like ole' Cutty Soames?'

'I'm nothing like that traitorous reprobate.'

'Aye? So ye did make a deal wi' him, then?'

She stared me down silently.

'Seems to me your people needed pies,' I said at last. 'Does it matter much how they got there?'

'Adds body to the meal. Really brings out the flavours of the meat,' I replied. The troll seemed satisfied with the answer, but disapproving. It picked up a bloody goat bone and crunched noisily on it behind me.

I tried to recall anything about the little time I had ever spent with my mother in the kitchen. I live out of cans and off takeaway menus these days, but I grew up with her cooking. I vaguely remembered something about Marmite being good for a meaty stew. I found a jar and dumped half of it in. My soup became brown sludge.

Carrots, I thought desperately. Carrots would brighten it up.

The troll was getting impatient.

'How long this gonna take? Want to be long gone before nasty sunrise.'

'Not long now,' I replied, still trying to delay the inevitable. I wished it were as simple as stalling until dawn. Trolls and sunlight, they don't mix.

As I gave the soup a final stir, I allowed the sprigs of deadly nightshade to fall from my sleeve into the concoction. While cooking is not one of my strong points, at least sleight of hand is. I hoped this would work.

Heaving the pot with both hands, I set it down by the troll.

'Tuck in,' I said.

The troll eyed the sludge dubiously.

A rattling noise that I had been trying to suppress suddenly grew louder in the background. With a bang the only other coblyn-sized pot by the stove burst open and out flew Ang. I cursed her skinny wrists.

The troll stared dumbly from Ang, to the soup, back to Ang. There was almost an audible 'click' as it pieced things together. It let out an ear-splitting roar and kicked over the pot of soup. Then it closed one beefy fist round my throat.

'You think I'm *stupid?*' it snarled, shaking me to and fro. My feet kicked helplessly off the floor while my lungs burned for breath.

I was dropped to the ground without warning. Through watery vision I could see the troll swatting something around its ankles, accompanied by Ang's croaky cussing. I fumbled in my coat for Plan B, the torch. I leapt up, dodged a wild blow, flicked the switch, and pointed the beam up into the troll's thick face.

The troll bellowed with pain. It drew up its hands to shield its eyes from the thin violet light of the torch, features twisting grotesquely as the rough skin began to harden and crack.

'Get it away!' it bawled. 'Away! Away!'

Another wild swing connected with my torso and swept me off my feet. The torch clattered to the floor several feet away. The troll advanced, teeth bared around cracked lips, eyes flashing like thunderclouds.

'Ang! The torch–!' I cried, and rolled just as the troll's fist came down.

It howled again as Ang pointed the torch at its back. It gave me time to scramble out of reach, gasping for breath on the other side of the room. There had to be something there, something I could use . . .

And suddenly, there it was – a glint of light drew my eye to the perfect thing, lying inconspicuously next to a notebook and a pile of mushrooms on the counter. Yes! I snatched it up like a lifeline. Thank whatever god was watching for the paraphernalia of witches!

The troll had turned, was stamping towards Ang as she tried to shrink away inside another cupboard. I picked up glass bottles and hurled them at its back.

'Over here, pig features!'

The troll laboriously turned its bulky frame toward me again. It shook off the glass like dust.

'Ang, the torch! I need it!' I'd lost sight of her; she'd burrowed deeper into the cupboards somewhere. I wiped the sweat from my brow and flung myself away from the troll again. I hoped Ang could hear me.

Now it was the troll's turn to throw things. It wrenched the heavy Belfast sink out of the wall and hurled it in my direction. Roll. Await crushing sensation. Breathe. Inwardly express gratitude for the troll's lack of accuracy.

I tried to dart forward but fell on my back. The tail-end of my coat was caught under the sink. If you have ever tried to get out of any item of clothing in a hurry, you will know that such an endeavour is impossible. I flailed frantically as the troll approached, tangling my arms in the sleeves.

And then the torch dropped into my lap.

The troll was upon me, one colossal fist rising in slow motion. I brought up my arms as if in a fighting stance, magnifying glass held in one hand and torch in the other. I flicked the switch, and felt as though I had just pulled the trigger of a gun.

There was no sound at first, just the slow spread of surprise across the troll's features. And then a crackling sound as the skin dried and split and gradually turned stony. It staggered backwards, arms outstretched, face turned entirely to stone. I used the violet beam to force it away, out the door and into the night. The troll ran, fled, into the dark.

I sagged, torch and magnifier falling from my hands.

I found Ang shivering under the table. She refused to come near me.

'Dirty trick, *gwas*,' was all she would say, giving me the dirtiest of looks. 'Dirty trick.'

'You should have trusted me. I had it all under control,' I tried to explain. But I couldn't really blame her – I wouldn't have taken well to being offered up as soup either.

Mark was the next problem to tackle. There was blood around his head, but it had congealed and I couldn't see bone. The dislocated shoulder took some effort to pop back into place, but at least he could be thankful that he wasn't conscious for that part. It would hurt like hell when he woke up, though.

* * *

When he did wake up, it was two hours later, and I'd managed to haul him onto the couch, inexpertly bandage his head, and make a cup of tea.

'Where's mine?' was the first thing he said to me.

'Make your own,' I replied, with a humourless smile. Everything still ached, and I couldn't help but feel that it was all his fault, somehow. 'How do you feel? Remember who you are? The date and all that?'

'Yeah, yeah.' He waved my questions away. 'What happened, Hansard?'

'There was a troll. Ate all your goats, I'm afraid. But lucky for you I happened by to save your sorry self. So, *you* tell *me* what happened. Bit unlike you to be taken off-guard, isn't it?'

He rubbed his head, grimacing in pain. 'I know. But, trolls, man. They keep to themselves, you know? Years since there's been any kind of troll attack. They can't stand human habitation. You tell me how I was meant to expect that.' He groaned, eyebrows knitting together. 'Seriously, could I get a cup of tea?'

I shrugged. 'Sure.'

When I returned, he was in conversation with Ang, who sat opposite nursing her own brew.

'This one tells me you threatened to make her into soup,' said Mark, raising an eyebrow.

'It was necessary. Honest.'

'She said you scared the troll off with a torch. Was it the black light?'

'Yeah.'

'Clever.'

Ang piped up from behind her mug. 'Why'd it burn the troll? Ain't sunlight.'

'Do you know what UV light is?' said Mark. She shook her head. 'It's invisible to the naked eye but is present in sunlight. It's the ultraviolet radiation that reacts with troll skin, creates a stony texture. The UV torch is called a black light. It's quite weak, I use it for fluorescence tests.'

Ang nodded slowly. 'And who're Baines 'nd Grayle?'

'What?' Mark's expression clouded.

'That's right,' I exclaimed. I'd completely forgotten. 'Baines and Grayle. The troll said it was working for them, or something like that. Any idea what it means?'

'Never heard of them,' said Mark. He held my gaze steadily, until I conceded and looked away.

'I guess it will remain a mystery then,' I said brightly into my tea.

'I suppose it shall.'

'Now, how do you feel about discussing the matter of remuneration? For our time, trouble, and bruises?'

'Don't think just because I've been hit on the head that I'm going to let you walk off with a steal, Hansard.'

'Wouldn't dream of it.'

* * *

We didn't walk off with a steal, but it was almost as good as. We opted to stay the night, ate out of cans, and even made an effort to help tidy the wrecked kitchen. Though tidying a witch's kitchen is a hazardous endeavour: you don't want to touch most of the stuff in case it does something nasty to you.

We retrieved the iron horseshoe from the remains of the door in the bush and hung it on a makeshift plank door, taking care to leave it the right way up. Good protection from most spirits and beasties, is a horseshoe. Iron in general, for that matter. Just make sure your horseshoe stays the right way up, otherwise all the good vibes will spill right out of it.

In the morning Mark gave me supervised free reign of his cellar store, which was jam-packed with long-life spells and potions. I came away feeling like a rich man, albeit a badly bruised one.

'I thought we was here to ask about missing coblynau, not fill our pockets,' said Ang, eyeing me critically as I packed a crate with bottles.

'Of course, Ang. But if there's one rule I live by, it's to never pass up a business opportunity.'

'There's a truth if ever I heard one,' Mark chimed in. 'What's this about missing coblynau?'

He listened with interest to Ang's account, how there had been whispered rumours of a group that wanted to leave the synthetic existence her tribe had created for themselves. One day the mine-dwellers awoke to find themselves five short, the rumours turned reality.

Ang said the group had taken their bluecaps with them – so she believed they had gone willingly, not forced out or kidnapped. The mines were in uproar over it for weeks, until the Gaffer brought his pickaxe down on the whole issue and deemed the missing coblynau outcasts.

'Which ain't the problem. They knew what they was askin' for by leavin',' said Ang. 'But we never heard from 'em after that. 'Tis awful strange. Coblynau always write home, even if they ain't welcome thesselves.'

'I know of your kind,' said Mark thoughtfully, 'but I've not seen a coblyn for decades. I understand you to be more reclusive than your knocker brethren. But, you are like cousins, after all. Could your friends have taken up with them?'

'*Knockers? Never!*'

'That's it then, is it?' I said distractedly. 'No word on the grapevine, as it were.' In truth I hadn't really expected any. My promise was a thin veneer under which I hoped to keep Ang happy while replenishing my stock.

'Have you tried seeking them with quartz?' suggested the witch. 'A simple searching invocation?'

Ang leered doubtfully from under her flatcap. 'Don't want none o' that devilry.'

'It's worth a try, Ang,' I said. 'We just need something that belonged to one of your friends. You know, something they've touched or worn.'

She gave me a contemptuous look. 'And where will ye be findin' that?'

'Well . . . you must have *something*. A keepsake of theirs? Something they gave you as a gift? I mean, you were close with these coblyns, right?'

Ang shook her head. 'No *gwas*. They liked to work wi' clay, where I preferred coal. Never spoke much.'

'But– but you said they were your kin!'

'Aye. Part of me clan. Don't mean I have to like 'em.'

I couldn't help but stare. 'So you've sacrificed your home and your way of life . . . for people you *barely know?*'

'Something's happened to 'em,' she said firmly. 'They got a right to be found.'

'Dutiful folk, aren't you?' said Mark, rubbing his chin. 'If I were you, I'd swallow my pride and visit the knockers down in Devon and Cornwall. You might find their ears are closer to the ground than ours. No pun intended.'

Ang was sniffy of the idea, but grudgingly agreed to set out on the road with me again. I showed her on the map how far it was to Devon

– some four hundred miles along my preferred route – and bargained for us to spend a few more days in the Lake District first so I could make a living. I daren't try to broach the subject of petrol prices. She'd probably tell me to put coal in the engine.

We set out around midday. Ang broke the silence between us once we were a few miles from the house.

'You really trust that witch, *gwas?*'

'Yup.'

'Why?'

'We've known each other a long time.'

'Would ye call him a friend?'

'Hard to have friends in this line of work, Ang.'

She went quiet again, clearly mulling something over. The pasty I'd bought her lay discarded to one side, untouched.

'What is it, Ang?'

She chewed her bottom lip. 'Don't y'think he's lyin' about that Baines 'nd Grayle? About not knowing what it means?'

'Oh, *definitely*,' I said cheerfully. 'That's all just part of the business, Ang. It's the number one rule on the Black Market: don't ask, don't tell.'

She seemed to reflect on this, and then said, half to herself, 'But what kind o' people can order about a troll? They take orders fr'm nobody. Fearful, is what 'tis.'

I wouldn't admit it out loud, but I agreed. Mark's reluctance to divulge what he knew had bothered me. He's a decent sort, and someone too sensible to get wrapped up in messy business. But this 'Baines and Grayle' thing stank of messy business.

I forced a smile and pressed my foot down on the accelerator.

'Cheer up, Ang. Lunchtime soon. Fancy soup?'

Episode 5: Shellycoat

Contrary to what you might think, the Black Market isn't centred on London. Seems strange, what with the capital being the living, beating heart of the whole country: it's the centre for *everything*. News, music, art. Sackfuls of culture churned out every second in an incestuous squall of creation and distribution. That's the problem, really.

The Black Market isn't based in London because too many other things are. Including the *other* black market. The one that peddles drugs and sex and ruined lives. Sure, our Black Market thrives on the same things, but it's a better class of ruination.

If your chosen method of degeneration had to be obtained by way of a hazardous journey into another dimension, wrestled from the jaws of an unspeakably monstrous beast and then brought back in a jar sealed with a maiden's kiss in moonlight – then you know it must be quality stuff. And a lot more exciting than a bit of white powder up your nose.

Of course, the maiden's kiss or suchlike is often replaced by duct tape. Duct tape can do anything.

The point I'm trying to make is that the Black Market is everywhere. It's more of an idea than a place, you see. You're just as likely to find a dealer of 'specialty' goods in the heart of Camden Town as you are in a sleepy Lincolnshire village. The Welsh contingent is particularly thriving. Lots of residual magic in Wales. Something to do with the sheep.

On a mild but drizzly day in March, the Black Market was thriving more specifically on the western edge of the Lake District, in a Cumbrian town called Cockermouth. I may or may not have decided to take up residence in this location purely for its delightful name. I am a child at heart.

''m hungry, *gwas*.'

And then, of course, there was Ang. Two and a half feet tall with pointy ears sticking out from under a flat cap, the little Welsh coblyn had been my travelling companion for a few weeks now. She didn't take up much space, but her debris sure did. Pie wrappers, beer bottles and spent tea bags – if it wasn't covered in pastry she wouldn't eat it, and if it wasn't ale or tea she wouldn't drink it. It may not sound like much, but when the entirety of your living area consists of one Ford Escort estate car, space fills up fast. And she snored like a wildebeest.

'We'll get food later, Ang. We need to make some money, first.' I emptied a crate of potion bottles and heaped them in Ang's skinny arms. 'Arrange these on the table, would you? Neatly.'

'I ain't doin' your work.'

'"My work' is how we fund all those pies you eat. If you want to keep eating, it's going to become 'your work' too.'

'Fine talk. We been out here all mornin' an' made no sells. Ain't no-one here's gunna buy your heathen magickry and cheap doo-dads.'

'Just be patient.'

'This's a farmer's market, *twpsyn*. People are here t'buy meat 'n' cheese, not charms 'n' potions.'

'Trust me, Ang. There's always a customer out there. You just need to learn to spot them.'

'There ain't none here.'

I met her sceptical gaze. Time, I decided, to give Ang some

instruction in the art of Black Marketeering. 'Listen up, Ang. You're going to learn a bit about our consumer base.'

'Our what?'

I scanned the crowd and nodded at a bloke with hunched shoulders opposite us. He was staring moodily at a selection of cabbages, brow furrowed as if trying to read a sign in a foreign language. 'See him? Creased up clothes, no ring, keeps scowling at pretty women? Screams 'divorce papers,' don't you think?'

'Does it? Mebbe his wife sent 'im to get cabbages because he broke the iron an' dropped his ring down the privy.'

'Aha,' I said proudly. 'I know he's divorced, because he was just telling the cabbage-seller all about it a moment ago.'

'That ain't no skill. An' it ain't right to listen in.'

'It's critical market observation.'

She screwed up her face. 'Right. An' what's his misfortune got to do wi' anything?'

'That's our target market, Ang.'

I picked through the bottles on the table and selected two distinctly different styles. I held them up for Ang's inspection. One, a simple curved flask with a pinkish tint, and the other, a mean little vial with an ugly green liquid inside. 'What do these have in common?'

'Them's potions.'

'They're *best sellers*,' I corrected. 'Love potions,' I waggled the pink one, 'and, broadly speaking, *revenge*. That chappie over there falls into the 'spurned lovers' category of our demographic.' I ignored her mouthing *'Demo-what?'* under the table. 'Desperate people, angry people, these are our favourite customers, Ang. They have an axe to grind and I'm here to provide the grindstone.'

I pointed out some of my favourite vengeance brews on the table. I stock the classics: tonics that cause warts and boils, minor accidents, money troubles, that sort of thing.

The most entertaining item was a tincture which effects a person's perception of their own genitalia. Lasts for a week, thoroughly freaks out the recipient and puzzles any doctor they go to, who of course can't see anything out of the ordinary. (Results may vary: it might appear larger, smaller, or have turned purple with sparkles. I once received the gleeful report that my patron's ex-boyfriend had become convinced it was singing to him. Had a voice like James Brown, apparently).

The trick is to identify the people who wish to buy these wares, and that's a skill all its own. Search for the sullen expression, the white tan line on the ring-finger. Listen for the conversation, the frustrated tone of voice and curl to the lip.

Ang looked distinctly unimpressed. 'I see. Ye take advantage of them's too downtrod to think better of it. Can't get upstandin' folk interested, eh?'

'To the contrary! I have a thoroughly upstanding and middle-class brand of customers too. I like to call them the hippies.'

The hippie, I explained, comes in several flavours. The most common is the young, earth-loving waif who, despite a strong abhorrence of the ecological impact of commercialism, is nevertheless able to stomach spending a great deal of money on outlandish jewellery and stylish tie-dye outfits made by children in Thailand (but in an environmentally *friendly* manner).

These ones are suckers for cheap and colourful jewellery, especially if you can claim it was made using 'traditional' craft skills in a poorer country (funny how no one considers 'traditional' to encompass slave labour).

Another type of hippie is the older, not necessarily wiser, New Age Wicca enthusiast. The ones who loudly proclaim the healing power of crystals and mud, and whose spells contain not a single ounce of blood or newt's eyeball. (Actually, crystals can be pretty magical in the right circumstances – but you have to do more than just pile a bunch of rocks on your body and hope.) Crystals and other shiny things sell well to these guys in any weather, but you've got to know your geology. When I first started this gig I quickly learned that 'this pink rock' and 'that greeny-blue rock' was not a satisfactory method of identification for even the most disinterested of tourists.

But every so often, lurking under the guise of the New Age Hippie is an actual, genuine witch. They are usually quite profitable – if overly sanctimonious. I've received no end of lectures about how one should not try to control the will of others through spells and potions. What are spells and potions for then, I wonder?

It's the love potions that attract the most ire: 'You can't just make people fall in love!' 'You can't force someone to do things against their will!' 'It's unethical to affect the fate of others!'

''Tis 'nethical,' observed Ang.

'Well, yes. But do you have any idea how much these things sell for? Besides, the naysayers are technically correct,' I said. 'You *can't* force someone to fall in love with you. At least, not with what I'm peddling. It's bloody hard to make someone do something they don't want through magic.'

'What do them potions do, then?'

I smiled slyly. 'Exactly what it says on the bottle. They boost feelings of love. Towards whatever the recipient already holds some love for.'

'This one says, *Imbue the object of yer desire wi' long-lastin' passion an' ardour.*'

'Now read the small print.

She studied it silently. 'That's tricksy, *gwas.*'

'I call it the Hobbyist's Infatuation.'

'Don't people complain, *gwas?*'

'Maybe. But I simply can't hear them over the sound of how much money I'm making.'

'An' how much money is that, *gwas?* Cuz I heard we can't even afford pies no more.' Ang leered at me over a box of voodoo dolls.

'We've just hit a slow patch. But rest assured there is never any shortage of spurned lovers or disgruntled employees, even in a quiet town like this'

'Hmph.' She dumped another box haphazardly on the table. Its contents – a fine array of Holy Grails, totally legitimate for a given definition of the word holy (i.e. with holes in) – toppled and crushed the display of enchanted (cursed) roses I had been working on.

'Tidy that up, please. Or there'll definitely be no – *watch the thorns!* – no pies later.'

'No pies at all, at this rate,' she grumbled. 'No hope if ye only sells to the desperate.'

I bristled. 'I'm a salesman, Ang. I can sell to *anyone.*'

'Aye? What about them?'

She indicated a gaggle of girls coming our way. They were late teens or early twenties, all blonde hair and pink lipstick, clutching large handbags and tottering in high heels over the cobblestones.

I squared my shoulders. 'Watch and learn.'

I picked up my tray of jewellery and thrust it forwards as they passed.

'Fine jewellery for fine ladies?' I said grandly. I whipped out a cheeky smile too.

They exchanged glances, then peered down petite noses at the tray.

'Mood rings? That's so retro!' one exclaimed. She held aloft a pink ring. 'Wasn't it, like, they'd be red if you're angry, blue if you're calm? Or green? I think mine were always green.'

'Don't they like, change with heat, or something?' said another.

'No miss, not these ones,' I interjected. 'These rings change your mood, not the other way round.' I held forth a sample of rings in the palm of my hand and selected them one at a time. 'The pink ones, like this, they encourage your feelings of empathy to surface. Red ones bring out feelings of stress and anxiety – a good gift for whoever's been irritating you lately. Green ones–'

'Oh, look at this cute necklace!'

'Let me see. Oh, isn't that the star of David?'

'No, it's a pentangle.'

'–inspire patience,' I finished wryly. 'It's called a pentacle, miss.'

'Don't witches wear these?'

'Yes,' I said. 'But so do lots of people. You see, it's a protective charm and–'

'Get it for Emma, she likes that spooky stuff.'

'Nah, it looks kinda cheap.'

Under the table, I heard Ang snort with laughter. I changed gear.

'How about this pendant?' I proffered a silver wedjat amulet: the Egyptian Eye of Horus. 'Sterling silver, comes with a delicate silver chain too.'

'Ooh, that is nice. Isn't that nice?'

'Yeah, definitely. Do you have any ankhs? Like, ankh earrings?'

I switched trays. 'Ankh pendants, yes.'

'But, like, earrings?'

'I'm afraid not. Perhaps instead I can interest you in–'

'Oh, hey! Look at this cute little rabbit foot!'

'Ew, get it away!'

'That's disgusting.'

'I think it's cute. Don't you?'

'Uh, *no*. I'm *vegan*.' This one rounded on me. 'Did you kill this rabbit?'

I kept my smile. 'No, miss. Wouldn't harm a living thing.'

'Well, you practically *did* kill it, because you're selling it. Fur is murder!'

She threw the rabbit foot on the ground. It bounced.

She picked it up and inspected it quizzically. 'It's made of rubber.'

'What?' said her friend.

'The fur's just stuck on. Look.'

'You mean it isn't even *real?*'

The group fixed accusative glares at me.

'Animal-friendly?' I tried.

They left without buying anything.

'That was sellsmanship, was it?'

'Shut up, Ang.'

One of the girls hung back, still idly pouring over my wares. I had mistaken her for part of the group, but in hindsight it was clear she'd just been hovering on the edge. She seemed older; had a more down-to-earth air about her. More patience in the eyes and thoughtful creases around the mouth. She was perusing the potions, discreetly arranged to the back of the table.

'Cleansing room spray?' she inquired, pointing to the label of one.

'Clears out negative energy, miss. Fills the air with harmonious vibrations and positive energies.' I adopted an easy smile. That's one of my own inventions. Plastic spray bottle filled with water, salt, and whatever perfume I can get my hands on. A few floating flower petals give it a nice aesthetic quality (pro tip: fancy petals are easily obtained all year round from supermarket flowers – security isn't looking out for a man surreptitiously filling his pockets with plucked foliage).

She set it down, disinterested, and picked up another, turning the angular glass bottle around in her hands.

'Careful there, miss. Pretty strong mixture, that one.'

Her thumb brushed over the label, and one delicate eyebrow rose as she read aloud: '*Hopping Mad Medley.* 'Convert the recipient's inner rage into an uncontrollable desire to hop?''

'Fun and harmless come-uppance for that person in your life with a bad temper. Satisfaction guaranteed.' I grinned broadly.

She returned my smile and picked up another bottle. 'What if I wanted something less . . . harmless?' Her eyes remained trained on the vial in her hand, as if she wasn't really interested in the question she was asking. Aha. Target demographic, sure enough.

'Might I suggest our *Odious Miasma*, for a stench that just won't leave? Or perhaps the *Hapless Harry*, for a bout of bad luck. But if you want to hit 'em where it really hurts, I'd recommend *Beggar's Fortune*, for a spell of money troubles.'

'Mmm.'

She appeared deep in thought, though it didn't seem like she was trying to decide on a manner of vengeance. There's usually a spark in the eyes, a little rush of excitement as they contemplate their revenge. But she stared at my wares as though merely comparing vegetables.

The thought turned over in my head: this one's no stranger to Black Market goods. A rare opportunity.

'Perhaps I could interest you in something a little more unique?' I suggested.

'What have you got?' she said, still distracted. Her attention flickered over the table.

I rummaged through my stock. 'Something like . . . a box of infinite compartments?'

'Dull.'

'Sacrificial ear spoon?'

'Common.'

'Aztec idol?'

'Last year.' She turned away and made to leave. 'I'm sorry to waste your time. I thought you might have something special.'

In a split-second I weighed the situation and found it to be a good one. From the depths of my trench coat I retrieved a tin box. 'You should have said so, miss! I can assure you, you have come to right place. I just so happen to have this one exceedingly rare and exceptionally beautiful commodity for sale. Have you ever heard of a bluecap?'

She looked at me properly for the first time. Now there was a spark in her eyes.

'No,' she said. 'What are they?'

I set the box down on the table and tantalisingly ran my fingers along the edge. 'Bluecaps are mining spirits, and they seek out treasure. One of these beauties will lead you to riches beyond your wildest dreams. Take a look.'

I pulled away the lid, and a soft blue glow illuminated the woman's entranced gaze.

'Oh, how pretty . . .'

Without warning, Ang reached up from under the table and slammed the lid closed. 'Not for sale,' she said sternly.

'Excuse me,' I said, smiling brightly to my almost-customer. 'Let me just talk to my associate here.'

I ducked down to Ang's level. 'What are you doing? We had a deal, Ang. Bluecaps for travel, and my generous assistance. They are *mine* to sell now.'

'To a good home, *pentwp*. Them's the terms.'

'And just what is a good home, huh? What does it matter to the bluecaps, anyway? They're dead! Spirits! They don't care!'

'Bluecaps need to work, *gwas*,' Ang growled. 'Not to be sittin' on a shelf for some stuck-up, soft-handed *ast* to gaze at of an eve.'

I grit my teeth and forced myself to speak calmly. 'All right, Ang. How about I ask her how she's going to look after them? I could even give her a set of care instructions if you like. 'Walk your bluecap at least once a day,' sort of thing, *all right?*'

'No deal, *gwas*. Don't like 'er.'

'For fu– heaven's sake. *Tough.* We already made our deal, Ang. I'm holding up my end of it.'

'Oh? Found a lead on me missing kin, did ye?' She glowered at me

74

until I looked away.

I rose, willing my face to relax and regain a friendly composure.

'Sorry about that. Now–' I closed my mouth, puzzled. The woman had disappeared. I exhaled my exasperation and thumped my fist on the table. 'Christ, Ang. Look what you've done. Scared her off.'

'Good.'

I wanted to throttle the snotty little creature. That sale could have made the day.

I reached down to retrieve the bluecaps, but my hand grasped thin air. I looked down in slowly dawning horror.

'Oh, shit,' I groaned.

'What?' said Ang suspiciously. She peered out from her hiding spot. From the look on her face, I gather my expression must have said it all. 'You best not've lost them bluecaps, *gwas*,' she said icily. Her normally pale features were slowly gaining colour.

'I can't believe she– I mean, she seemed quite nice.' I desperately scanned the crowd, but I knew she'd be long gone. 'What a, a–'

'*Ast*.'

'What?'

'Bitch.'

'Yeah. Exactly that.'

'It's your fault,' hissed Ang. Her ears might as well be steaming, she had turned so red. '*Twpsyn*. You utter *twpsyn*.'

'If you hadn't distracted me–'

'Then she'd've still made off with 'em! Right under your nose! *Ffwl!*'

'Stop shouting, Ang. We'll get them back. I'll find a way.'

'How?'

That was a very good question.

* * *

'We've been at this for an hour, Ang. Are you sure this is working?'

'*Cau dy geg.*'

'What does that mean? It's no use talking Welsh at me.'

'*Shut up.*'

I observed her for another minute, watching her brows knit closer and closer while her eyes and mouth screwed up into tight wrinkles in her face. You'd think her features were being sucked inwards by the force of the world's most bitter lemon.

We'd retreated to a deserted car park to start our search for the missing bluecaps. So far, I had been allowed to sit on the tarmac to say and do bugger all.

'Ang–'

'Oh, *cach*. I give up.' She flung her cap on the floor and stamped one heavily booted foot as she rose from her seated position. As far as I could tell (seeing as she wasn't talking to me at the moment) she had been staring intently into the blue flame of her old miner's lantern. Or at least, she had started with staring. After a while she'd begun tapping carefully on the glass, which progressed to an insistent knocking, then a frustrated rapping; finally, she'd shaken the lantern about and shouted at it in Welsh. Clearly, none of this had had the desired effect.

She gave the lantern a half-hearted kick and stuffed her hands in her pockets. 'Dunno what's wrong. They just ain't talkin' t'one another.'

'What aren't? The bluecaps?'

'Aye.'

'Are they connected to the one in the lantern?'

She flashed me a condescending glare. 'O'course. Wha'did I tell you them bluecaps were? Mine own kin, souls o' coblynau past.' She tapped her lantern. 'This were me mother, once. This spirit should be able to feel where its kin are, same as it can feel the whereabouts of a good vein o'coal.'

'So what's the problem?'

'Dunno. It just don't seem to know where t'go.' She scowled, kicking at the dirt. The anger washed out of her face and was replaced by gloom. 'S'your fault,' she muttered dejectedly.

I frowned. This wouldn't be so bad if it were only a tin of baubles I'd lost. Trinkets go missing all the time, you can't get attached to things in this business. But no, this was a box of Ang's ancestors that had been stolen away. Not to mention an incredibly valuable investment. Those bluecaps would sell for hundreds. No, maybe thousands!

It made me feel rather gloomy myself, thinking of that sales opportunity sitting on a pretty shelf in some oblivious girl's home. I bet she had no idea what she'd made off with.

Well, we'll see about that.

'C'mon Ang, it's not over yet. I've got methods too, you know.'

She regarded me doubtfully. 'Like what, merchant man? You a thief-tracker too, now?'

Ignoring her, I opened the boot of my car and rummaged inside until I'd made enough space to open the secret compartment. You know, that compartment you're meant to store your first aid kit and emergency tools in. Mine contains different kinds of tools.

'Grab the road map out from under the seat, would you?'

'Do it yeself.'

'Spread it out on the bonnet, please.'

'Oh, I'll do what I'm tole, shall I? *Cer i grafu.*'

'And don't swear at me, please.'

'*Cont.*'

'I'll pretend I didn't hear that.'

I emerged with the small quartz crystal and silver chain I had been searching for. Ang was already waiting by the front of the car, scowl still in place. It turned to a sneer when she spied the crystal dangling from its chain.

'Scryin'?' she said. 'I ain't using that witchery. Them heathen crystals ain't right.'

'You've got a weird idea of what's heathen. You keep the soul of your dead mother in a lantern, for crying out loud.'

'S'different. Things in the ground be pure. Shouldn't be taken out and tinkered with.'

'You used to be a miner! Your entire job was taking things out of the ground so that they could be tinkered with!'

She shrugged. 'S'different. Coal 'n' iron is safe. But crystals . . . They got them vibrations, you know?'

I did know, sort of. Some crystals and other rocks are good at resonating with the things around them, and they can be sort of, *tuned* to mimic certain vibrations. And if you think of these vibrations as types of energy, well, it means you can do all sorts of things with it. Take the crystal in my hand, for example. When it came out of the ground, it was just a lump of quartz. But after several weeks of fine tuning in a crystal smith's workshop, it can now mimic the resonances of objects and people – and with a bit of practice you can use it to find those things on a map.

You must let the crystal 'tune in' to the correct vibrations first, though. To find a missing person, you need something like a scrap of their clothing or some of their hair – anything of theirs that might still hold those residual vibrations. To find the missing bluecaps, I knew just the thing we'd need.

'Ang, are you able to get that bluecap out of your lantern?'

'What for?'

'Do you think you could make it, sort of, sit on top of the crystal? It needs to know what it's looking for, you see.'

'No way, *gwas*. I ain't letting it near that thing.'

'C'mon, Ang. Do you want to find the others? This might be our only chance to find them before they're out of reach.'

I could see worry and reluctance battling it out over her features. She'd retrieved her flat-cap and was wringing it through her hands.

'I promise it'll be fine, Ang,' I said soothingly.

'Your promises ain't worth much, *gwas*.'

'That's unfair. I don't lie. Often.'

'Yet somehow ye still manage to steer well clear o' the truth.'

'We all have our flaws.'

'Hah!'

She chewed it over, tapping her foot and wringing her cap. I glanced pointedly at sky, where the sun was well on its downwards arc to meet the horizon. Ang exhaled noisily and fetched her lantern.

'Don't make me regret this, *gwas*.'

'Stop worrying. Can you get it to hang onto the crystal, somehow?'

She unscrewed the lantern's cap and held out her arm. The bluecap flame noiselessly drifted upwards and wrapped itself around her wrist. It was an eerie sight. The blue flame flickered on her skinny fingers as she reached towards the crystal. It slid off, folded itself around the sparkling quartz and hung there, dancing and shimmering in the breeze.

I turned to the map spread on the bonnet, with the silver chain clutched tightly in my fist. The town of Cockermouth lay just to the north-west of the Lake District and sat upon the River Derwent and River Cocker (this place is a giggle-a-day for me). I held the crystal over the centre of Cockermouth and tried to focus. Or rather, unfocus. The less *there* you are, the better – means you're not providing as many distracting vibrations, or something. I breathed out and let my edges unravel.

'You sure you know what you're doin'?' said Ang, eyeing the crystal suspiciously.

'I'm not an expert, but I know the basics. So just be quiet and let the crystal do its thing, all right?'

She folded her arms grumpily but kept quiet. As I relaxed, the crystal began to stir.

It was the gentlest of movements at first, barely a back and forth. Then it grew into a slow, swinging circle above the town. Our eyes followed it keenly as the circle grew broader, faster. Faster still, and wilder. The chain wrenched on my grip as it dissolved into a frenzied whizzing to all corners of the map.

A biting pain shot through my hand and up my arm. I yelped and yanked my hand away, dropping the crystal onto the tarmac.

Ang darted forward and scooped up the fallen bluecap, which shrank into her embrace like a frightened child. She glared angrily at me. 'Look what you did! Did you know it was going to do that?'

'No,' I said, sucking my fingers. They ached.

'I *tole* you it wasn't right messin' with them tinkered crystals. Got us nowhere, eh?'

'I wouldn't say that.' I picked myself up and gingerly plucked the crystal from the ground. It was hot. 'We now know that the woman who stole those bluecaps is no amateur,' I said darkly.

'What's that supposed to mean?'

'It *means* that she probably has a spell or talisman hiding them from prying eyes. Something that muffles the signal. She knows *exactly* what she stole. Probably knows what they're worth, too.'

I could see the panic in Ang's eyes as this sank in. 'How we going to find them now, *gwas?*'

'I don't know,' I admitted. I'd used up my ace and now I was back to square one.

I didn't really want to say it, but our chances of ever finding the bluecaps had become extremely slim, because the wards hiding them must be powerful. The signal hadn't just been muffled; it had been completely drowned out by something so loud it hurt – the crystal had been desperate to be *anywhere* but over the map.

So this woman, this thief, could be anything. Witch, maybe. Perhaps not even human. Plenty of strange beasties have picked up the knack of walking around in human skin.

In Ang's arms, the bluecap suddenly glowed brighter.

'What's it doing?' I asked.

'Dunno,' said Ang, equally puzzled.

The flame leapt from her arms and floated in the air for a moment. And then, with a quiet *pop*, it shot off into the distance.

'Follow it!' screamed Ang.

I was already running. Around a corner and down an alleyway, then out into a wide street where perplexed shoppers became angry shoppers as I crashed through their midst. The blue glimmer weaved in and out of sight ahead of me. The second wave of startled cries from people behind told me that Ang was hot on my heels.

We turned into an emptier road, and then I was hopping over a fence – *oh, that must be Cockermouth Castle up ahead* – we barrelled past the ruins and into the trees following the line of the castle walls. The trees ended abruptly, and so did the ground.

I caught myself on a low branch and flung out an arm to catch Ang as she flew past. We clung to the tree and fought to regain our footing. We were inches away from slipping down the muddy bank into the swirling waters of the Derwent.

'Where's . . . where's th' . . . bluecap?' Ang spluttered in-between heavy gasps for breath.

I pointed. It was hovering about a metre above the river, where a pile of rubbish was floating on the surface.

'You don't think she chucked 'em in the river, do ye?' said Ang, horrified.

'I highly doubt it.' I peered closer at the mass underneath the bluecap. 'Look at that rubbish in the water. It's not moving.'

'So?'

'See the eddies around it? There's something solid under there. Like it's anchored in place.'

Ang looked at me anxiously. 'We're not gunna have t'swim are we, *gwas?*'

I cast around for a large rock and found one to my liking. I hefted it in one arm. 'I hope not.'

The rock curved in a nice arc and dropped down right on top of the floating rubbish heap. I wasn't sure what I was expecting, but the pile didn't sink. Instead, it rose.

'*Gwas,*' whispered Ang fearfully. 'What is that?'

I've never encountered a rubbish monster before, but I had no other name for what emerged to face us. A sentient pile of rubbish. It turned, appeared to spot us, and was now swimming – or wading? – in our direction. We remained frozen, clinging to our tree as the creature reared up in front of us.

From within the depths of weeds and trash a deep, slow voice emanated:

'*Did you throw that rock?*'

'Uh, yes,' I replied.

'*Why did you do that?*'

'I was trying to see what you were. Sorry about that.'

'What are ye, y'big pile o' *ysbwriel?*' said Ang from her branch.

The thing seemed to sag, and sadness filled its voice.

'*You would know what I am if I had my coat. They call me Shellycoat, for my beautiful coat of shells.*' It let out a sigh that sounded like waves.

'Looks like a pile o' rubbish to me,' said Ang. I shot her a chiding look, but she paid no mind. 'Where's your shells now, Smellycoat?'

The shellycoat sagged further, so that it was only just above the water it sat in. The mass of trash rattled as it moved: tin cans, plastic bottles and sweet wrappers glinted in the dying sun.

'*Stolen,*' it said mournfully. '*By a lady with quiet eyes.*'

Easy connection to make there. Spot on about the eyes. Her gaze had been so . . . patient.

'Funny you should say that. We've also had something precious stolen by a lady today,' I said. 'Perhaps you've seen it?'

'Many things float down the river. What does it look like?'

Ang opened her mouth. 'It's a–'

'Bit hard to describe, really,' I butted in. 'Maybe you could show us the things you've found today? Could be a bit of a reward in it.'

The shellycoat sighed despondently. Then it seemed to shrug – a ponderous, undulating movement – and several objects rose to the surface of its matted coat. Among them were an ornate bollock dagger, a very intricate (if damp) Japanese *omamori* amulet, and, best of all, a plastic bottle containing one glowing bluecap. I had to grab Ang by the wrist to stop her diving straight for it.

I pretended to inspect the array of items. I rubbed my chin thoughtfully and said, 'You know, this is a very exclusive mix of things. I have trouble believing that they all just washed down river.'

The shellycoat sighed again. *'I met the lady again. Moments ago. I have been waiting for her to pass by my river for many days. I asked for my coat back, but she refused. I dragged her into the water, but she stung me. These things fell from her bag before she got away.'*

A picture was starting to form of this woman. I could bet all these curious items were stolen from someone else. I bet it's how she makes her living. No amateur, indeed.

'Say, what's the blue thing in the bottle?' I asked.

'It's a pretty light. It floats in the air and the water, but I put it in a bottle so it won't get away. It lights everything up nice underwater.'

'That's pretty clever.'

'Yes.'

'Thing is, it looks to me just like one of them bluecap things. You ever heard of them?'

The shellycoat swayed in a way that I took to be a shake of the head. 'Well, they're ground-dwelling spirits, see. Very unlucky to have in the water. They'll drag you down into the depths of the earth if you let them.'

'Into the earth?'

'Yep, where it's cold and dark–'

'I like cold and dark.'

Ang nudged me. 'Mines are bloody warm, y'know.'

'Warm, I mean,' I continued, back-peddling. 'Humid. And oppressive, all those tons of earth weighing down on you. Not like the cool, free-flowing waters of a river.' I shrugged. 'Just saying. It pays to be careful around these things.'

'I like the light,' said the shellycoat, doubtfully.

'Yes, but one day that light may lead you into places you wish you'd never gone.' Now there's a piece of generalised truth if ever there was one. 'Anyway, I'm not interested in the bluecap. I don't want that kind of misfortune for myself, no sir. But I might be interested in taking the other items off your hands. For a price, of course.'

'A good price?'

'A fair price. Quite a bit of water damage, from what I can see. That dagger's going rusty – you can see it's obscuring the fine detail there. And that soggy amulet is only made of fabric and paper – the colours are starting to run, see. It might even be unreadable!'

The shellycoat shifted, or rather, *undulated* in thought. It wondered aloud, *'Is it enough to buy a new coat?'*

'A coat?' I repeated. 'Made of shells, you mean?'

A few shiny foil wrappers peeled away in the breeze as the mass nodded.

'This is a poor replacement. I miss the rattle of shells, not the clanking and rustling of this . . . this . . .'

'Rubbish,' said Ang flatly.

'Well, Shelly – may I call you Shelly? – I'm afraid I don't have a coat of shells to sell you. I do have some interesting charms and potions though, but, oh dear, I've left them all behind. It's a long way back, and I really can't stick around. Is there perhaps a favour I could do for you as payment?'

'A favour?' said Shelly in a slow, bewildered manner.

'It's the traditional on-the-spot payment for these sorts of things. I don't suppose you have any thorns you need pulling out of your paws? If you even have paws. Maybe a nasty bit of fisherman's netting we could remove for you?'

'No.'

'Dang. And I rather fancied that dagger, too.' I tapped my lips, eyes raised to the sky, then snapped my fingers. I suspect it made the shellycoat jump. 'Here's an idea, we could get rid of that bluecap for you. It's not a risk I'd like to take, having that thing about my person. But seeing as there are no other alternatives, I'm happy to offer it as payment. What do you think?'

'For all of these things?'

'I would settle for just the dagger.'

'No.'

Ang let out an exasperated sigh next to me. 'Can't we just–'

'In a minute, Ang.' I placed a soothing hand on her shoulder. I turned back to the shellycoat. 'What do you think my offer is worth?'

It spread itself wider and bobbed up and down in the water. For a moment I worried it was going to sink and take the bluecap with it. Then it said, 'The paper charm. You may have that.'

'What!' I exclaimed. 'That's daylight robbery, that is! I offer you this good service – which most people would be loath to undertake, mind you – and all you want to offer me is a bit of soggy paper!'

The bobbing became more agitated. 'Won't sell the dagger. You think it is valuable. I will trade it with someone who can give me a new coat.'

The dagger sank back into the mess of weeds and rubbish. *'But I offer you one further item. Your choice.'*

I cast my eye over the remaining trinkets. Largely worthless, but I selected a ring, anyway.

'This will do,' I said begrudgingly. 'This ring and that charm, so that I may dispose of your bluecap problem.'

'We are agreed.'

Wiry green tendrils, which I had assumed were just weeds, now grasped the amulet and bluecap bottle and held them out to me. They felt somewhat slimy in my hands.

'Pleasure doing business with you,' I said as the shellycoat disappeared beneath the water. The surface bubbled for a moment, and that was the last we saw of it.

Ang put the rescued bluecap away safely in her pocket. The other one zipped along behind us as we walked back to the car.

'That was mean, you know,' she said, after a while.

'What was?'

'The way you tricked that ol' Smellycoat. Bluecaps ain't no burden o' bad luck.'

'They do lead you underground, though.'

'Not in the way that you meant, *gwas.*'

'Doesn't matter what I meant. Didn't lie, did I?'

'Didn't tell the truth, neither.'

She ducked behind me as some people passed us in the street. It's easy for such a small creature to go unseen. Half the time people don't see her simply because they don't look down. She continued wandering behind me until we reached the car, all the while a distracted look of deep disquiet on her face.

I gave her a friendly pat. 'Don't worry about Shelly, I'm sure it'll be fine. As for us, we're more than fine, we just recouped our losses today!'

'We only found one bluecap,' she said icily.

'Yes, and we *also* found this incredibly valuable *omamori* amulet! Normally they're ten-a-penny from Japanese Shinto shrines, like your basic good luck charm. But this one is far more complex, a strong protection ward, I think. Probably antique, too. A lot of money in that.'

'Thought ye wanted the dagger?'

'So did Shelly,' I said smugly. 'Just an ornamental knife, nothing special. We got the real prizes today.'

Ang retrieved her lantern. The floating bluecap slid inside without prompting. 'Ye think that pile o' rubbish will find a new coat?'

I shrugged and started to re-arrange my wares in the boot. Probably best to move on from here, ASAP. 'Surely all it's got to do is collect some more shells. Plenty of them about.'

'Plenty o' bluecaps, too. But only a few of 'em are mine.'

I stopped and turned to look her square in the eye. I thought about crouching down to her level, but knew she'd consider it to be the condescending gesture it was. 'Look, Ang. No one is sorrier than me about your bluecaps. That's a tidy of sum of profits I'll never see again; I wish I hadn't let them out of my sight. The fact that we recovered one bluecap today was just a piece of good luck. I'll be honest – I don't hold any hope of finding the rest.'

'What happened to 'I'll find a way'?' she said accusingly. I winced.

'That was before I knew what we were dealing with. This thief clearly has some power behind her. You saw the size of that shellycoat. She *wrestled* with it and *won*? She's stolen all these valuable things – *priceless* things – and has the ability to keep them hidden? I don't know what kind of aces she has up her sleeve, and I don't want to be the idiot who finds out the hard way. Not to mention the fact that she's probably skipped town already. I would, if I'd just had a brush with a dissatisfied customer.'

Ang's eyes narrowed. 'Ye a coward, *gwas?*'

'I'm *alive*, Ang. And I intend to stay that way.'

She turned quiet, but it was that loud kind of quiet that lets you know a sulk is brewing. I awkwardly tried to pat her shoulder. 'C'mon, Ang. Let's get something to eat. I'm famished.'

She nodded sullenly. Looks like I was going to receive the silent treatment again. I didn't much mind, it would be nice to have some peace.

Ang might think me a coward, but I had good reason to be cautious. Spend any amount of time in my world and you quickly learn there are some very big fish sharing the water with you. I'm not exactly one to preach about looking before you leap – heaven knows I've jumped headlong into my share of dangerous situations – but even I know to back off when the fall looks too high. And to me, something about this thief smacked of a very, very long drop.

And normally this would be the end of it. I'd cut my losses and move on. But something kept dragging my thoughts back to it.

You see, I had this awful, troubling notion bubbling away in the back of my mind. Somehow, I knew that this wasn't the last we'd seen of the woman with the quiet eyes.

Episode 6: Black Market

I was still in the Lake District when I heard that the annual Market was to be held in Hull. I've said before that the Black Market doesn't exist in any one place alone. This is true: it is a concept in aggregate, an abstract collective of mercantile bodies who may stake their claim to a particular territory or wander aimlessly across the country. All of them seeking out the next big opportunity.

But every once in a while, *the* Black Market comes to town, and this is the biggest opportunity of them all. There's a childish excitement that surrounds the event, as may be expected of a massive underworld party, and of course it's the only chance we get to show off to all our peers. Vendors of otherworldly goods will flock from miles around for the chance to be noticed by new customers – and to one-up their competitors. It's the only time you'll find so many of us in one place, and it only happens once a year.

No one really knows how it happens, either. The word simply spreads among traders up and down the country: The Market is being held. The time and location are passed along like a hot but sweet potato.

I don't know who decides on these details. Maybe nobody decides. It has crossed my mind more than once that the Market is so loaded with magic and occult power that maybe, in a disturbing sort of way, it might be alive.

Maybe we're all tendrils of this great amorphous beast stretching across the country, like the tentacles of some immense, preternatural octopus. And once a year it pulls us all inwards to feed on the things we've gathered. Or maybe it's more like a colossal, slow heartbeat, pulsing outwards and inwards to the tune of the seasons.

But that's just my fancy. I have a lot of time to think to myself during those long car journeys.

'Why we gotta go all this way just for a market, *gwas?*'

Car journeys have been less peaceful of late.

'It's only three hours, Ang. And it's not just any market. It's *the* market.'

The coblyn dropped her greasy pie paper in the footwell, where her dangling feet were just beginning to brush the top of a rising layer of garbage. If she slipped off the seat, I was sure she would drown in it.

'Ye should do somethin' about this rubbish,' she said, as if reading my thoughts.

'I'm not your housekeeper.'

"Tis your car.'

'It's your mess.'

'Your problem.'

I changed gear somewhat roughly, then winced at the resulting *crunch*. I shouldn't take out my frustration on the old girl. My car that is, not Ang.

'Have you ever considered that you should try to pull your weight around here? This isn't a free ride, you know.'

'Nope.' She leaned back and tipped her flat cap over her eyes. 'I already paid.'

We'd had this conversation a dozen times or more, and I already knew how it ended: Ang would berate me for not yet having found any information on her missing coblynau brethren, and then she would helpfully remind me that I had lost five of her prized bluecaps to a thief, and *then* I would stuff another pasty in her mouth just to shut her up.

But, for once, I had a counter argument.

'Let me tell you why you should be interested in the Market, Ang,' I said. There was a disgruntled noise from under the flat cap. 'Once a year, for three days, everyone who's *anyone* attends the Market.'

'And you're 'anyone', are ye?'

'Only the finest purveyor of occult goods in all of England!'

'Aye. I read yer business cards. *Twpsyn.*'

'My point, Ang, is that the Market is the biggest melting pot of otherworldly citizens you will ever come across. For just three days a year we're not hiding in shadows or keeping our heads low. We're big and loud and we love to *talk.* Everyone's bragging about their biggest sales, their newest finds, and possibly about any *weird new species they've met.*'

'Ye better not be callin' me a weird specie,' Ang grumbled.

'I swear you miss the point on purpose. Ang, your kind aren't exactly common in the world any more, y'know? We don't even see knockers that much these days–' she bristled at the word *knockers,* '– so I'm convinced that if anyone's come across a coblyn in their travels, this is where we'll hear about it. Heck, maybe your friends will come to the Market themselves. There's always something that we've never seen before. Maybe coblynau will be the next big thing.'

This is perhaps the most honest guarantee I have ever given. It's a foregone conclusion at each Market that there will be *something* you've never seen before. It might be some precious, mythic artefact (last year there was a furore over the bones of a lost saint), or some new type of tincture (love potions and youth tonics are old hat), or maybe some bizarre creature scarcely caged (although this often ends horribly – the imbecile who introduced us to piskies ought to be shot).

My mind had been racing for weeks over the prospect of what the

Hull Market would bring. And what I, in turn, would bring to it.

Since meeting Ang, I'd been euphoric with the knowledge that I now possessed six bluecaps: fiery spirits usually seen only in the hands of knockers and other mine-dwelling goblins. Knockers and coblynau don't part with these things easily – bluecaps are, after all, the spirits of their ancestors. So, I was understandably aching with anticipation for the opportune moment to show off my amazing catch. I, Jack Hansard, had *bluecaps* for sale, which is something that no other trader could boast.

Or at least, now I had blue*cap*.

Blast that thief. One moment of distraction, and I'd lost the biggest opportunity of my life to some woman with a nice smile and quiet eyes. Her eyes, I couldn't get them out of my head.

So now I had one bluecap to sell, which was substantially less exciting than six bluecaps. Ang still had the one in her lantern, but she wasn't letting go of it for love nor money. Still, one bluecap was better than none, and it was worth smiling about. I decided I was going to make some *waves* this year.

* * *

When we arrived in Hull, it was well past midnight. Just as well, because the Market doesn't open its doors to anyone before the twelfth hour. Sort of traditional, you know.

We pulled up at a warehouse on the river front. An innocuous, blocky building nested in a cluster of identical warehouses, it was the perfect venue for a three-day gathering of the country's underworld.

Now we just had to find the door.

As we circled the building, I concentrated on unfocusing myself. The trick is to become as fuzzy as the hidden door – to slide into the same space it occupies. I could feel the edges of it as we drew closer.

'What are ye waiting for?' said Ang, giving me a curious look. 'Door's right here, *gwas*.'

'One moment,' I mumbled, gritting my teeth with the effort of concentration. The wall in front of me shimmered, and within a blink it was a door, as it always had been.

'Ye got rubbish eyesight, *gwas*,' Ang said, shaking her head.

'It's a human thing. You ready for this?'

'Aye.'

I pushed open the small door and was hit by a crashing surge of noise. Ang followed, dumbfounded, as she took in the vast crowds swarming between rows upon rows of traders.

I grinned like I was home. In a manner of speaking, I was. 'Welcome to the Black Market.'

I hefted my bags over one shoulder and grabbed the fold-up table, armed and ready to claim a small square of this bustling territory as my own. The warehouse had appeared small on the outside. On the inside it was palatial, just like that alien doctor's time travelling spaceship thing (I've never really watched television). Around the edges of the room was a thriving trade in comfort where several bars, eateries, and bunks-for-rent had set up shop.

The rest of the hall was taken up by the chaos of the Market. I leaned down to Ang.

'Try not to smile at the people you pass. And try to ignore the ones who don't look like people.'

She nodded mutely and followed my weaving trail.

The centre was where I really wanted to be, in the very hub of all that commotion. It sucks people inwards like a black hole, so all the best stuff is found in the very middle. I've never had a spot even close to it.

Today would be the same. I'd have to be content with my humble pitch on the end of an outer row. Table out, curtains up, let's put on a show.

'Ang, pass up those bottles, will you?' I looked around for the little nuisance. 'Ang?'

She poked her head out from under the table, large ears quivering. The noise around us was thunderous with the stamping of boots, humming of voices and clinking of coins.

'You're not going to hide down there, are you?' I said, a little surprised. It wasn't like her at all, she was usually so brash and full of herself – I normally have trouble convincing her to keep a low profile when we're out on the streets.

Then it occurred to me that Ang has only dealt with humans before, and she's used to lording it over them. Men used to fear and revere coblynau in the mines, even leaving out food to ensure their continued affability. But at the Market you had to pay attention to the shape of your customer, and many of them were pretty monstrous.

There was at least one lumbering troll in the crowd. Granted, it was on a leash, but that was no less reason to be worried about it. There were plenty of figures that looked human-shaped at first glance. But out of the corner of your eye you'd see the flick of a tail, or the glint of much-too-sharp teeth. Or perhaps you'd smell the stench of rotten meat, or the taste of seawater in the air.

'C'mon, Ang. Work to be done, eh?'

She nodded reluctantly and began handing up stock to the table. 'You know many people here, *gwas?*'

'Oh, nearly everyone,' I said modestly. 'Extensive list of contacts. You've got to know who's who in this business.'

'Who's 'im, then?' She pointed at the trader across from us. He had no table. Instead, a stack of glass tanks filled with murky water and suspicious seaweed made up his pitch.

'That's Tony Gill,' I replied. 'Deals in aquatic . . . creatures.'

''E looks slimy. And 'e stinks o' fish.'

'He catches them himself.'

A similarly slimy customer approached Gill's stall. Ang watched in rapt fascination as the two conversed before exchanging currency and handshakes. She flinched as the customer stuck his head deep into one of the tanks. The water gurgled, and the man emerged with a splash. Three flailing tentacles were briefly visible before they were sucked into his mouth. If you looked too closely you could see movement under the bulging skin of his throat.

Ang looked too closely.

'Try not to throw up on anything valuable,' I said. I didn't bother hiding my grin as I went back to arranging my display. Pride of place would go to the bluecap, my big score. But I'd wait awhile first, build up a crowd – and then a big reveal. *Waves,* I tell you!

'Hansard! How do, mate?'

My hand was gripped in the firm handshake of one surprisingly tanned Irishman.

'Tracey!' I responded warmly. 'Didn't know you were back over here, good to see you in one piece. How was the continent?'

'Full of competition.' He grimaced. 'Got a few more songs in my belt, for what it's worth. Not much call for a traditional siren these days. Too many of my kind have packed it in for bloody pop stardom.'

'Can't say I blame them,' I mused. 'Who wouldn't want a life of fame and fortune?'

'Someone who doesn't want to be hunted down for singing people to death.'

'Ah.' Fair point. Can't say I envied his situation.

Ang re-emerged looking a little less green and began digging around the bags for a stray pasty.

'Who's the kid?' exclaimed Tracey. 'Don't tell me you've picked up some foundling?'

Ang turned her wizened face on him, her gaze chilly and unimpressed. Tracey took a step back. 'Hey now, didn't mean any harm. Didn't realise you were a knocker, that's all.'

I stepped between them as fire lit up Ang's eyes. 'You see, it's–'

'*Not knocker.*'

'–a bit tricky because–'

'*Nor knacker.*'

'–she doesn't–'

'*Coblyn,* I am!'

'–like that word,' I finished lamely. I leaned closer in a conspiratorial manner. 'Between you and me, she's given me my biggest score ever. She can call herself what she wants.'

Tracey's stunned expression twisted into amusement. 'What score would this be? You've never had a good sale as long as I've known you.'

'All shall be revealed in good time.' I knew I sounded smug. I didn't care; I was enjoying myself too much.

'You sure you're not going to reveal yourself to be a prat?'

'Have some faith!'

'Well, it wouldn't be the first time.'

Ang popped up between us. 'Thought you said ye were some kind o' big man here, *gwas?*' She regarded me with a very critical gaze.

'I am! Or, I will be. Soon. Very soon.'

Tracey shook his head disparagingly. 'Your problem, Hansard, is that you don't have a niche. Just look at this mishmash of crap you're selling.' He waved his hand at my entire pitch.

'You're wrong there,' I said. 'I've had lots of niches.'

'I mean you need to have a niche for more than five minutes.'

'Ye do seem t'get bored o' things real quick,' said Ang.

'Oh, shut up, both of you.'

'You ain't really anything here, are ye?' she continued, and her gaze soured further. 'Tupenny merchant o' tat is what you are. 'Anyone who's anyone', my arse!'

'Why don't you take a walk!' I spat back. 'Go and eat somebody else's food for five fucking minutes!'

Despite the incessant roar from the throngs of people milling around us, it was like a little bubble of silence had bloomed in our tiny circle.

'That's how't is, is it?' said Ang slowly. I suddenly found myself recalling the old stories of rocks inexplicably falling on miners' heads when they were rude to the spirits of the mine. I tried not to instinctively duck.

Ang readjusted her cap over her dishevelled curls, picked up her lantern, gave me a final unforgiving look, and disappeared into the crowd.

'Looks like you're in the doghouse,' murmured Tracey.

'Pretty sure I've been living there for the past month,' I said gloomily.

'Drink?'

'Ought to sell something first. Anyway, there's my big reveal. I'm not joking, you know.'

'Of course you're not,' said Tracey, with more than an ounce of pity in his voice.

'Shouldn't you be working?' I said irritably. 'Singing happiness at people and what-not?'

'Just browsing. I'll earn my living later.' He broke off, distracted by a group of women passing by my stall. 'Ladies,' he said, in his most charming voice (which, for a siren, is about as charming as you can get).

They flashed large, dark eyes at him and batted their ridiculously long lashes. They had a barely-there, waif-like quality about them. The tallest of the three picked out a ring from my table and offered it forward. In a rich, breathy voice she said, 'How much for this?'

'A kiss and it's yours, fine lady,' said Tracey, stealing my cue.

She twirled mossy hair in her fingers. 'Surely not enough for such a pretty thing.' She paused, lips parted, pink and inviting. I looked on, bored. 'Perhaps I give you a better price?' she said, with a deep sigh that sounded like the wind.

'I would be honoured to . . . *barter*, with you.' Tracey bowed, like the ludicrous poseur he was. 'Devin Tracey, at your service, fine lady.'

She giggled and held out a beckoning hand. I pulled Tracey back and whispered in his ear.

'You saw she's a huldra, right?'

'Of course. How could I resist something like that?'

'Cow tails turn me off.'

'Your loss.'

'I've heard their backs are covered in tree bark, as well.'

'How about I tell you later?'

I watched him saunter after the seductress and her companions, unsure whether I should be envious or not. I can't say I've particularly experimented in the non-human area of the bedroom. Too much chance of something weird or painful happening to your valuables, if you catch my meaning.

Now that all the distractions were gone, I could finally turn my full attention to *sales*.

I'd rolled up my shirt sleeves and was just launching into my patter when I heard the commotion. I would have thought nothing of it, if it weren't for the screeching Welsh insults that punctuated the uproar.

I groaned and vacated my pitch, then fought my way through the rabble (which was quickly turning into a mob at the prospect of a fight) towards the source of the ruckus near the centre of the Market. As I leapt over the last table (and the shoulders of an angry Sandman) I found Ang ferociously grappling with two men trying to hold her down.

'*Basdun!*' she screamed. '*Give them back!*'

'Hold it!' I shouted, just as one man raised a club, ready to crack

Ang upside her head. I ran in, hands held out placatingly. 'Hey now, what's she done, eh? No need for this, she'll be quiet– right Ang? Ang! *Ang.* Be quiet.'

She shut up long enough for one of her assailants to answer me. 'Caught the little goblin stealin' shit,' he said. 'You know the rules. Hands to y'self.'

'I'm sure there's been a misunderstanding here,' I assured. 'Ang isn't the thieving type, honestly.'

'*He's got my bluecaps! That* basdun *has my bluecaps!*'

'What?' I looked round, startled. Sure enough, there were five bottled bluecaps sitting proudly on a table not three feet away.

'*Whose* bluecaps?' said another voice. This one I recognised. It was almost as charming as Tracey's, and it made me want to punch it repeatedly. Its owner ambled forwards and leaned down to stare into Ang's eyes. He smiled condescendingly. 'My dear, these are not *your* bluecaps. You see, they are in my possession. That makes them *my* bluecaps.'

'You thieving *basdun! Cer i grafu!*'

He straightened and turned to me. 'Is this chap with you, Hansard? You should teach him better manners.'

I clenched my jaw, politely refraining from knocking the smug smile off Edric Mercer's face. I cannot fully express how much I hate this man. He wears a stupid, long red leather coat. I bet he thinks it makes him look cool. I also wear a long coat, but mine is completely practical and necessary for my work. I'd be nothing without all these pockets. And he has a hat. Big floppy thing with a wide brim and a feather in it. A feather, for goodness' sake!

'Where did you acquire those bluecaps?' I asked, biting back the insult my mouth was begging to tack on the end.

The smug bastard tapped the side of his nose and smirked. 'You know how it is, Hansard. Can't go revealing tricks of the trade.'

'Tricks like stealing from other traders, you mean?'

He merely smiled and waved graciously at his two lackeys. 'You can let the little one up. I hardly think we need to fear such a small menace.'

I managed to grab hold of Ang before she could lunge for Mercer's knees.

'You should keep an eye on him,' Edric continued. 'Wouldn't want any more misunderstandings. Such things can be fatal, you know.'

'Indeed.' I squared my shoulders. 'I'd hate for you to be implicated in a similar kind of . . . misunderstanding.'

I moved to leave, but he stopped me with a hand on my shoulder and murmured, 'You should watch your back in this pond, Hansard. You're such a little fish.' He smiled again and turned away.

Bastard. He always has to have the last word.

'Why are we leavin'?' hissed Ang. 'We need to get them bluecaps back!'

'Are you nuts? They string people up for thievery around here.'

'He's the one should be strung up.'

'Can't say I disagree. Are you certain those bluecaps were yours?'

Despite being so much shorter, she managed to look down her nose at me. 'I *know* them's mine. What kind o' coblyn would I be, if I couldn't recognise mine own kin?'

I didn't doubt her.

It felt like too much of a coincidence, the bluecaps turning up right in front of our noses. And how did the quiet-eyed thief at Cockermouth fit in? Did Mercer hire her? Or maybe she only sold him the bluecaps? Either way, he'd be making all that money which should be rightfully mine.

But that wasn't the worst of it. Suddenly, I found myself robbed of my thunder. My one bluecap was nice, but not as nice as five. And all anyone would remember was that Edric Mercer had them first. He's always first. *Bastard.*

Gloom enveloped me as we both walked back to my pitch. So much for waves. So much for glory and a fantastic tale to tell. So much for my chance in the spotlight.

Sod this Market. Maybe I'd just pack up and leave so I didn't have to see Mercer's smug face again.

I looked up, trying to shrug off the descending melancholy.

And then, across the crowd, I saw patient, quiet eyes.

* * *

I crashed wildly through the hall. Snarls and growls followed in my wake – what's a few trampled toes and elbowed faces? – I was too intent on my goal to pay them any mind. I reached the spot where I'd seen her and spun round in desperation.

'Where'd she go?' I shouted frantically. I threw myself into a nearby cluster of people, certain she must be hiding amongst them.

'Watch yourself, mate,' said one of the surly men as I broke through.

I grabbed him by the shoulders and screamed into his face. *'The woman. Did you see her?'* With a stunned expression, he dumbly shook his head.

'What woman?' said a less easily fazed member of the crew.

'She was right over there! She has these . . . eyes,' I floundered. Their blank faces told me I sounded as mad out loud as I did in my head. I shoved past them and into a new stream of people.

'Slow down, *twpsyn!'*

A tug on my coat had me stumbling. Another step and I was flat on my face. I groaned, little sparks of pain igniting in my wrists and knees. Small but heavy work boots came level with my face, and then Ang's piercing grey eyes came into view.

'Ye want a hand up, *gwas?'*

'Please,' I mumbled.

She walked out of sight and began to kick me in the side. 'Get up,' she said. 'Get up, get up, get up.'

'Ouch, *stop that.*' I picked myself up and rubbed what was probably a blossoming bruise.

'What you chasin' after, anyways?'

I scanned the swarming crowd distractedly. 'That woman. The thief. You know.'

Ang looked confused for a moment, then my words sunk in. '*Where?*' she hissed. 'Wait 'til I get my hands on that light-fingered *ast.*'

There were too many people. You could have your eyes trained on one figure and lose sight of it in an instant. It's the kind of crowd I usually love: easy to hide in.

People meander around markets in streams. They weave in and out like the currents in a river, and they create swirling eddies where two opposing courses meet. The biggest, most famous traders are like islands, and the currents part around them – even if the island decides to go for a walk.

People knocked my shoulders as they pushed by. I'm more of a pebble than an island. But the lady with the quiet eyes, she might as well be a grain of sand.

I laid a hand on Ang's bristling shoulders. 'We're not going to find her now. It's too easy to disappear here.'

'Well, we'll *un*-disappear her,' Ang seethed. 'We'll make her regret–'

'Later, Ang. Let's go back to the stall, make some money. We've got three nights here, and plenty of people to speak to. *Someone* will know who she is.'

'Y'reckon?' she said doubtfully.

In truth my sense of self-preservation had just caught up with me. Chasing after that thief? Was I mad? We already knew from experience that she must be powerful – she had the ability to hide from scrying stones and she'd bested a big old shellycoat on its home turf. I'd sworn off further attempts to try and locate her. Not worth it.

'She might have a reputation,' I said, despite myself. 'People with reputations cause a lot of gossip.'

'Like that Mercer.'

'Yes, like– What do you mean?'

'Heard others tellin' tales about him. When I was looking o'er his goods and saw mine own bluecaps there. Lots o' gossip about him, it seems. What's his reputation?'

'None worth talking about,' I muttered. 'C'mon, let's go.' I steered her back the way we'd come. Her boots thumped on the tiles as she kept pace.

'I hates 'im much as you, *gwas*. But I wants t'know what sort o' man he is. Can't size up an enemy based on size alone. Is he known t'be a thief?'

I considered this, reluctantly. 'Sort of,' I decided. 'Look, I'm not saying any of this is true, but they say he's stolen all sorts of impossible things from impossible places.'

'How impossible?'

'Oh, I don't know. They *say* he's been to the underworld and wrestled treasures from the jaws of Cerberus. They say he's played dice with gods and won; he's eaten fey food and lived to tell the tale. He's caught wild nightmares bare-handed, and apparently ridden every type of supernatural horse you can imagine – even a feral hippocamp, and I've no idea how he managed to breathe underwater to do that. They *say* he can acquire anything you want, whether it's dragon gold or a lock of Samson's hair. No challenge has got the best of him yet. You see? Complete bastard.'

Ang glanced at me sidelong. 'You wish ye were more like 'im, eh, *gwas?*'

I stiffened. 'Who would want to be like him? He's a ponce. He's arrogant, pretentious, manipulative, and . . . and have you seen his hat? It has a *feather* in it.'

'Not like ye at all, then.'

I resisted the urge to throw something at her.

'I don't want to be anything like him,' I said, half to myself. We reached our table, which remained right as I'd left it, happily untouched.

It's an interesting thing about the Market, there's a code of sorts. Everything is fair game if you're out on the road. Woe betide you if you loudly proclaim that you're travelling to such-and-such a place with something rare and valuable on your hands. You may as well order yourself a personalised mugging on the way.

Different matter altogether at one of the big markets, like this one. Steal from a trader *here* and you risk the wrath of an entire mob falling upon you. A mob which has been drinking and looking for an excuse to have a fight, no less.

Anywhere else, leaving your wares unattended is an invitation for thievery. Here, it just looks like a trap. No one is that stupid. Especially with so many watchful, suspicious eyes at every turn.

And the Regulators make up some of those pairs of eyes. These are the serious individuals in sombre grey suits, holding clipboards and asking penetrating questions. There are, if you can believe it, items that are banned from sale on the Black Market. It's a very short but very dangerous list of things, and the Regulators make sure none of them turn up at the annual Market.

At least, they don't turn up for very long. Regulators have very direct methods. A long drop with a short stop, if you catch my meaning.

Nothing gets in the way of their job quite as much as uncontrolled violence, so they're quick to nip situations – like thieving – in the bud. And it's my fear of their direct methods that makes me think twice about stealing our bluecaps back from Edric Mercer. Unjust as the situation was, it was too risky to try anything here.

We could go after Miss Quiet-Eyes, instead, I thought. *Track her down, maybe find some leverage against her or Mercer. There must be someone here who knows who she is.*

I couldn't believe I was considering this.

Now if only I could remember what she looked like.

Next to me, Ang yawned and smacked her lips loudly. 'How long we gunna be at this, *gwas?*'

I checked my watch. Half past two in the morning.

'People will probably start bedding down in about five hours.' I grinned at Ang's disbelieving expression. 'It's a nocturnal market, Ang. People have travelled a long way to get here. Everyone wants to mingle and drink and party.'

'I notice you ain't mingling.'

I pretended not to hear and busied myself with re-arranging the artefacts on the table. Customers, that's what I wanted. A good distraction to stop me from stewing over the fact that somewhere in this crowd was a thief, and that thief had given my property to Edric bloody Mercer.

'*Myttin da*, friends,' said a voice, apparently from nowhere. 'Down here.'

I peered over the table and saw a pointy-eared man, almost three feet tall. He wore a grimy hard-hat with a flashlight attached, and equally grimy overalls. He cracked a friendly smile and stuck out a hand.

'Name's Goron. *Da yw genev metya genes!*' It took me a moment to realise he was speaking primarily to Ang. She stared at his outstretched hand with bewilderment, and then shook it, uncertainly. '*Pyth yw dha hanow?*' said the stranger. Ang looked at me for help; all I could do was shrug. I didn't understand either. He looked at us, from one to the other. '*A wodhes'ta kewsel Kernewek?*'

'Sorry,' I began, 'we don't really understand . . .'

'Ye don't speak Cornish?' he said, giving Ang a look of surprise.

She remained puzzled for just a moment longer, when it finally dawned on her. '*Knocker*,' she rasped, getting riled up all over again. 'Thought ye were coblynau, I did.' She spat at his feet, for good measure.

He seemed quite taken aback by this. 'Coblyn?' he said, aghast. 'I heard ye'd all hid ye'selves away! We 'aven't heard from our kin in those parts fer years.'

'Do I look hid away, ye *drewgi*? Take yer eyes and scratch 'em somewhere else.'

The knocker, far from looking insulted, actually appeared amused. He extended his hand once more. 'Sorry for me brash introduction. I saw ye o'er by the bluecaps held by Mercer. Did he really steal them from ye?'

'Aye,' said Ang, angrily batting his hand away. 'And it's no business of yourn.'

'Cretinous, that is,' Goron continued conversationally. ''E should be strung up fer it. Especially for vexin' such a handsome woman.'

'Eh?'

'Ye have eyes as slick as slate, girl. Strong arms, like a real putter. And a feisty temper t'boot. I'd like t' take ye fer a drink.' He doffed his hard-hat to her, leaving Ang wide-eyed and open-mouthed.

Coblynau, spending all their time underground, naturally have a very pale complexion. The blush creeping up Ang's cheeks was quite a brilliant contrast.

'Off with you, ye soft-headed *ffwl!*' she said.

'I think she means she'll think about it,' I said brightly. Ang shot me a dirty look.

Goron the knocker placed his hat back on his head at what he probably thought was a jaunty angle. He winked at Ang. 'I'll ask ye again tomorrow, lass. You're the finest *bal maiden* I ever did see.'

He strutted off with a huge smile splitting his face in half.

'What's a *bal maiden*?' Ang asked me, after a while.

'Dunno. Haven't picked up any Cornish. I think *bal* might mean 'mine'? You hear knockers talking about home a lot and the word crops up.'

'Hm.'

'You going to see him, you think?'

'No,' she replied vehemently. 'Not some nasty knocker.' She grew thoughtful for a moment. 'Mind you, always thought knockers were s'posed to be ugly.'

'Don't you know what they look like?'

'Everyone knows what knockers look like. Warty and long-nosed and fat like a ball o' lard.'

'You both look very similar to me.'

'*Twpsyn.*' She grabbed a wrapped pasty and the flask of tea. 'I'm going t'sleep in the car. Away from knockers and thieves and other nasties.'

I tossed her the keys and watched her slip away through the crowd. It was thinning out as people drifted towards the bars at the edges of the room. Probably Ang's admirer was having a drink at one of them. It made me chuckle – I had told Ang that she was bound to see something here she'd never seen before.

* * *

By the leaden light of morning I had a headache and hadn't found out a single thing about the lady-thief with the quiet eyes. I'd tried speaking to other traders, but quickly realised that it was going to be difficult to get information on a person I couldn't even describe. The only thing I could pinpoint was the way her eyes looked. It bothered the hell out of me.

I slept fitfully through the daytime, wrapped in a blanket under my table in the massive warehouse. The Market never quite slept, but it did lower the volume from roar to hubbub, with a baseline of snoring all across the room.

When the sun dipped outside, it was our cue to return to business. The night brought with it a few late arrivals to the Market, and there was a burst of squabbling over what little space was left. One latecomer in particular caught my attention, and revived my hope of finding our thief.

'We're going to seek some professional help,' I told Ang.

'Thought you was the professional, *gwas*,' Ang snorted, mouth full of pastry. She'd decided the best way to adjust to staying up all night was to eat constantly and drink endless cups of tea. I felt it was making her more irritable than usual. I hoped she wouldn't discover coffee.

'Yes, well, sometimes even the professionals need professional help. To find our thief, we need a specialist.'

'Hah.' She sprayed crumbs over the table. I brushed them off with a grimace. 'You said ye had 'contacts', *gwas*. None o' these lot seem eager to be in contact wi' ye, 'cept this Irish fella.'

The Irish fella was Devin Tracey, who had taken to lounging by my stall when he wasn't chasing not-quite human ladies into bed. I think he was fascinated by Ang (and I hoped it wasn't for the same reason he was fascinated by other non-human ladies).

'I don't see why you're having so much trouble,' he said amiably. 'You know she's *here*. Do some proper detective work. Ask around til you find someone that matches her description.'

I sighed. 'That's just the problem. I don't have a description.'

'Oh, come on now. What does she look like?'

'I don't know.'

'Rubbish. What colour was her hair?'

'I don't know.'

'Style, then. Long? Short? To her shoulders? Mohican?'

'*I don't know,*' I said in frustration. 'Tracey, it's like she occupies this black hole in my head. There's just empty space where she should be.'

He turned his attention to Ang. 'How about you, little coblyn? You got a better memory than our friend here?'

She slowed her chewing and looked thoughtful, and then confused. 'I . . . remembers her eyes,' she said. 'Sort of, calm, like. Peaceful, I thought.'

'Yes!' I exclaimed. 'It's the one feature I can recall. I've started thinking of her as Quiet Eyes, actually.'

Ang nodded. 'Yeah, that's right. Buggered if I can remember anything else though.'

'That's all?' Tracey rubbed his chin. 'Must have been beautiful eyes, then. I'd like to help you find her, I really would.'

'Ye can't do a worse job than this *mwnci.*'

'Look here, it isn't my fault–'

'Aye, it never is.' She pointed an accusatory digit at me. 'Yer too busy makin' excuses to do any good, an' too full o' lies t'be worth anything. You told me ye could find my missing kin – and so far we gots nothing! Why would ye be any better at findin' a thief? I bet you ain't even looking. Too 'fraid to find her.'

'I am *not* afraid,' I said firmly, failing to convince myself of the lie. 'So everyone's going to stop criticising my abilities, and we're going to talk to a specialist.' I stood up, grabbing Ang by the arm. 'Watch the stall for me, Tracey. Won't be long. Don't give my stuff away to girls just because they're pretty.'

'What about men?'

'What?'

'Men can be pretty, too.'

'Don't give my stuff away. Let's go, Ang.'

The latecomer we were looking for was easy to find among the hodgepodge of colours and shapes that made up the rows of traders. For a start, her pitch protruded higher than anyone else's, and it stood out with bright reds, greens, and gold ornamentation. There's also the fact that it was a caravan, which was pretty distinctive in itself.

It was a traditional horse-drawn Romani caravan, owned by one Reva Longley. The advantage of a caravan is that you have the upper hand when it comes to claiming territory, and Reva had muscled her way in-between a seller of theurgical perfumes and a carver of sentient woods. Her horse stood in the middle of the aisle, a peaceful, immobile giant, contentedly munching in its nosebag while the perfume seller argued with the wood carver over who would have to clean up the freshly deposited manure.

'We're goin' to a gypsy?' said Ang. 'Them's as bad as witches.'

'How would you know? You've never met one.'

'Heard stories,' she said darkly.

Ang wasn't entirely wrong. Old folktales give plenty of warning about 'gypsies' who place curses on unwary travellers and anyone foolish enough to cross them. But history – and folklore – is often unkind to outsiders, which the travelling Romani peoples usually were wherever they went, and the myth of the 'gypsy' had followed them like a curse of its own.

So perhaps it was an interesting parallel with Ang's comparison that the Romani, like witches, had also suffered a long history of persecution – and perhaps it's natural to assume they might have become gifted in the arts of revenge magic as a result. But if they were, then you wouldn't buy such a thing from Reva. Her specialisms lay strictly in the removal of enchantments rather than in the placing of them.

She is also well-known for her spectacularly good eyesight. I mean, she doesn't even have to unfocus to see a pixie – it's just *there*, to her.

And woe betide you if you try to lie to her face: your words are as transparent as glass. So, I reason, if there's anyone that could see where our thief is hiding, it's got to be Reva.

I hopped up the steps and rapped my knuckles on the gaudily painted wood.

'Enter.'

We ducked through the curtain and into the dark, smoky interior. Incense, the rich and sweet scent of vanilla. Reva sat gracefully on the other side of a slim table, the smoke curling about her long black hair. She gazed at me with dark, soulful eyes.

'Mr Hansard.'

'Reva.' I felt like bowing, but there wasn't enough room. A respectful nod instead, then.

'Who is your friend?' Her eyes flicked to Ang by my side.

''m Ang,' said the coblyn. She seemed a little awestruck. Most people are, when they meet Reva for the first time. She has a real talent for creating atmosphere, and this tiny room was full of it. Add in the vision of herself: the billowing folds of satin that embraced her tawny skin, the small beads that caught the light around her neck, and the petite gold chain that glittered on her head . . . and then she'd smile at you, and it would give you this lovely warm glow inside like suddenly you're the luckiest person in the world to be at the centre of her attention for just this moment.

She smiled.

'It's nice to meet you, Ang. And to see you again, Mr Hansard. What can I do for you?'

I shook myself. 'Hm? Yes, right. I'd like your help. I was hoping you could help me find someone.'

'A woman?'

I don't know why, but I blushed. Maybe because Reva had a way of insinuating a whole lot while saying very little. 'Yes. A thief, as it happens.'

'She has wronged you?'

'Yes.'

'Very well.' She nodded to us, and we moved to take a seat on our side of the table. She held up a hand. 'Fifty pounds, Mr Hansard.'

'Thirty.'

'That's a shame. I thought you wished to do business?'

'Thirty-five.'

'Fifty.'

'Forty.'

'Fifty.'

'Forty-five?'

'Fifty.' She smiled sweetly. 'You are not in a position to haggle, am I right, Mr Hansard? You wish to find this woman?'

'I do,' I said, defeated. 'Fifty.'

'Thank you. A girl needs to make a living.'

'You seem to be living pretty well already,' I said, eyeing up the gold leaf decoration inside the cabin.

'We will consult cards,' Reva declared, pulling out a pack.

'That tarot witchery?' said Ang suspiciously.

'Tarot is for tourists.' She splayed the deck on the table. Every card was blank.

Ang stared at her incredulously. 'How you meant to read 'em if there's nothing there?'

Again, that sweet smile. 'Practice.' She turned to me. 'Do you have anything that has been in the possession of this woman?'

'Yes.' I rummaged in my coat pockets.

'Do we?' said Ang. 'How come you've got– Oh, I see.'

I proffered the bottled bluecap, the only one we had rescued from the clutches of the thief. I hoped it would be enough.

Reva passed her hands over it, closed her eyes, and nodded. It would be enough.

She shuffled the pack and began to deal the cards one by one.

'So what's she doin' now?'

'*Shush,* Ang,' I said.

We watched in silence as each card was laid down, gradually filling the surface of the table. No mysterious marks or other signs appeared to us, but Reva leaned over and inspected them intently. A sharp intake of breath suggested she'd seen something we couldn't. Her hand hovered over the card in question, and she extended one slender finger to tap it. She drew her hand away and looked up at us through long lashes.

'You know she is here?'

'Yes. But I think she knows we know, and she's hiding. I want a name, and anything else you can tell me.'

Reva's features were unreadable, though I sensed she was mulling over her response. She knew something, all right.

Eventually she spoke, and I hated the answer. 'Mr Hansard, you must not try to find this woman.'

'What? But–'

She held up a finger, silencing me without a word.

'It goes very bad for you, I think, if you find her.'

'But why?'

Reva hesitated, as if trying to decide how much to tell me.

'I want my fifty pounds worth,' I said petulantly.

'Then perhaps your money buys you protection, instead of information.'

I was gobsmacked. 'I'm sorry, let me get this straight. You want me to pay you to tell me absolutely nothing, is that right? No deal, sister. No way.'

She pursed her lips and drew in a deep breath. 'Then let me tell you this. She is not hiding. She does not fear you. She is bad news, and so are her associates. You should forget about her, Mr Hansard. She is out of your league.'

That got me. Like a punch in the gut.

'What 'ssociates?' said Ang. I'd all but forgotten she was beside me.

'You should be fearful of them.'

'We don't know who they bloody are!' I snapped. 'How can we stay away from someone we don't know? Stop wasting my time.' I snatched the bluecap up from the table. 'We're done here, Ang.'

'Wait,' said Reva, as we reached the door. There was clearly a battle inside her head, and a little bit of it had spilled onto her face. 'Hansard . . . Have you heard of Baines and Grayle?'

Something clicked in the back of my mind. They were familiar words. 'No, I don't think so.'

'Now you have. And you should stay away.'

She looked at me kindly, and I recognised the look for what it was. It's the look you give to a child who wants to go and play with the big kids on the swings. It's a look that says, 'you're too little for that sort of thing', and it made me feel small as hell.

Little fish, Mercer had called me.

I threw open the curtain and marched angrily out into the thronging masses.

At first I marched without purpose, and then my feet took charge and turned me round towards the centre of the Market. And suddenly I knew exactly where I was going, and I was going there with the rage of the righteous on my side. I could hear Ang struggling to keep up, but she sounded muted, far away and drowned out by the blood boiling in my ears.

I clenched my fists and marched right up to Edric Mercer and his fancy table, right there in the very centre of the Market, right at the centre of everyone's attention, just like he always is.

He caught sight of me, that smug, slightly amused smile sliding straight onto his face, and before I could think about it I had thrown the first punch.

The world went very loud and chaotic, and then totally black.

Episode 7: Quiet Eyes

Clanging. My head. Like a bell. Exploding. Like a melon full of . . . of . . . fire. All mushy. No, not mushy. Hard, like a bell. *Clanging.*

With what felt like Herculean effort, I levered my eyes open. I discovered that the world was swaying, and apparently upside-down. I groaned, or tried to. It came out more like a gurgle.

'Nice of you to join us,' said a dry voice to my left.

I turned my head and saw the face of Edric Mercer about a foot away, at the same orientation as myself. Warm satisfaction flowed through me as I noticed the purple bruise under his eye. I was vaguely aware that I was the cause of it.

'Ah, you're awake. Good,' said another voice. It spoke in clipped tones and belonged to a woman who, despite being the wrong way up, was clearly a Regulator. Mercer groaned for the both of us. 'You will answer when I call your name.' The Regulator consulted her clipboard. 'Albert Two-Toes?'

'Here,' said someone gruffly.

'Berlinda Bloodhorn?'

'Yes,' moaned another.

'Edric Mercer?'

'Present.'

'Jack Hansard?'

'Mm.'

'Kale Stevens?'

'Here.'

'And what is the knocker's name, please?'

'Coblyn . . .' Ang responded, feebly.

'What was that?'

'Her name's Ang,' I chipped in. 'She's a coblyn, not a knocker.'

The Regulator peered at me over her glasses. 'What's the difference?'

'She's Welsh.'

'I see.' She made a note on her clipboard. Probably adding Ang to a list. Regulators love lists. 'I trust you all understand you are being held here due to your involvement in the fracas earlier this evening. Tell me please, who started the fight?'

Despite the growing ache from the blood pooling in our heads, no one spoke up. We all knew what to do; like chastised schoolchildren, we stuck to our silence. You don't grass up your enemy. You just beat him up later, in a quieter location.

The Regulator knew this too and wasn't about to waste effort on a small bust-up. At least, I hoped it was only a small bust-up. I hadn't been conscious for most of it.

She exhaled in an exasperated but resigned manner. 'All right, then. You will be given permission to leave once someone has come forward to vouch for your character. You will be released on the understanding that you will not be involved in any further disturbances. All future infractions will result in a far more *permanent* solution. Have I made the situation quite clear? Please affirm your acceptance of these terms.' This was met with a chorus of groaned assent. 'Good.'

She motioned to a snub-nosed troll loitering nearby. It stepped forward, raising a giant cleaver in its enormous fist. We shrank back as much as a collective of hanging bodies could. The troll swung, and Mercer hit the ground with a thump.

'Mr Mercer, we have already received your character reference. You are free to go.'

He picked himself up, unsteadily. He must have been quite dazed, because he staggered off without throwing one witty quip behind him.

The Regulator cast a cursory eye over her remaining captives. 'As for the rest of you, you will remain hanging until I receive a reference, or you suffer a brain haemorrhage. Whichever comes first.'

A small crowd had gathered around us. We were the free entertainment for the evening. A stone bounced off my head. Ang squeaked somewhere to my right.

I scanned the upside-down faces of the mob for one I recognised.

Front and centre in the crowd, one gaze met mine.

A calm, quiet gaze.

I couldn't believe my own eyes. She was still here – she was *right here!* I tried to call out, but my voice was strangled in my throat. I tried to take in her face, her features, her hair, every identifying mark and crease in her skin, and tried to burn the image onto my retinas. All the while her cool, quiet eyes followed me. I think there was a smile on her lips, but I couldn't say for sure.

With a flick of her hair, she turned away.

'Wait,' I croaked as she slipped into the crowd. '*Wait!*'

She was gone. Again.

My head was thumping. I felt like I might pass out.

'*Dydh ha,* my lovely,' said a familiar gravelly voice. Through the descending haze I could just make out a grimy yellow hard-hat. ''Scuse me, I'd like ta vouch fer the lady here. She be of fine and stalwart character.'

'You vouch for Ms Bloodhorn?'

'What? Nah, ye blind *bobby.* This lady, the fair coblyn.'

'I see. And you are?' said the Regulator.

'Name's Goron. Blacksmith, I am. Enchanted iron and the like.'

I heard the scratching of a pen on paper, followed by a soft *swish* and *thump*.

'Ye alright, lass?'

'Get y'smelly hands off me. Go away.'

''ng,' I implored. It was getting harder to breathe.

'Oh. Could ye vouch for him, also?'

'D'int 'e get ye into this trouble?'

'Avenging my bluecaps, he was.'

'Ah, say no more!'

Black clouds were edging in on my vision. My cheeks felt puffed full of cement, trying to drag my head clean off my neck.

There was a *swish* and a *thump,* and a great deal of pain.

'Nngh,' my throat articulated.

'Don't do it again,' said the Regulator, standing over me. 'We keep track of offences, you know.'

'Nngh.'

'C'mon lad, up ye get.'

Two pairs of wiry hands gripped me under my shoulders and hauled me to my knees. They couldn't really haul me much higher than that. I lurched to my feet and patted down my pockets. Everything in order, nothing broken, except . . . oh. I withdrew my hand from inside my coat and shook the sticky residue from it. That was the last of my discount Invincibility Cordial. Ironic, that.

I took stock of my other essentials: my jaw felt swollen, my left shoulder was on fire, every bit of me ached, and I discovered a nasty cut across the palm of my hand.

'You any good with a needle, Ang?' I asked blearily, pressing my coat sleeve into the cut.

'I can darn socks,' she said uncertainly. 'More at home with a pick, really.'

'I'd like t'see ye at work wi'a pick, lass,' said Goron.

'You ain't gonna see nothing of the sort!' Ang replied hotly.

'Calm down, both of you. Let's get back before more trouble finds us.'

Ang threw me a sidelong glance. 'With respect, *gwas*, ye went out of your way to find that last spot of trouble.'

I rubbed my aching jaw, trying to recall the events that had led up to it. I remembered visiting Reva, and I remembered the way she had looked at me, and the bitter anger that had propelled me all the way to Mercer's pitch. And, with a dark satisfaction I hadn't felt in a long time, I remembered finally giving in to temptation and punching the smug git square in the face.

'How big was the fight, in the end? Six of us strung up, were there?'

'Them's just the ones that were too slow,' said Goron cheerfully. 'Most of 'em legged it soon as the Reg'later turned up. Ye shoulda seen that troll o' hers in action. Well, ye were on the receivin' end, so I'd wager ye saw enough.'

My shoulder twinged louder. 'I suppose I'm glad I don't recall the details. Were they all Mercer's boys?'

'Naw. Most were just passin' by. Jumped in fer the fun've it. *Bobbys*, the lot of 'em.'

'*Bobbys?*'

'Idiots, lad. Who's fool enough to join a fight in this place? Ye'd have t'be a bleddy great *dobeck* to risk bein' noticed by one o' them Reg'later types.'

''Twas a damn *ffwl* thing, *gwas*. Didn't think ye had it in you,' agreed Ang.

'All right, everyone makes mistakes,' I said irritably. 'Mercer had it coming, anyway.'

'Aye, he did,' said Ang. 'But mebbe ye should have picked your moment, like.'

'Next time git yeself hid first. Come at 'im sideways,' suggested

Goron. 'If 'twere me, I'd pick me a good high spot, then *caggle* 'im proper!'

Ang and I exchanged looks. It was nice to not be the only one lost in translation for a change. Ang was the one who asked. 'What's *caggle?*'

'Means t'cover 'im in filth! Pour a great ol' tub of muck on 'is 'ead!' Goron exclaimed gleefully.

Ang cackled loudly. 'I'd pay t'see that thievin' *basdun* wallowing in muck, like a pig in a pen. Ha! Fittin' for such a colossal *pen pigyn!*'

'Ee, I do love a maid that can cuss.' Goron reached into a pocket in his overalls and pulled out a small parcel of brown paper. He held it out to Ang. 'I 'spect ye be famished after that quarrel. I brought ye another *hoggan*, lass.'

Ang's eyes lit up. She greedily snatched the package from his hands, then tried (and failed, miserably) to conceal her delight.

'Gifts be getting ye nowhere,' she said loftily. 'I just don't like things t'go to waste, is all.'

Goron cracked a smile as he watched her rip into the paper. The smell of warm pastry reached my nose. She bit into the shell of the *hoggan*. Meat juice dribbled down her chin.

'He give 'em to me this mornin',' she whispered to me, around mouthfuls. 'He's a smelly ol' knocker, but his pasties ain't half tasty.'

I think Goron may have fathomed the path to Ang's heart. I wondered if that was the traditional way to woo a knocker. Maybe their version of a romantic, candlelit dinner was a good solid Cornish pasty shared by lamplight in an intimate corner of the mine. Maybe next to a good seam of coal to provide the romantic backdrop.

We reached my pitch. It stuck out on the end of the row: less like a sore thumb, more like a broken one – at an odd angle and going slightly green around the edges. Despite my best efforts it was still woefully full of stock, and some of it was starting to go off. The *Odious Miasma* in particular was trying to escape its bottle. Mind the smell.

'Aieee! Big man!' guffawed the trader next to me. 'Broke out of lock-up, eh? Fancy yourself a fighter now, ah?'

'Shut up, Gary,' I muttered.

'You wanna pick a fight with me, big man?' he continued, grinning. 'I got these dancing sparrows here, they'd be a good match for ya!'

'My money's on the sparrows.' Tracey sauntered over, bearing a mug of foaming yellow beer and an amused expression. 'So, you're a fighter now, are you? That your new niche?'

I squared my shoulders. 'Mercer had it coming.'

'Maybe. But from *you?*'

I deflated. 'Shut up, Tracey.'

He winked and offered me the beer. 'Don't say I never do anything nice for you. That's a fair bruise you have there.'

'Covers up 'is ugly *fizzogg*, aye?' snickered Goron. 'A definite improvement. Maybe you should have a go at Gary's singing mice next time. I reckon you could take them.'

I scowled inwardly. Sure, everyone laugh at the one man who tried to stand up for something today. Admittedly, that man may have chosen a rather dull-witted way to do it, and may actually be somewhat unclear about the thing he was standing up for, but at the very least I was the only one in this circle who could say that he had punched Edric Mercer in the face today. That had to be worth something.

'I saw that woman again, if anyone cares,' I said moodily. 'She was watching while we were strung up, you know.'

'The lady with the eyes?' asked Tracey, with renewed interest. 'Did you work out what she looks like, this time?'

I shook my head. 'That's just the thing. I saw her, completely. I mean, I was looking right *at* her. But I don't know what she looked like.'

'Hmm. What colour were her eyes?'

'I don't know.'

'What? But earlier you said her eyes were the only thing you *did* remember. You're not trying to pull my leg, are you?'

Ang spoke up. 'Said she had calm eyes, *twpsyn*. Di'n't say nothing about the colour. Buggered if I could tell ye.'

That's right, calm. Horribly calm, the more I thought about it. Eyes that viewed the world as though it was of complete irrelevance.

Calm, perhaps, because there was never a reason not to be. Patient, because the owner of those eyes doesn't have to take risks. Quiet, because this person could slit your throat in front of all your friends, and not a single one of them would be able to recall her face. They were the eyes of a woman who was safe and comfortable in the knowledge that she would slip out of your mind as easily as a dream.

'Some kind of spell?' mused Tracey. 'There's this chap a few rows over who sells budget glamours. You know, make yourself handsome for a day, that sort of thing?'

'You're a regular patron, are you?' I said sourly.

'Darling, I'm his *inspiration*.' He unloaded his best grin – it dripped with charm almost as much as Ang's pasty dripped with gravy. I tried to hold back my smile but failed.

Bloody sirens. If we weren't friends, I would deeply distrust the man. Tracey's intrinsic charm was so thick you could bottle it like a sauce. Not a bad thought that, could be an idea worth pursuing: a brief image of Suave Condiments flashed through my mind. Fancy a splash of Debonair on your chips? Maybe some Poise to spice up your salad?

I shook my head to clear it. Later.

'So, what you're saying,' said Tracey. 'is that despite seeing your lucky lady twice at the Market now, you're *still* no closer to tracking her down? Good grief, it's like having the needle jump out of the haystack at you.'

'Except the needle is invisible.'

'Or you're just bad at catching. Now, if you want some tips on how to really reel a woman in–'

'Not your sort of tips, thanks. Although,' a thought struck me, 'I don't suppose you have a song that would, I don't know, make her come to us?'

'Oh, *lots.*' He smiled lazily. 'Trouble is, my song would also attract all the other ladies in the room. And then it would draw them into a stupor. And then they would die of fatigue, or malnutrition, or some other thing. And then probably some Regulator would hunt me down for it, as if it were my fault that people would rather die than stop listening to me. Your call, though.'

'Let's not.'

As much as I hated to admit it, Tracey was right. We were back to square one, and I was out of ideas. We had no leads on our thief. Except–

Perhaps it was the knock I'd received to the head. What else could have made me forget Reva's words?

'There is something else,' I said, then leaned in conspiratorially. Gratifyingly, everyone else leaned in too. I lowered my voice to a whisper. 'Have you heard of . . . Baines and Grayle?'

Tracey shrugged. 'Nope.'

'Really? Nothing?' I failed to conceal my surprise, and my disappointment. Tracey usually had his finger on the pulse – a lot of gossip seems to be passed on in the bedroom.

'Been out of the country, mate,' he reminded me. 'Now, if you wanted to know about the rise of this mysterious new power in Bavaria–'

'No,' I said flatly.

He shrugged. 'Suit yourself. There were heroes and sword fights and everything.'

I became aware that another conversation was happening down by our knees. Goron was shifting uneasily on the spot while Ang nudged and cajoled him.

'I can see it in yer eyes, ye old *ffwl*,' she said. 'What is it that ye know?'

Goron bristled under our combined stares, but I think it was Ang's pleading that swayed him.

'Don't know nuthin' much,' he said hesitantly. 'Never met these Baines 'n' Grayle folk meself. They seems to come as a pair, never heard of one nor t'other by hisself.'

'Are they traders?' asked Tracey curiously.

'Dunno. Only heard o' them from other knockers, see?' His brow creased. 'Some talk of work for knockers who wants it. Good money for good metal, so's they say. Trouble is, the few who went, ain't come back.'

'Maybe they decided to stay there?' I suggested.

He gave a worried, humourless smile. 'Could be. Could be.'

'You don't think so.'

He fidgeted with a loose thread on his overalls. 'Knockers don't like t'stray from home, 'cept for good work. Mebbe it is good work, so they stay. But they ought've sent word home. They left a month agone, and we've had no word as yet.'

Ang's gaze flicked to mine, and suddenly I knew she and I were thinking the same thing.

'Are they family of yours, these missing knockers?' I said carefully.

'O' sorts, o' sorts. I don't know 'em well, like, but they still be kin to me and mine.'

'And how did you – and how did *they* – hear of Baines and Grayle in the first place?'

'Already said, *bobby*. Other knockers come by our home, tellin' of good work. Most din't care fer it, but a couple of the young'uns thought it an adventure, see. So, they go off together with this woman and ain't heard of again–'

'What woman?' said Ang sharply.

'I dunno. Some human woman. She was with the knockers that come to us.'

'What did she look like?' I pressed.

Goron fixed me with a pointed stare. 'Ye all look alike t'me.'

'*Try*, would you?'

'Please,' said Ang. I think it may be the first time I've ever heard her use the word.

Goon shook his head. 'Wish I could, lass. Like I say, more'n a month's gone since then, and in truth I barely noticed she was there.'

'That's a bit strange, don't you think?' I said. 'I mean, humans tend to stick out amongst knockers.'

'Aye,' said Goron. 'Yer uglier.'

'Hmm.'

Ang was tapping her foot. 'There weren't no woman come to us,' she muttered. 'But s'posin' they ran into her and them Baines 'n' Grayle on the road?'

'What's that, lass?' said Goron.

'Mine own kin be missing, too. Was meant to ask ye and yer fellows if any coblynau had passed by, but it was plain when we met that ye hadn't seen a coblyn in years.'

'Y'are the first I've laid eyes on in near a century. And it be a great honour, may I say.'

'Away wi' yer worthless flattery,' said Ang, but it didn't sound like she meant it. She nodded at me. 'Anyways, this *pentwp's* meant t'be helping me find 'em, but he ain't been any use yet.'

'Now wait a moment!' I cried. 'Haven't we just found a *clue*? I *told* you we'd find a lead here.'

'Aye, and what lead's that, 'xactly? 'Cuz I still feels no closer, *gwas*.'

I was still working it out. It wasn't enough to give us the whole picture, but it was a small piece in the puzzle. Ang had echoed my own thoughts. Were Baines and Grayle to blame for the disappearance of Ang's coblynau as well as Goron's knockers?

Whoever they were, whatever part they played, this Baines and Grayle were sounding very suspicious indeed. It was an odd thought, but the names had the ring of, well, partners in a legal firm, or something like that. Maybe they were just two mercantile black marketeers in business together. Or maybe they were something worse.

'You remember where we first heard of Baines and Grayle, Ang?' I said thoughtfully.

Her brow furrowed. 'That troll, weren't it. The one that beat up yer witchy friend.'

'That's right. And my 'witchy friend' emphatically didn't want to talk about it afterwards. From what Goron's said, it sounds like maybe these people are either employing knockers or capturing them. And now, thanks to Reva – or should I say, thanks to *my idea* to see Reva – we know that our bluecap thief is *also* linked to Baines and Grayle somehow.'

'Ye think she works for 'em?'

'It's possible. But who *else* is here that has a connection with our thief?'

Ang looked blank for a second, then angry. 'That smarmy *basdun* wi' the hat. Ye think he's behind it all? Is that what yer gettin' at?'

'Only one way to find out. Who's up for a chat with Mercer?'

'You're joking,' said Tracey. 'Haven't you had enough punishment for one day?'

'I need to ask him a pressing question,' I replied grimly.

'With your fist? It won't work out any better a second time.'

'I've decided to change direction.'

* * *

127

'You want to *trade?*' Mercer said incredulously.

'Certainly,' I responded, with my most jovial smile in place. It may have looked a tad skewed due to my swollen jaw. 'I'd like to offer an apology for earlier, of course. Been under a lot of stress lately, don't quite know what came over me.' I lowered my voice so that his three bald cronies couldn't hear. 'A mere miscommunication. Baines and Grayle send their regards.'

He flinched. I don't know what I was expecting – it was a stupid ploy, a mere shot in the dark – but the flinch took me entirely by surprise.

I suppose I had expected one of two reactions. Either I would be faced with sneering disdain (which would tell me that Mercer knows more about Baines and Grayle than I do) or I would be met with a sudden blank wall of ignorance (which would tell me that Mercer knows a *lot* more than I do). Either he's working for them, or he's working with them, and I'd hoped to find some small indication as to which it was.

But a flinch? A flinch holds bags of information. It holds *fear.*

I smiled again. 'About my business here. I would like to buy my bluecaps back. I'm sorry, I mean I would like to buy *your* bluecaps. Just a coincidence that they look so similar.'

'They've already sold,' Mercer snapped. 'Not that you could have afforded them.' He seemed to regain his composure. He adjusted his stupid hat. 'I have no business with you, Hansard. You are lucky we are in the open, like this. With . . . witnesses.'

'Well, we both know someone who doesn't need to worry about witnesses, don't we?' I said brightly.

It wasn't exactly a threat. But if, for example, you had previously made the acquaintance of one quiet-eyed thief and, just supposing you knew that she was as dangerous as she was sly, then you would be forgiven for taking it as a threat. Something flickered in Mercer's eyes.

'What do you want?' he hissed.

I teetered on the verge of showing my hand. If I asked him what he knew about Quiet Eyes, the jig would be up. At the moment, he thinks I'm in on whatever it is that he's hiding.

I tested the shape of a question on my tongue and settled with, 'How did you acquire those bluecaps in the first place?'

His eyes narrowed. 'They were traded for. In the usual way of things.'

'And may I ask what was valuable enough to offer in trade for them?'

'No, you may not,' he said tartly. But then, in a surprising spirit of reconciliation he added, 'I will say that I did not know their provenance before they came into my possession.'

'So you *admit* they were stolen!'

His eyebrows raised incredulously. 'Hansard, you do *know* what business you're in?'

Damn, he'd knocked me onto the back foot. I changed tack quickly to keep him talking. 'Who bought the bluecaps from you?'

'Some knocker. Paid good money.'

'Who?'

'Who cares? They all look the same.'

'Didn't you get a name?'

'Why would I care what the wretched creature's name was? Doubtless the little rodent will scurry back to his hole in the ground. If you want to find him, try digging in the dirt.'

Ang's ears pricked. Goron laid a hand on her shoulder.

'Who ye callin' rodent ye rotten *diawl bach*–'

'What did he pay?' I cut in quickly.

'*–rydych chi'n haeddu cael eich gorchuddio â budreddi–*'

Mercer sneered at Ang. 'What *is* the horrid thing saying? Make it stop.'

Ang broke out of Welsh and shouted, *'How came ye to know the woman? What business has ye wi' Baines 'n' Grayle an' coblynau an' knockers an' bluecaps? Ye comes clean now!'*

There was a ringing silence that spread in a circle outward from Ang. The nearest traders were suddenly quietly preoccupied with rearranging their tables, very deliberately not-paying-attention in a way that was designed to pay as much attention as possible.

'You don't know anything about Baines and Grayle, do you?' Mercer said, very slowly. His voice almost had an edge of amusement in it, except that it was about to turn nasty.

The air seemed to heat up around us, swelling like the air before a heavy storm. Some of Mercer's men squared their shoulders. I tensed.

'Gentlemen.'

We froze. The sound of a pen tapping on a clipboard filled the sudden, empty silence.

The Regulator stared at us impassively over her glasses. It was a look reminiscent of a stern librarian, and just as terrifying. Her pen scritched across the paper. When she was finished, she tore off a strip and handed it to me.

The words: 'ORDER TO VACATE PREMISES' glared up at me.

'Sign here,' she instructed, pressing the pen into my hand. I signed to acknowledge my receipt of the note – in triplicate, obviously. While I complied, she addressed the whole group. 'You are in direct violation of an order given not one hour previous, to wit: stipulated adherence to peaceful behaviour while in attendance of this Market. You were warned that further violence on your part would result in drastic action on ours.'

'But there hasn't been any violence,' I said, puzzled.

She fixed me with her cold stare. 'There will be if you don't vacate the premises.'

Ah. Straight to the point, Regulators. Very efficient.

She ripped off another ticket and handed it to Mercer.

'You don't expect me to leave as well?' he said indignantly. 'Do you know who I am?'

Her hard gaze turned on him. 'Indeed. You are an individual who is complicit in the aforementioned contravening behaviour. If you do not accept my terms, then you will be a deceased individual who *was* complicit in the aforementioned contravening behaviour. And, consequently, no longer my problem.' She held out the pen. 'Sign here.'

As much as I wanted to savour the sight of Mercer being knocked down a peg, it was time to make an escape. The key now was *speed*.

'We leavin', *gwas?*' said Ang, trotting beside me.

'Yes. Time to make tracks. I want to be far away by the time Mercer sets off.'

We collared Tracey and cajoled him into lending a hand. Bottles disappeared into their cases, jewellery was unceremoniously stuffed into boxes, and the ceremonial boxes were rapidly encased in bubble wrap. Powders, gems and knick-knacks were stowed in their pouches, and the stuffed barn owl that I had picked up somewhere along the way was perched precariously on top of the heap.

I felt strangely alive. I've never been thrown out of a Market before. It only ever happens to people who get noticed.

'*Hansard!*' bellowed someone behind us. A glance revealed three bald-headed, ugly buggers wading through the crowd in our direction.

'Run?' I suggested.

We ran for it.

'Excuse me,' said Tracey, and slipped behind us.

On the edge of hearing I thought I could hear music. *Ohshit.* 'Don't listen!' I yelled to Goron and Ang.

We burst through a throng of people and out of the doors and slammed them shut behind us.

Ang banged on her ear. 'Sounded like someone singin', *gwas.*'

I found myself rubbing my eyes, weirdly drowsy. As we collected ourselves, Tracey strolled outside. He gave a mock salute. 'No need to thank me.'

'What were you playing at?' I said angrily. 'You nearly caught us up in that!'

He had the gall to look hurt. 'Give me some credit. It was only a little lullaby, just enough to knock out your friends back there. Even caught me a smooch off one before he went down.'

'Stupid,' I said, but with no real malice. 'What if a Regulator had snatched you?'

'But they didn't,' he replied brightly. 'Now, are you leaving or what? I've got places to be, too.'

'What places?'

'Well, I've got me a warm bed to go to tonight. After that, who knows?' He shrugged happily.

No doubt his warm bed came with a lady attached. I wondered vaguely how the life of a drifter came so easily to him, happy not knowing where it would take him next. Then I remembered that's basically how I live, but with fewer warm beds and nice meals. Living two sides of the same dream. Somehow his side looked classier.

We reached the car and swiftly loaded it. Goron was trying to persuade Ang to stay.

'It's not an abandoned mine,' he was saying. 'The big folk abandoned it, but we're still there. Smithin' when we ain't minin'. Produce the finest enchanted metals in the whole country, so we do. We could go there soon as the Market's over.'

Ang actually seemed unsure of herself. 'I dunno, Goron. I'm a coblyn, me. Never smithed in me life.'

'I can teach ye,' he replied encouragingly. And then, slowly, his face fell. 'Ye ain't stayin', are ye?'

Ang wouldn't meet his eyes. I nudged her with my foot, but she wouldn't look at me, either.

'G'bye,' she muttered, turning away.

'Wait.' Goron grabbed her hand. 'Wait awhile. I've got somethin' for ye. Stay there.' He scampered off back inside the warehouse.

I frowned. 'He better be quick. Those goons won't stay asleep forever.'

'We're waitin',' said Ang firmly.

When Goron returned, he was holding a crate of bottles, each lit with a gentle blue glow. Ang's eyes widened. She looked from the bottles, to Goron, and back again.

'Them's mine,' she said faintly. Goron nodded and placed them at her feet.

'Safe an' sound,' he said. 'Didn't want some unworthy beggar t'be makin' off wi' 'em. Bought 'em, legal like, so that Mercer won't be after ye. Well, not because of these, at any rate.'

Ang picked up the bottles, one by one, turning them over in her hands.

'*Diolch*,' she said gravely.

'Eh?'

'Means thank you.'

'Ye welcome, lass.'

She placed them back in the crate and held it out to the knocker.

'Take 'em. You'll give them a good home, and good work. I knows it.'

At first he looked taken aback, but then he accepted the crate with a solemn expression.

'I will at that. Ye have my word.'

'Could we maybe discuss some financial compensation . . . ?' I tried, but I knew I was being ignored.

'*Hyns diogel*,' said Goron. 'Means good journey.'

'*Da bo chi,*' said Ang. 'Means goodbye.'

I sighed. 'Look, this is all very touching, but if we don't leave soon then we're going to have to deal with Mercer and his boys. I don't know about you, but I'd rather not end the night as a smear on the pavement.'

'I'll write ye,' said Ang. They nodded to one another, and that seemed to be that.

'Safe travels,' said Tracey.

We were on the road again, heading into the faded grey light of dawn.

I wasn't sure whether the night could be counted as a win. We'd got the bluecaps back, briefly, sort of. Ang was happy with their new owner, though we hadn't been paid for them. We had a little more information on the quiet-eyed thief, and the two mysterious names she related to, and we knew that Mercer was afraid of them.

It didn't sound like much.

At least I was certain that Mercer hadn't hired Quiet Eyes himself – why would she worry him, if she was on his payroll? And as for Baines and Grayle: what kind of person is so dangerous as to frighten a man who has traversed the underworld and fought monsters? And there were the missing coblynau and knockers too, all wrapped up in the same mystery.

Despite these new leads, it felt very unsatisfying to only have more questions, rather than real answers. Quiet Eyes was at the Market the whole time; I'd seen her twice yet was still no closer to knowing who she was.

Does it matter any more? asked a faint voice in my head. *We got the bluecaps back. Sort of. They're the only reason we were trying to chase her in the first place. None of our business now, is it?*

True, true. But what about my promise to help Ang find her missing people?

Well, she's given away my bluecaps to a knocker she got all gooey-eyed for. Why should I continue to care? None of my business.

Ah. But you see, I'm not in this business for the sake of keeping to my own business, am I? I wouldn't have gotten anywhere in this world if I didn't like to know the answers to questions like 'What does this do?' and 'What price could I get for that?' and 'How did that strange man in the coat suddenly disappear when the coins he gave me turned to dust in my hands?'

If you find out the answer it means you can pull the same trick on some other bugger down the road. Practically karma.

At least there was one question I could get an immediate answer to. 'Why didn't you stay?' I asked Ang. 'Goron seemed all right.'

'Not ready yet, *gwas*,' she said distantly.

'Oh? I thought you might have preferred his help tracking down your missing friends. Seeing as you consider me no help at all. And, frankly, you gave him my payment.' I glanced at her. 'Wouldn't you be happier with your own kind?'

She stared out the window, watching the twilight scenery roll by.

'I seen things,' she said thoughtfully. 'I seen trolls and witches and a river-dwellin' smellycoat, and a gypsy who reads blank cards and a thief with uncanny eyes, and a knocker who's all right and does good pasties. Can't find none o' them in a mine. Well, 'cept the knocker and the pasties.' She paused. 'Life's intrestin' round you, *gwas*.'

Somehow, that felt like the biggest compliment anyone had ever paid me.

'Even if y'are a big liar and rubbish at detectiving.'

Less complimentary.

'How are you going to keep in touch with him?' I asked.

'Same way I keeps in touch with coblynau back home.'

'You do?'

'Course, *gwas*. I sends letters, reg'lar.'

'I've never seen you post a letter,' I said doubtfully. 'And I'm sure the Royal Mail doesn't deliver to mines located in dimensions hidden within the folds of reality.' Actually, I wasn't sure on that last point. It would explain a lot about the British postal system.

Ang fixed me with the glare she reserved for when I was being particularly dense.

'Rats, *gwas*. They go *everywhere*. Reliable delivery if you got the grub to pay 'em. They likes ham best.'

'Huh.'

We drove in silence for a while. It felt heavy on my shoulders.

'*Gwas?*'

'Mm?'

'Where we goin' now?'

I don't know.

'Next sale, Ang. Next opportunity.'

'What about them Baines 'n' Grayle?'

They're sharks. We're fish. Tiny, tiny fish.

'Ain't we goin' after them, *gwas?*'

The sky paled around us, bringing the world into gradual focus. I felt myself awaken, sharpened by the light of dawn. The path was becoming clearer.

I took a breath. 'How far are you willing to go to find your kin, Ang?'

Our eyes met, and I knew the answer.

'As far as the road is long,' she said.

'It'll be dangerous, you know. We might get into real trouble. I mean, *real* trouble.'

My eyes were back on the road, but I could feel hers boring through my skull.

'What's in it fer you, *gwas?*' It was a question with a blade attached. 'You ain't exactly done your utmost up til now, have ye?'

I considered my answer carefully.

'I want to catch that thief. I want to know who Baines and Grayle are. I want to know why everyone's so afraid of them. The way I see it, we've got a common enemy now, right?'

'Oh? And I can rely on ye against a common enemy, can I?'

'I'm *in*, Ang. From now on, I'm in, and I'm serious.'

It was like a knife slowly turning in the side of my head, that was the nature of Ang's stare. I wondered if maybe my thoughts were spilling out of the wound for her to measure.

Then she turned away and tipped her flat cap down to her nose.

'Good,' was all she said, leaning back into the seat.

'Okay then,' I said. 'Okay.' I wasn't certain if I was reassuring her or myself.

I focused on the tarmac, the never-ending vein of grey that gave the lifeblood to my living. The sun was up, and the sky was so blue.

Under my breath I said, *'Let's hunt sharks.'*

Episode 8: Informant

On a cold, cloudless summer night, two grumbling figures huddled over a tiny flame in the middle of a harbourside car park in Bristol.

'*Cach*. It's gone out again, *gwas*.'

On a cold, cloudless summer night, two grumbling figures huddled over a complete *lack of* flame in the middle of a harbourside car park in Bristol.

'Damn. I think that's the last of the fuel, too.'

Ang and I both stared sadly at our dinner perched on my ancient camping stove.

'Dun't fancy cold soup,' groused Ang.

'I don't think it's a matter of what either of us fancy, right now.' I passed her a spoon. 'Eat up.'

In fact it turned out to be lukewarm, if slightly gloopy, and chicken soup comes with the inbuilt quality to be comforting no matter the temperature. It was welcome, at any rate. We'd been waiting in this one spot for hours, and the night was now so late that it was practically early.

On the opposite side of the harbour, the grid of yellow lights from the boxy, identical flats had long since winked out, leaving us with only the ambient radiance of streetlamps.

A few yards in front of us, sleeping boats bobbed gently in the water, tucked up for the night with ropes and tarpaulins. They made for unsettling company. The way their black shapes blocked out the starlit surface made them look for all the world like lurking aquatic monsters – some spindly, some squat, some long and narrow. I was briefly put in mind of shellycoats and wondered what kind of debris would go into their mantles around here. A lot of disposable coffee cups, if I'm any judge, and probably the odd tarpaulin snatched off an unwary vessel.

This waterfront was significant. It was a long, man-made channel that connected to the River Avon and was lined with more quays and wharfs than you could shake a fish at. Boats were always moored here. It was called the Floating Harbour, and to most people this was because ships would always be afloat in it – due to some genius of engineering that went beyond both my understanding and interest. But there was another reason too, and only people like myself knew about it.

'This best be worth it, *gwas*.'

'It will, Ang.'

'And what if our man don't even know anythin' useful?'

'Then we'll just have to find someone else,' I said firmly. But I sincerely hoped otherwise. I'd burned through a *lot* of favours to get this far, and possibly a few bridges, too.

Ang yawned. 'S'it time yet?'

I checked my watch. 'Twenty minutes.'

'Never heard o' ghosts keepin' a schedule,' she muttered.

'What about ghost trains?' I said absently.

'Don't be daft. Why'd a train be a ghost? Ain't got no soul.'

'I'm sure there's someone who'd argue with you on that, but I'm not qualified to say either way.'

We were waiting for three A.M. Commonly called the Witching Hour, though I don't see why witches should get all the credit. If you indulge in my ramblings on the nature of reality, I reason out the Witching Hour as a kind of temporal bridge. Just as bridges themselves may act as a bridge across reality – being a space where the fabric of our world wears just a little thin – then so too can this strange pocket of time. It's no coincidence that so many ghost sightings take place between the hours of three and four A.M., and likewise why the hour has percolated into our collective consciousness as a time for magic.

I stared across the water, waiting.

Perhaps it was the peculiar way the starlight reflected in the ripples, but it seemed to me that the air began to shimmer.

'Ugh,' said Ang. 'Itches.'

There was a sense of fizzing in the air. I hurried to the edge of the harbour and looked down. My eyes widened with delight. 'Ang! You have to see this!'

'What are ye gettin' all excited abou– Oh.'

From deep under the dark water, a soft glow emanated. If you unfocused and looked carefully, the glow became the outline, the shape, the shadow of a boat, many boats, anchored along the bottom of the channel.

'Them's some big barges,' said Ang. She knelt and peered into the water. 'Reminds me of the trows what used to sail up an' down the Severn wi' all their cargo. Sometimes they was pulled along by men, when the waters were too low to sail proper. Real work, that was.'

She shook herself out of reverie and glared up at me, as if it were my fault for catching her in the middle of a memory. 'Why're them boats underwater, *gwas*? Ain't natural!'

'That's the Floating Harbour,' I said grandly. 'It's a place without a place, if you catch my meaning. Or rather, it exists in many places at once. It's a location that . . . floats, for want of a better word, through ethereal and corporeal states and, therefore, reality.'

She squinted at me. 'Yer making that up jus' to sound clever.'

'I am not. I spoke to an expert. I've been assured it's something to do with quantum.'

'Gibberish.'

It possibly was gibberish. But it made a sort of sense to me. You could travel on the Floating Harbour without having to, well, travel. Step onto a boat in one location and step straight off it into somewhere else.

Trouble is, you might not know *where* you would be stepping off into. Could be the bottom of the ocean, for all you knew. I've heard of one sorry chap who stepped right into the middle of a warzone. Some other bugger stepped into a different timeline altogether. Apparently, you either need to have a ticket that confirms your destination, or you need to be really bloody good at steering.

I told all this to Ang.

'Ye've *heard*,' she repeated shrewdly. 'Ye never actually seen it before?'

'Oh, I've *seen* it,' I said. 'Just like this. Plenty of times.'

'But you ain't travelled on it?'

'I have never purchased a ticket.'

'And ye don't know how to, neither,' she grunted, though it was tactfully under her breath.

I ignored her with equal tact and bounced lightly on my heels. I wouldn't let on just how excited I was. Because we *did* have a ticket. We might not have bought it, exactly, and in truth, Ang was right that I had no clue how to go about obtaining one. But I had *wanted* one. Ever since I'd first seen those spectral boats gliding underwater in their silent and eerie majesty, while standing under the light of a full moon and in the company of–

But that was a long time ago.

We had a ticket now. It had been sent to us in a carefully blank envelope, dropped by a crow. I didn't exactly know who had sent it, or where it was going to take us, but I needed to find out.

I felt for the slim piece of card in my pocket. It seemed to have become heavier with the arrival of the boats. I pulled it out. Despite the added weight it had lost a sense of physicality, as if I was holding merely the ghost of a ticket. What had been gold embossed decoration now glowed in faint blue lines. I fancied I could see my hand through them.

'Look, *gwas!*'

I followed Ang's pointing finger to where the shape of a phantom ship was becoming larger and larger in the water. Coming closer, I realised.

'Must be our ride,' I said, barely keeping the glee out of my voice.

It didn't surface, but a tall mast had broken through into the air and the prow of the ship was left resting just proud of the water, lapped at by dark little waves.

'We're never gettin' on that.' Ang's voice dripped with terror.

'We are.'

'We'll *drown.*'

'We won't. Because we have a ticket,' I said confidently.

'But how'll we *get back?*'

'It's a return. Look, it even says so here.'

Even so, with one foot hovering over the edge of the concrete, I hesitated. The water was quite a bit further down. It would be embarrassing to break a leg on your first Float.

I opted instead for a graceless bum-shuffle off the side, hauling Ang onto my shoulders at the same time. My feet caught the prow and slipped; there was a sudden rushing, horribly fluid sensation as we both plunged, and the water closed over our heads.

I tried to breathe. Water filled my lungs.

I'm drowning.

I'm DROWNING!

And then it was rushing *upwards* again, and I surfaced with a gasp and grabbed at the nearest solid object, which turned out to be the prow. Ang, in turn, had grabbed onto me. We both spluttered, hawking up a pint or so of fetid water and retching for air.

''m gonna kill ye, ye wretched *celwyddog*,' Ang moaned. 'That's 'liar', but I reckon ye'd put claim t'knowing that already.'

I saved my breath. I was too busy choking on it.

A furtive, croaky voice called above us. 'Mr Hansard? You mustn't waste time!'

Still reeling from the non-journey, I struggled to make immediate sense of the situation. A hand was offered and I gladly took it, though the body on the other end seemed too weak to actually be of any assistance, and I dragged myself and Ang to shore.

It turned out that our boat was moored (I presume) on the edge of a silver lake in the middle of a sparkling field. It looked like a meadow, if grass were made of glass. Glass that could shift and bend under the weight of a breeze. A gentle tinkling sound accompanied the wind.

'Di' we drown?' said Ang damply.

I patted myself down and noted a distinct lack of water weighing me down. My clothes were covered in a thin layer of droplets, as if we'd just walked through fine mist or a splash of sea spray.

'How does that work?' I asked aloud.

'There's no time,' said the croaky voice. I looked around into an unpleasant, sunken face, lined with deep shadows and streams of sweat.

I forced a smile. 'Mallory, I presume?'

* * *

I had never heard of Mallory, until ten days ago.

For a month, maybe more, Ang and I had chased rumoured nothings around the country for information about Baines and Grayle.

143

From my list of business associates (or at least, the ones who were currently on speaking terms with me) it seemed the vast majority were completely oblivious of the name, and I began to wonder if we were just too far down the food chain. Sharks pay no mind to plankton after all, and probably vice versa.

But the very few who had heard of them, had also heard enough to only speak in whispers. No one seemed to understand my description of Quiet Eyes, but nevertheless word got round that I was looking for some invisible thief, and that information attached itself to the words Baines and Grayle, and finally we were nudged in the direction of a horse-ish vet called Sumi.

I'd wondered about the 'ish' part right up until we caught up with Sumi on the job. She was described as slender, Korean, and usually dressed in brown overalls. She was outside when we'd pulled up at her stable yard, engrossed in cleaning the hooves of a tall black stallion.

I had Ang throw a scarf round her head in case there were any normal folks about, and we strode across the yard.

'Good day.' I gave a friendly wave. 'Would you be Sumi, the horse-ish vet?'

She ignored me just long enough to make me consider repeating myself, and then said, 'I am,' while still industriously scraping a hoof.

'Who's this clown, then,' said the horse.

I had to double-take. I opened my mouth.

'Everyone knows horses can't talk,' Sumi said calmly, without looking up.

'But it just–'

'Nope.'

I glanced at Ang. She raised an eyebrow.

The horse snickered.

I glared at it. 'I don't believe you.'

'Really?' said Sumi. 'That's unusual. I notice you don't have a horse with you.' She wiped her hands on a towel and moved to the next hoof. 'So? What can I do for you? If you're willing to accept a talking horse, then you must be here on ish business.'

'What's ish?' said Ang, beating me to it. Sumi finally looked up from her work. The presence of a coblyn seemed to gain her interest.

'Everything that's sort of, but not,' she answered vaguely. She pointed at the stallion. 'This one is sort of horse, but sort of not.'

'I am a pooka,' said the horse proudly. I noted it spoke with an Irish accent. 'Today I am a horse, to run freely over the fields. Tomorrow I shall be a fox, slinking in warm burrows. Maybe after I will be a raven, soaring untethered over all of creation.'

'He likes to go on a bit,' said Sumi.

'He's a shapeshifter, then,' I said in awe. I wondered if it would be rude to ask for a sample of his tail-hairs or a portion of hoof-clippings. Someone would want to buy them, for sure. Genuinely horse-ish.

Ang nudged me. 'We gots other questions to ask, *gwas*,' she said tiredly. We were both running on empty.

'Right. You're right.' I turned to Sumi. 'We're here because we've heard you know something – or rather, you know *someone*, who knows something about . . . Baines and Grayle.'

The words dropped into the air like a lead weight. I fancied I heard them bounce.

'Hark at him,' said the pooka. 'Sounds like he's looking for mischief.' Sumi dropped the hoof. 'Off with you, Killian. I'll finish this later.'

'What? But I had an appointment.'

'Later.'

The horse clopped around the corner, trailing sounds of indignation.

'Why?' Sumi said, so quietly I almost missed it.

Ang took this one, explaining brusquely. 'We're lookin' for 'em. An' I'm lookin' for some o' my people. Thinks they be mixed up together, an' not in a good way. If ye knows anything, I hopes to find out before any harm comes of it.'

Sumi looked distinctly uncomfortable. 'I see. You are looking for trouble, then?'

'Just information, right now,' I interposed. 'But from what little we know, it certainly sounds like trouble. We hope to avoid it and, ideally, rescue anyone caught up in it.' A bit of a grand over-statement that, but it seemed to do the trick.

'I might know a guy,' Sumi said uneasily. 'Look, I'm not promising anything. I don't know anything about this Baines and Grayle except that they're bad news. I had a friend who . . .'

I saw the hesitation and leapt into the gap. 'Did this friend get mixed up with bad news?'

There was the shadow of a nod. 'I . . . think he took a job with them. But he never told me the job and wouldn't speak about it. Things got salty between us after that, and I haven't seen him for a few years. But last I heard he wasn't doing too great.'

'That's great! I mean, not about your shattered friendship. But what's his name? Where can I find him?'

She winced. 'That's the thing. He's hard to find now, by his own design. He's gone slightly . . . strange. He thinks someone's out to get him. Do you know what a pocket dimension is? Apparently, he went to the trouble of getting one made and now doesn't leave it, for anything.'

Ang nudged me. 'She mean like what me and my kin did wi' our world o'er the bridge?'

I nodded. 'I think that's right. He's locked himself in his own little fold in reality, then? How do we get to it?'

'You don't.' She sighed. 'At least, not without an invitation. I've tried. He won't believe me, though. Apparently, a friend reaching out is too unlikely a scenario for him to accept.' She glanced at us. 'But maybe he'd meet you. I can't help but feel like Baines and Grayle have something to do with what's messed him up. Maybe if he knew you were trying to help someone else . . . I don't know for sure. Like I say, no promises.'

I pretended to mull this over. Of course, there was no chance I was going to walk away from an opportunity. We'd already wasted enough time getting this far.

'I can get a message to him, that's all,' Sumi said. 'It's up to him whether he wants to meet you. He goes by Mallory.'

And about a week later Mallory's crow found us. Dropped the envelope right in through my car window. There was no message inside, just the ticket, a time, and a date.

* * *

Now, in the middle of the needle-point meadow, Mallory's crow dropped from the silver sky and alighted on his shoulder. The man had backed off from us, his eyes flicking between Ang and me in a constant rhythm.

'You're Hansard?' he rasped. It sounded like he was struggling to get the words out of his throat.

'That's me–'

'Show me your ticket!'

'Why?' I waved it anyway. 'We're here, aren't we?'

'Could be anybody,' he muttered, then snatched the ticket from my hand. He held it up to the silver light, and his face suddenly contorted. His gaze snapped back to us with an ugly expression. 'You might've stole this! How do I know you're you? How do *you* know you're you? *Stay back!*'

'Hang on, here!' I fumbled in my pockets and pulled out a grubby business card. 'See, that's my name. And this is Ang. She's my associate.'

'Why isn't her name on the card,' he said doubtfully.

I felt my polite smile was turning into a rictus. 'We're not business partners. She only helps out a bit.'

Mallory took the card from me and squinted at it very close to his face. I wondered how well he could see out of those sunken eye sockets. He still seemed unconvinced. 'Are you *sure* you're yourself?'

'Who *else* would I be?'

'They have ways,' he muttered under his breath. That was the only way he talked, really, in surreptitious mutterings.

'As for the 'they' in question . . .' I prompted, in what I hoped was a gentle manner. I felt a single wrong word could spook him. And he was looking increasingly unwell. Sweat poured off him in rivers. At moments it seemed like he was struggling to breathe and might faint. 'Do you maybe want to sit down, first?'

He lunged forward, grabbed me by the shoulders. 'What they? Are you with *them*?' He looked quickly side to side then said in a whisper, *'Baines and Grayle.'*

I plucked his hands off my coat – they were cold and clammy. I worried he'd lost the plot completely. 'No, Mallory, we're not *with* them. We're here to find out *about* them. From you. Remember? Sumi sent you a message.'

He stared. 'How do you know my name? I didn't tell you my name.'

I tried not to groan. 'Listen, Mallory – may I call you Mal? Mal. Ang and I have come all this way to listen to your story. You invited us. But, if you don't actually have anything to say, we'll be leaving.'

I turned my back and walked slowly to the lake. Ang dodged in front of me, her expression irritated and confused. 'Wha–'

I motioned quickly for her to shut up and keep walking. Please, please, let the man not be so off his marbles that he doesn't pick up on this . . .

'Wait,' said Mallory.

Aha. My mouth twitched into a small smile of relief. I turned around with a tolerant expression. 'You changed your mind?'

Mallory nodded, and coughed. He swallowed – or tried to – and clutched his throat. Was he choking? I ran to his side and slapped him hard on the back. He made a sound between a grunt and a gasp and seemed to be breathing again.

'You don't seem well, old fellow.' I glanced again at the prickly landscape. The grass crunched into glass shards under my shoes. I wondered where he slept. If he slept. 'Are you sure this is the best place for you to stay? It can't be good for your health.'

'*I won't leave!*' he shouted, suddenly furious. 'They can't reach me here. They'd need a ticket. Oh yes.'

'How does yer bird get in then?' said Ang flatly. I gave her a sidelong glance. It was such an astute question I wish I'd thought of it.

Mallory leered at her. 'It's a *trans-dimensional* crow. *Obviously.*'

Ang and I exchanged a look. 'Nutter' was what it said.

'Her name's Barney,' he continued, oblivious. 'She's my only link to the outside.'

'An' what if someone tampered wi' it?'

Mallory almost laughed. 'With Barney? I'd like to see them try. She's a loyal old crow.'

'That's as may be,' Ang said slowly. 'But that bird there be a raven.'

Our eyes swivelled to the bird on Mallory's shoulder. He reached a hand up to it. 'Barney . . . ?'

The bird squawked and clamped its black beak on his finger. He yelped and madly flailed his arm. 'Get off you devil! *What have you done with my Barney?*'

The bird came free and soared upwards. It produced a *caw* that echoed strangely across the glass landscape, and disappeared into the sky. Mallory stared after it like a bereft man. I assume the bird had been his only company.

'Found me,' he warbled in a nonsensical way. 'They found me.'

I saw the fear clouding his eyes and acted urgently. 'Talk to me, Mallory. Is it Baines and Grayle you're hiding from? Tell us what you know. We want to help.' That last part may have been a generous bending of the truth; I suspected Mallory might be some way beyond help by now.

'It's 'cuz I left them. Said I wouldn't do it no more,' he burbled. 'Told them it was cruel. They didn't like that. The *alternative* is cruel, is what they said. But what they did to those little goblins . . .'

I *felt* the temperature drop in Ang. It wasn't his choice of misnomer that had chilled us both to the bone.

'*What* were they doing to them?' I urged.

He turned his sunken eyes on me. There were such shadows in them that I wanted to recoil.

He opened his mouth to speak, but his face suddenly looked strained, as though he couldn't get his jaw muscles to move right. He spasmed, a shudder that travelled from his stomach right up into his neck and kept going.

'Shit.'

'What's happening, *gwas?*'

'I think he's having a seizure.' I yanked off my trench coat and threw it on the ground. My mind raced. 'I think we have to lie him down, or something.'

He convulsed again, this time arching his back and opening his mouth wide to the sky. His eyes were streaming. That's when his throat began to bulge.

His skin stretched taught over a lump that grew to the size of a rugby ball wedged in his oesophagus. It was pulsing.

I backed the hell away.

'How's he still breathin', *gwas?*' Ang whispered in horror.

'I don't know.' *Maybe he's not.*

The bulge started to slide upwards in Mallory's throat. His mouth remained open in a painful 'O'. And then an oily red mass wriggled out of it.

Ang screamed. I don't think I'd ever heard her scream in anything other than anger before. But this was genuine terror. I realised I was also screaming.

It was like a maggot, as thick as an arm, with black veins bursting underneath its crimson skin.

It happened in seconds.

Mallory – or Mallory's body – lurched towards us in horrible jerky movements, like a puppet. The monster, the worm, whatever it was, was disgorged from his mouth, and in a lurid slippery motion it lunged for Ang's face. I punched Mallory out of instinct – I didn't realise until later that he was already dead – and he crumpled like an empty sack.

For an instant I was paralysed, watching the scene in slow-motion. Ang was trying to get a grip on the slug as it forced its way *into her mouth*.

I sprang, tried to grab at the glistening monstrosity, but the tail end was already disappearing down her gullet. Her eyes filled with panic. I was sure she couldn't breathe. It was now a bulge in her throat. I was on the verge of grasping her by the neck and trying to squeeze the thing back out, but then as I watched it slid down and disappeared into her stomach. She heaved one urgent gasp and collapsed.

'*Ang!*'

I shook her frantically. Her eyes were closed, and her skin was turning an ugly grey. But she was breathing! At least she was breathing.

'Fuck,' I said, except it was barely a word. I was still catching my own breath.

We're miles from help, I realised. *More than miles. Worlds.*

Ang was shivering. I wrapped her carefully in my coat.

We had to get home. Find help. Who'd help? Who could? Who would? My garbled thoughts struggled to string any plan together. Someone would. Someone would help.

I picked Ang up and carried her to the lake. She was heavier than I expected.

We need the ticket, I remembered just in time.

I left Ang on the bank and approached Mallory's body. I've seen dead bodies before. It's an unfortunate hazard of the job. But this one looked . . . empty, like a husk. Like it was missing some essential person-ness that at least made other corpses human. I wondered how long that slug had been inside him. The body looked like it had been sucked dry.

I shuddered and prodded it with my toe. Thankfully, it didn't move.

I didn't want to touch it, but I did anyway. He was wearing what might have once been a suit but was now so frayed and threadbare that it had lost any sense of style or definition. I found our ticket in his trousers, and then because I was there already, I riffled through the rest of his pockets. The search turned up nothing useful: an old handkerchief, some sticky boiled sweets, and a bag of birdseed. I had a vague idea that I was looking for clues about Baines and Grayle, but mostly I was trying to stop myself from thinking about Ang. About that slug forcing its way down her throat. About it sitting in her gut. Doing what? Feeding?

I stared at nothing for a moment.

Had Baines and Grayle sent that thing to kill Mallory? Was it meant to kill us, too? Did they *know* about us? We had been asking a lot of questions.

We're plankton, I reminded myself. Why should they care about bottom-feeders like Ang and me?

Whatever the case, Mallory was clearly right to have been so paranoid.

I almost left him there, in his sparkling cage of glass. But something about that didn't feel right. Once I left, probably no one would ever be able to reach this place again.

Maybe I could return the body to Sumi or something. Perhaps she could send him home, if he had one.

And anyway, suggested a darker part of me, *we might need it.* The word 'autopsy' had already crossed my mind, and I'd never forgive myself if the key to saving Ang somehow lay in the corpse, and I'd left it behind.

I'd forgotten about the raven. It landed several yards away. If I'd had anything to throw at it, I would have.

The bird ruffled its feathers. 'Didn't expect to run into you clowns here.'

My head snapped up. *'What* did you say?'

It clicked its beak. 'Mallory has a limited supply of those tickets, right,' it continued conversationally. 'Well, *had.* Didn't expect him to waste one on you two.'

I leapt to my feet. 'How do you know that? Did you cause this?' I swiped at the bird, but it took off easily and circled overhead. There was only one person I'd spoken to about Mallory. But, ha, Sumi may have been the only *person* present, but it didn't mean she was alone. 'Are you the pooka?' I yelled into the sky.

The raven landed lazily, just out of lunging distance. 'So what if I am, mister?'

I pointed at Mallory. *'Did you do this?'*

'Think you'll find the worm did that, mister. What do they say about early birds and worms?' The pooka turned its head from side to side, fixing me with one eye then the other. 'You might say in this case, the early bird *delivered* the worm.'

'Did Sumi send you to do this?' I demanded.

'You're dense, aren't you?'

I paused, and stole myself against the simmering anger. Of course it wouldn't be Sumi. She was probably just an unwitting point of access. Mallory himself knew who was out to get him. 'You work for Baines and Grayle.'

The raven scratched its beak. 'Not work for, exactly. Contractor, right. They like contractors. And contracts. Hate people who break 'em, though.'

'People like Mallory?'

'What do I know. I'm just a bird. Squawk.'

I narrowed my eyes. 'But you found him through Sumi.'

'Oh, sure. Sumi's a sweetheart, real good on the grooming. Been watching her for months, right. You guys were a right stroke of luck though. There's no way *I* could have got her to contact Mallory. Do you know she asked me to do it for her? She knew that I had the knowing of the boats. Asked me to carry your message for her, so she did. Gave me a line right in. Still,' it faltered, stretched a wing, 'didn't expect you two to actually turn up here.'

'Why are you *telling* me this?'

It shuffled on the spot, which is a strange thing to see a raven do. 'Wasn't expecting collateral casualties.' It nodded at Ang. 'Not in the contract, that. Can get into a lot of trouble, doing what's not in the contract.'

My skin prickled. As if the thing was judging Ang's life by a contract. 'Can you get that worm out of her? Tell me how to save her.'

Again, the bird contrived to look awkward. 'Thing is, I was just to deliver the worm. Back when it were a tiny thing. Then to keep an eye and confirm when Mallory fell dead. I don't rightly know what it actually is, right. But even my bird brain is baulking at the thought of eating anything off that corpse, and for a raven that's being *absurdly* picky, what with fresh eyes going to waste and all.'

'Don't you dare eat him!'

Episode 9: Nether

'**D**o you know how fast you were going, sir?'

The red fuel light blinked at me accusingly.

I grimaced. 'I suppose it was a bit fast. Sorry about that. I'll take the ticket and be on my way, shall I?' I tried to surreptitiously knock the pile of other unpaid vehicular fines off the passenger seat.

The police officer, a no-nonsense brunette with an impassive expression, pulled a notebook from her vest and wrote something down. If I were in a better frame of mind I'd have been entertained by her uniform. It had this severe hi-vis on black thing going on, very respectable and authoritative, but in my view it was ruined by the silly white top on her police hat. Almost as if someone had said: 'How can we make this intimidating uniform suddenly look like a children's costume? Bam! White bowler hat.'

Although, faced with the forbidding countenance of this unamused officer, I was re-thinking my stance on the issue.

Under the not-at-all-comical hat, her eyes surveyed me and my scruffy suit, then moved to the tattered maps spread across the dashboard and the half-finished bag of yesterday's chips nestled in the open glove box. 'I'll need to see your license, sir.'

'Of course. Right away.'

I groped in my pockets. I hoped she wasn't going to try to search the car. I really didn't want her to find the body in the boot.

She took my license and stared intently at it. 'Why were you in such a hurry Mr . . . Jones?'

'It's pronounced *Joh-nes*,' I said. I feel it adds a bit of authenticity. My tired brain grasped for a suitable lie. 'I'm on my way to a party, running late. I didn't mean to be careless, won't do it again, officer.'

It was immediately obvious I'd made a horrendous mistake. Her expression said it all: I didn't look fit to be seen panhandling on the street, let alone attending any kind of social event. It occurred to me that I probably didn't look like the kind of person who even ought to be at the wheel of a car right now. My hair still had weeds in.

And why would you be going to a party at the crack of sunrise, anyway? my fried brain berated itself. As if on cue, the dawn chorus launched into a mocking tune from the nearest hedgerow.

The officer's hard gaze fixed with mine and I'm ashamed to say my smile faltered.

'Could you step out of the car for me, sir,' she said, in no way meaning it as a question.

Ah.

'No problem,' I replied, perhaps a little too cheerily.

Then I turned the ignition and slammed my foot down.

This was exactly the wrong time to stall the car.

She was quick to reach through the open window and grab me by the wrists. Argh, tight grip. Her partner, who had been busy eating a biscuit in the car behind, spat custard cream and frantically jumped out.

I struggled for a moment but she wasn't letting go for anything. There was nothing else for it. I yanked as hard as I physically could and pulled the policewoman through the window.

It caught her by surprise and she landed with a yelp, sprawled half on the passenger seat, half across me, and legs sticking out the window. Her partner made it close enough to slam his hands on the side of the car just as I floored the pedal once more. He rebounded off, stunned, while I tore away down the empty country lane.

'You maniac!' screamed my captive. Her head cracked against the dashboard as I sped round a sharp turn.

'Sorry,' I said. And I meant it. No one deserved to encounter me on a day like today. And I didn't deserve to be having a day like today.

I shouldn't have been speeding, I thought glumly.

Now, speed was the only option. And it was proving exceedingly difficult to steer with someone's legs in the way.

She squirmed the rest of the way inside and dizzily hauled herself upright in the passenger seat. Out of the corner of my eye I watched her take stock of the situation.

Madman driving. Doors unlocked. But driving very fast. Jumping out not an option. No sign of her buddy in the rear-view yet, but I could hear the sirens. She eyed my grip on the wheel.

'It'd be very stupid,' I said. 'Y'know, if you were thinking about trying to take control of the car. We'd just crash, and probably die, and neither of us want that.'

'What do you want, Mr Jones?'

'For you to fasten your seatbelt? If I have to brake suddenly I really don't want to see you flying through the windshield. Honestly, it would ruin my day.'

Tall hedges flashed past on either side; they obscured every bend. I felt my gut lurch every time we turned a corner, certain it would be our last. It was a blur of green and tarmac.

She reluctantly snapped the buckle in place.

'I think you should calm down and consider your position, Mr Jones,' she said, with remarkable composure for someone who had just been kidnapped.

'Mm.' I was rather more concerned with concentrating on the road. And the foliage I was driving into to avoid oncoming traffic. We swerved violently, narrowly missing a tractor.

'My partner won't stop tailing you, and he'll have called for back-up.' A sharp intake of breath as we bounced over a pothole. 'They'll have a helicopter on us in no time. And you've abducted a police officer, Mr Jones, so they'll be calling in the big guns. Who have actual guns, Mr Jones. It will go a lot better for you if you stop the car now.'

'Shut up,' I snapped. The blue lights were now visible in my rear-view mirror. But that was okay because I'd just spotted our ticket home.

'Mr Jones, I can see you're low on fuel. It really will be better for you to give yourself up now, rather than let this situation get any worse. My partner isn't going to stop following you, Mr Jones.'

'Well, he's not going to be able to follow us much further.'

'Why? Where are we going?'

'Over the bridge,' I said grimly.

'What?'

Now this was going to take some doing. Crossing a bridge takes time and focus. I didn't have the luxury of time, and all my focus was currently on steering. So let's turn all that focus into steering *across* the bridge, into the space beyond space beyond it. It's an old bridge made of stone, only wide enough for one vehicle at a time. And there was already a car in the way – *there was already a car in the way.*

'Stop,' she said urgently. 'Stop, you'll crash!'

So what we have to do is focus on steering *around* the car in the way, squeezing into that tiny gap, squeezing *through* that gap–

'Stop!' she shrieked. 'Stop the car!'

–into that space where the shape of reality warps and bends, with a screech of wheels and a scrape of metal–

'*No!*'

–and through the other side, across the bridge.

The car trundled to a halt.

I turned to the officer who, white-faced, was clutching the sides of her seat.

'Sorry about that,' I said, a tad shakily. 'All over now, promise I won't do it again.'

She was trembling. So was I.

'What,' she said, in a hoarse voice, 'was that?'

'That was us crossing a bridge. Now look, Miss . . . ?'

'That was insanely dangerous,' she said. Before I knew it, she'd lunged and grabbed me by the collar. She cursed as the seatbelt locked in place. I took my chance and gave her an elbow to the jaw. I wrenched myself out of her grip and gracelessly fell out of the car.

'I shouldn't run if I were you, Mr Jones!'

'I don't intend to.' I fought to regain my breath and held out my hands in a placating gesture. 'It's Hansard, by the way. Jack Hansard. And I should look out the window. If I were you.'

Her lip curled with suspicion, but she looked anyway. The blanket of thick rolling fog had its desired effect. Her jaw slowly dropped.

She twisted in her seat and stared out the back window. One end of the stone bridge could be seen, the rest of it stretching away into a thick grey shroud of mist.

Before I could stop her, she'd flung herself out of the car and stood staring in bewilderment at the foreign surroundings. Gone were the trees, the grass, the sky, the sun. All was fog.

'Please don't move, miss! It would be a really, really bad idea!'

'What happened to everything?' she said, stupefied.

She started towards the bridge. I dashed around and grabbed her by the shoulders.

'Let go! Or I'll–'

'Please listen to me,' I implored. 'I'll explain everything, but you mustn't move away from the car. You'll get lost in the fog.'

Her eyes seemed to come back into focus and her mouth set into a hard expression. In moments she'd thrust both my wrists behind my back and shoved me hard against the car. *Ouch.* I dimly noticed there was a horrific gash in the paintwork.

We'd nearly crashed. Just another second, just another millimetre, we'd have been smears on the road . . .

I came back to earth with the sound of her reading my rights. 'Mr Jones. Hansard. Whoever you are. You are hereby under arrest. I advise you to remain still–' I heard the clink of handcuffs.

'Won't you hear me out?' I pleaded. 'Look, I know this is all very strange, but trying to arrest me isn't going to solve anything.'

'I disagree.'

Damn, I couldn't get free of her. I tried to kick behind me, and she evaded it with ease.

'If you don't stay still I'll be forced to use, well, force!' she snapped. 'So stop struggling and– What is that?'

She stiffened. So did I. For we both heard the low, menacing howl rumbling out of the fog. We peered into the wall of white, which suddenly seemed more solid than it had before. The fog began to move. Or perhaps 'writhe' is a more appropriate description. Indistinct, stumbling shadows were forming in the murk.

'I think,' I said, voice a whisper, 'that we should get back in the car.'

Wordlessly, we did.

Outside, the howling turned to a kind of sighing moan. Tendrils of fog snaked towards us like outstretched limbs.

My unintentional captive turned from the window to me, her cheeks pale. 'You said you had an explanation?' she said through gritted teeth.

I nodded. 'This might take a moment to sink in, but I'll try to keep it as short as possible.'

'Don't patronise me.'

'I'm not! I won't. Look, imagine . . . imagine there are lots of different planes of existence – let's just call them other worlds for now, shall we? – and they all exist at once. And let's say that it's possible to cross into these other places at certain locations. Bridges, for example.' Her eyes narrowed. I ploughed on. 'What I'm saying is, a simple bridge in our world can act as a bridge to a whole *other* world. And so, knowing that all these other places, these other worlds exist, then there has to be something for them to exist *in*. There has to be something, sort of *around* them, to make sure they don't go bumping into one another.'

'You're going to tell me that's where we are now.'

She was quick on the uptake, at least. 'Yes. That's where we are now. Most people call it the Nether. Horrible foggy place of nightmares. But you can think of it as being a sort of reality-cushion. Hardly as scary, being inside a cushion,' I added brightly.

I watched her digest the information. She seemed to be taking it remarkably well, though I suspect the constant unearthly moan outside was providing a lot of support for my story. As if on cue, another howl rolled out of the fog.

She closed her eyes for a moment, breathed in deeply, exhaled, and when she opened them they were sharp once more.

'How did we get here?' she asked grimly.

'Funny story,' I said. 'There was this copper who tried to search my car and–'

'The *bridge*,' she said impatiently. 'How does that work? I thought we were going to crash.' Another thought apparently hit her square in the face, as her next question had more than an ounce of fear to it. 'Are we dead?'

'No! Far from it,' I assured. *But not necessarily for long.*

'You're sure?'

'Yes!'

'Fine. If we're not dead, then take us back. *Now.*'

I tapped my chin thoughtfully. 'Back isn't really an option for me. I have a horrible feeling I'm going to get shot if we go that way.'

She took another deep breath. 'Mr Hansard, are you sane? Do you understand that you have taken a police officer hostage?'

'I have bigger problems,' I said quietly. 'Look, we should at least be on first name terms. I'm Jack. Who're you?'

She considered me sullenly for a while. Then she pulled out her little black notebook, and I'm pretty sure she wrote my name in it.

'Age?' she said.

'You're kidding. I'm not telling you anything else.'

'Mid-forties.'

'How dare you! I'm thirty–' I caught myself. 'I don't look forty.'

'Have you *seen* what you look like?'

'I've had a rough week,' I grumbled. 'Would you put the pen down, please?'

She didn't, but she told me her name. 'Officer Neills. And we'll keep it at that.' She watched me fumble with the ignition, stalling the car again. 'If we're not going back, then where are we going? What's got you so spooked, Mr Hansard?'

I leaned my forehead on the steering wheel for a moment. How many hours ago had I set off on this mad race across the country? How could I explain the reason I was pelting down a quiet Lancashire lane at ninety miles an hour at seven o' clock in the morning?

I decided I would have to show her, if I had any hope of getting her on my side.

'Lift up the blanket on the back seat,' I said.

She did. At first she recoiled, mouth twisted in a mix of confusion and astonishment. Then she leaned in, inspecting the small quivering thing under the covers.

'What is it?' she asked.

'A friend of mine.'

Her brows knitted together. 'It looks like a goblin.'

'How would you know what a goblin looks like?' I replied sourly. 'Her name's Ang, if you care.'

'*Her*?' She shook her head. 'All right, but what *is* she, then?'

'A coblyn. They like to live underground in mines and other dark places.'

'Like a goblin.'

'Well, yes. But don't let her hear you say that.'

'What's wrong with it– her?'

I hesitated. How much could I say without breaking the poor woman's mind? Just because she hadn't suffered a nervous breakdown yet didn't mean she wasn't going to. She already had that distinctly frazzled look of someone approaching the edge of their mental capacity.

'She's . . . dying,' I said slowly. 'I'm trying to get her to someone who can help. At least, I hope he can help. I don't think she has much time left. Look, that's why I was driving so fast. I'm sorry you got caught up in all this, but you didn't really give me a choice.' I studied her face as I spoke. She seemed to be coming round. 'And that's also why we can't go back, you see. I might get shot, or at the very least people are going to want to ask a lot of very serious questions, and Ang might not survive. Forward is the only way. But I promise, once we're out of the Nether, you're free to leave and we'll be on our way. You don't have to see us ever again.'

That last bit was more of a hope on my part. I hoped she would decide to leave us alone.

She considered this while staring fixedly out the window, where dark shapes still moved in the mist. She seemed to reach a conclusion.

'How about you get us out of this fog, Mr Hansard?' Her voice was carefully level. 'Forward, or whichever way you need to go.'

'Gladly.' I smiled, though she didn't return it.

'But I'd also like you to answer some questions.'

'Ah, yes. I thought you might.'

'Starting with *exactly* who you are, and how you know about all these . . .' she waved a hand in a gesture that broadly encompassed everything around us, '. . . things.'

'That might take a while.'

'How long will it take to get out of here?'

'Uh. A while.'

'Then get talking.'

I refrained from saying that I actually had no idea how long we would be stuck here. As I started the ignition, successfully this time, I finally acknowledged the thin thread of worry winding its way round my own thoughts.

I had never meant to end up in the Nether, you see. No one ever does.

I've never seen it in such detail before. It's a world that you glimpse as you're passing between worlds – a curl of fog and a fleeting suggestion of shadows. Maybe crossing the bridge had been a stupid idea. I knew it was reckless, but at the time it seemed like the only option. You need time to unfocus, to aim yourself in the right direction – and at the time, I hadn't really thought about what I was aiming for. And that's how you end up lost in the Nether.

Lost. Now there's a horrible thought.

Still, I thought, with momentary pride, I did manage to pull not only myself across the bridge, but two other living bodies as well. Not to mention an entire car. That was pure skill, that was. Even if my bones now ached and my head pounded from the exertion.

I peered through the fog, trying to make out the shape of the road. Not that it was a road: more like a space where the fog was thinner, and hopefully safer to travel through. The fuel light blinked at me.

What a mess. Trundling through the Nether with a near-empty fuel tank, one abducted police officer in the passenger seat, and a dead body in the boot. At least she hadn't found out about the body. I hoped it would stay that way.

Worst of all, I was sure she was still going to give me the speeding ticket.

* * *

There is nothing quite so effective at putting your nerves on edge as the absence of sound.

There was the noise of the car engine. The presence of our breathing. The occasional creak as we shifted in our seats.

But no reassuring sounds of rubber meeting tarmac. No crunch of gravel under the wheels. Nothing at all to suggest we were driving on anything but air.

'I suppose there is a road under us?' Officer Neills said after a while.

'Best not to think about it.'

'Oh.'

Moments passed, as we stared ahead into the grey fog. The world outside was formless; it was hard to tell if we were making progress. Neills squinted through the glass.

'Are you sure we're moving?'

I considered the possibilities. 'I'm sure the wheels are turning.'

'That's not the same thing.'

The woman was tougher than she looked. I suppose you need to be, to make it in the police force. She was a constable in a Lancashire Road Policing Unit – that, and her name, was all she had told me outright. I'd pried a first name out of her too, and it turned out to be as plain and straight-forward as I'd expected: Jo.

Although she looked to be in her mid-twenties, Jo's slight build and young face were deceptive. I'd already learned from experience that a lot of strength was compacted into those lean muscles.

Her mind had turned out to be similarly tough. Once she'd gotten to grips with the situation – that she had been transported to the void between worlds and was surrounded on all sides by nightmarish shadow creatures – she'd handled the rest of the information with a calm matter-of-factness which frankly put me on edge. She had even taken out the notebook again and was jotting down notes.

As she shifted in her seat, her knee knocked an old carton of orange juice into the foot well.

'Leave it,' I said, as she bent to retrieve it. 'Doesn't matter.'

'Is this one of your business cards?' She waved a square of card which did, indeed, bear my name and esoteric profession in a fashionably gothic script. *Jack Hansard. Purveyor of Occult Goods.* 'How are people supposed to find you? There's not a phone number or anything.'

'Why would I want to be found?' I said, perplexed. 'Sounds risky to me.'

'Then what's the point of having business cards?'

'It looks good. Makes a statement.'

'You're an odd man, Mr Hansard.'

'What gave it away?'

'You do know you have dirt and weeds and all sorts in your hair?'

'Yes. Thank you.'

She pursed her lips and wrote another note in her book.

'Explain again how you got us here?' she said. 'I understand about the bridge and passing between realities. At least, I think I do. But I don't understand *how* you do it. Surely this should be common knowledge if it's as easy as you suggest.'

'It's not easy,' I pointed out, secretly glad to have more conversation to take my mind off things. 'I call it unfocusing. Oh, how do I explain this? So, think of there being walls that separate one part of reality from another, all right? Now, is it possible for a person to pass through a brick wall?'

'Sure. If you've got a big enough hammer.'

'. . . Right,' I conceded, after a moment's thought. 'I suppose that's one way. But you'd need a really *big* hammer. It'd be a lot easier if you just weren't so solid, right?'

'You turn yourself into air?' Her tone was unimpressed.

'Sort of. Look, even a good brick wall will have some tiny, porous holes in it. So you need to think yourself *unsolid*, as far as reality is concerned. Then you can fit through those holes. Now this place, the Nether, is sort of like the gap inside the wall.'

'I see. We're stuck in the insulation.'

'Ha. Yes.'

'Okay. Let me get this straight. A bridge in our world is like a really thin wall, right? And you thought us unsolid in order to pass through that wall.' I nodded. So far so good. 'So what's stopping you from thinking us the rest of the way through to the other side?'

'Ah,' I said. 'You might say I'm looking for a suitably sized hole.'

She seemed to accept this explanation, and I was really quite proud of it. There are lots of analogies you could use to describe the process of unfocusing, and none of them are wholly accurate. Still, you don't need an engineering degree to pilot a plane; likewise, no need to study metaphysics in order to traverse the realms of existence.

She tapped the pad with her pen, staring keenly into the fog.

'I don't understand why nobody's been policing you people,' she muttered.

'We're good at keeping a low profile. Being able to hop outside of reality helps.' The irony of my current situation wasn't lost on me as I said this. 'Besides, we police ourselves.'

'That's called vigilantism. It's against the law.'

'But we're *outside* the law, do you see? You show me any law, any statute, that makes it illegal to sell potions that turn people's arms purple.'

'I think Trading Standards would have something to say about it.'

'Sometimes people *want* their arms purple!'

I saw the pen move again. I wanted to throw the thing out the window. Who did she think she was, coming into my world and trying to make it fit with hers?

'And what happened to the goblin?'

'Coblyn,' I corrected irritably.

'You said she was a friend?'

'Yes. Look, we had a run-in with an unsavoury individual, all right?'

'Do you often run into unsavoury individuals?'

I pressed my foot down on the accelerator, willing the car to go faster. It didn't.

'Do you often get into this kind of trouble, Mr Hansard?'

'Is this what they teach you in police school?' I said peevishly. 'Keep asking questions until your suspect pleads guilty out of frustration?'

'Do you often have friends dying in the back seat of your car?'

My knuckles whitened on the wheel. How dare she. This snotty police officer with her calm voice and her black notebook and her pen. How dare she be so aloof, so insincere. What was it to her if Ang lived or died? *How dare she.*

Jo carefully folded the book into a pocket on her hi-viz vest. 'Struck a nerve?'

'Just be quiet,' I said, and realised it had come out as a snarl.

She did, for a whole three minutes. And then she said, 'Is there anything I can do?'

'No.'

'I could look over her if you like. I'm a certified first responder, after all.'

'What does that mean?'

'It means I have advanced first aid training. I don't know anything about coblyn physiology, but there might be something I can do.'

I scowled. 'You don't have to pretend to care.'

'What makes you think I don't?'

A snide laugh burst from my mouth. 'You're a traffic cop! What kind of person chooses the spiteful career of needling people for being five miles over the fucking speed limit? Someone small who likes to feel big. I'll bet you wanted to be a detective or something. No, worse! I bet you're the kind of person who *likes* to write passive-aggressive notes and make up rules and hand out little tickets just because it makes you feel a bit more powerful than everyone else. You and your fucking tickets. All in the name of feeling more important than you really are.'

Neills didn't answer at first. The atmosphere in the car was oppressive, like the fog had found a way in and was slowly suffocating us. When she did speak, it was in such an offhand manner that it caught me off balance.

'About seventeen hundred people die in road accidents every year in Britain,' she said, as casually as if she was pointing out the colour of the sky. 'And somewhere around twenty-five thousand serious injuries. Give or take a few hundred.'

'So what?' I got the feeling I would hate where this was leading.

'We're first responders.'

'Right.'

'And we carry teddy bears in our vehicles. Standard issue.'

'What?'

'For when we encounter an incident involving a child.'

'An incident.' I couldn't help the way my gaze slid across to her carefully poker-faced expression. The self-righteous anger drained from me like blood from a wound and left me similarly pale and queasy.

'Do you want to know the numbers?' she said. 'Or would you like to tell me again why speed limits are petty?'

171

I had no words left.

Well, I could manage one.

'Sorry,' I mumbled. She nodded, and that seemed to be that.

My thoughts, still tumbling over one another, tried to reconverge on the road ahead. The lack of road ahead. The fog still rolled on by, featureless and grey. I couldn't tell how far we'd travelled. Maybe we really hadn't moved at all.

'Have you and your friend been in business long?'

'I thought we'd finished the interrogation.'

She shrugged and turned to the window. 'Just trying to make conversation. It's not exactly stimulating scenery.'

I rolled the muscles in my shoulders. I was stiff all over, sat at the wheel for too many hours on end. 'Ang joined me a few months ago. We're not in business together, exactly. Well, we are, in that she employed me, you see?'

This seemed to puzzle Jo. 'Really? You're working for that little creature?'

'Sort of.' I relented, too exhausted to find another lie. Talking seemed to ease the tension between us. I gave her a run-down of Ang's deal with me, some snippets of our efforts to find the missing coblynau.

'So you're like a private investigator, or something?'

I puffed my chest at that. Jack Hansard, Private Investigator. That would make a great business card. 'Something like that,' I said loftily.

'When you're not scamming people with illegal magic junk?'

There was the shadow of a smile behind her lips. My mood started to pick up. Just as well, it had been hovering down in the dirt recently. 'Nothing illegal about it. I doubt you could find a judge willing to convict a man for selling nightmares in bottles–'

'He would if I could prove you were selling a harmful substance, or selling under false pretexts. Or if, as I strongly suspect, you don't pay taxes . . .'

'All right, all right. But there's far worse out there than me, and that's the truth.'

I could *feel* her resisting the urge to ask. Her fingers drummed against the door.

'Go on,' I said. 'I know you want to.'

'What kind of worse?'

Reflexively, I glanced up to the rear-view mirror. Jo caught the motion.

Ang was just a heap of dirty cloth in the reflection. *I should have found a better blanket for her,* I thought.

Jo frowned, and I could see the question she was framing in her head. I'd been stalling her interrogation with fanciful ramblings about the nature of reality and the cosmos, hoping to avoid this part altogether. But I knew she'd get back round to it eventually.

'Hansard, what were you *doing* before I arrested – tried to arrest you?'

'Running very fast,' I said, staring dead ahead. 'And then driving very fast.'

'Was someone after you?'

I sighed. 'Look, miss. You won't understand if I tell you, so it's best not to ask.'

'I seem to be understanding the rest just fine. Black Market: occult marketplace. Nether: trans-dimensional cushion. Hansard: man who owes me answers.'

She fixed me with a grim stare, which I steadfastly avoided by keeping my eyes on the non-existent road. She let the silence draw out. Exhaustion welled up in me.

I knew I had kept talking because I was trying to avoid the seriously distressing thought that I wasn't ready to contemplate. I no longer had a choice, and the thought sidled into my head like a petty thief nudging an unlocked window.

I don't know how to get out of here.

I was shot to pieces. There was no way I'd have the energy unfocus again. And even if I did, could I really pull all three of us back out of the Nether? I wished I could think like Jo. If only taking a hammer to the walls of reality really worked.

I opened my mouth, ready to let the whole story about Ang, Mallory, and the demonic worm all come spilling out.

'Hansard.'

'Hmm?'

Jo had gone rigid, all systems suddenly on alert.

With a sinking feeling, I registered the *thump, thump, thump* now emanating from the rear of the car.

'It's important to stay calm,' I said carefully. Drat. How long had the tire been leaking? I slowed the car to a crawl. It just made the *thump, thump, thump* sound louder.

'I am calm,' said Jo. Her expression returned to one of blank composure. 'We should fix it, don't you think?'

'That would mean stopping.'

'So?'

'Things might become . . . interested in us, if we stop.'

'Oh. What if we're quick? I can change a tire in five minutes flat.'

'I haven't got a spare,' I lied.

'Are you scared?'

'Of going out there? Definitely.'

'Stop the car, Hansard. I'm taking a look at that tire. We might be able to patch it up at the very least.'

'No. Why bother? Leave it be.'

'Hansard, I could walk faster than this. If we get chased by something, I want to know we can get away from it. Fast.'

'Nothing's going to chase us.'

'What about the thing that's been following us for the past ten minutes?'

Ah, hell. She'd noticed it too. There was a large shape hanging behind us in the fog. It gave the impression of loping, like an animal not used to legs.

'Ignore it,' I said. And then realised I had said it to thin air. Jo had flung open the door and hopped out. I slowed the car from a trundle to a halt. 'What are you thinking, jumping out of a moving car?'

'I would hardly call it moving,' she retorted.

I stepped out to find her crouched by the back wheel, examining it intently.

'All right, all right, if you're going to be difficult. Just step away. All the way. In fact, go right round the front.'

'Why? What don't you want me to see?'

'I keep all my stock in the back. Strange things, weird things.' I waved my hands vaguely. 'I'm afraid it would break your mind.'

She snorted. 'Try me.'

I hesitated. She had a sensible head on her shoulders, maybe she would understand.

Ah, but sensible is the problem, the other part of me thought. *A sensible person objects to the sight of a corpse. You need an insensible one to embrace it.*

'How about–' I began, but she pushed past. 'Hang on. Wait!' I tried to shove myself in front of her, but it was already too late. She pressed the catch on the boot.

Mallory's pallid, sunken face stared out at us. Well, not stared in fact, as I'd closed his eyes, but it still certainly gave the impression of staring. His head hung limply from a crooked neck, wedged in amongst the pre-packaged curses.

Jo stiffened. 'Is he dead?'

'Don't reach for the handcuffs just yet, all right?'

'Jesus, Hansard, I was just starting to trust you!'

I backed away. 'Calm down! This isn't what it looks like!'

'*It looks like you've packed a corpse in your car!*'

'I know it *looks* that way– All right, yes, it is technically the case, but he's in there for a very good reason! Just let me explain.'

'Explain fast.' Jo's expression was dangerous.

'This guy is the reason Ang's fighting for her life right now. Just meeting him put both our lives in jeopardy–'

'*So you killed him?*'

I looked appalled. 'Do you really think I'm capable of that?'

'I don't know what you're capable of.' Her hard stare kept me pinned, searching the lines in my face for some evidence of my character. She seemed to find something there that satisfied her because she relaxed, just a little, and said, 'No. I don't think you are. But you need to be honest with me. How did this man die?'

'Honestly? I think he was murdered.' I exhaled the rest in a rush. 'And the murder weapon was a demon slug that exploded from his mouth and now the same demon slug is sitting in Ang's stomach and I have to get her to someone who can stop it *before she dies too.*' I paused, noting the fascinated horror on Jo's face. 'Could you imagine me trying to report this to the police?'

'I can imagine it going badly.'

We were cut off by the low moan rising all around us. The fog seemed to become denser. Jo exchanged a tense glance with me.

'You said you could change a tire in five minutes?' I said. She nodded mutely. 'Make it thirty seconds.'

I struggled to roll Mallory out of the way. Jo dived forward and grabbed his legs. I shuddered at the stiffness of the limbs. It was a grotesque feeling, pulling on unyielding flesh. We manhandled him out of the boot and dropped the body to the ground. There was no thump – there was no ground, really – but I saw his neck contort to an even more gruesome angle as it hit whatever we were standing on.

I plunged back into the boot, frantically throwing boxes and bottles and the bloody stuffed owl out of the way. I heard the crack of breaking glass and vaguely hoped it wasn't one of the expensive ones. As we uncovered the spare tire in its cubby-hole, the first of the shadows emerged from the fog.

'Hurry!' I croaked. Jo was already setting the jack under the car. There hadn't been any sensation of heat in this place, but suddenly it felt like a tangible cold was wrapping itself around our throats, though I could still feel sweat beading on my brow.

The dark shapes were slow, stumbling, and they advanced with the wall of fog. There didn't seem to be any body to them, yet they conveyed a sense of heavy mass condensed into shadow. Later I would remember them with arms reaching out to us, though I'm certain they had no real limbs. I couldn't even tell you if they were truly person-shaped at all.

There were no distinct silhouettes, just smears of darkness undulating forwards. Perhaps there weren't hundreds of them like I imagined; perhaps it was all one mass encircling us.

Kneeling beside me, Jo wrestled with a corroded lug nut. I leant my weight to hers and together we wrenched it free. We rose to find the shadows, and the fog, almost on top of us.

Jo lashed out at a shape with the steel wrench. It passed right through. The shade didn't even waver, but part of it, a bit like a hand, but definitely nothing like a hand, reached out and enclosed Jo's wrist. She dropped the wrench.

Blue veins pricked up under the skin of her arm. Shock etched on her suddenly rigid features. She looked like the corpse, I thought.

I dashed to the boot and grabbed the one thing I hoped would work. I swung round, iron crowbar in hand, and thrashed blindly. There was some soft resistance, like slicing through a wall of butter, and the shadowy mass in front of me pulled back noiselessly. The low moan intensified, rising from below our feet.

I swung at the thing clutching Jo, and she collapsed to the floor gasping for breath. Her right arm, I noticed, was sickeningly blue. I hauled her upright and thrust the crowbar into her good hand.

'Just keep swinging!' I shouted.

I dropped to my knees and fumbled with the wheel. Old one: off. Spare: on. *On,* I said. God damn these things. Behind me, I heard Jo grunting with the strain. Just a few more minutes. Just a few more.

'Hansard.'

I jerked round again. 'What is it?'

She pointed with the crowbar. I followed it to the large, loping shadow towering out of the grey haze. It was like a coiled storm cloud gradually unfolding itself in our direction. The smaller shadows scattered and merged back into the mist.

'Help me with this!' I cried, desperately screwing lug nuts back into place. Jo didn't move, instead transfixed on the uncurling behemoth. I leapt up and shook her by the shoulders. 'Don't crash on me now! You were doing so well!' Snapping my fingers in front of her face, I realised it wasn't fear that had set her features so firmly. Rather, it was a look of intense concentration, even though her eyes were glazed over. She muttered something under her breath.

'What is it?' I pleaded. 'Can you hear me, Jo? *Jo!*'

'It's just a wall,' she murmured.

'Snap out of it!'

'We need a bigger hammer.'

I saw her fist clench the crowbar. She pulled it up, high above her head as if she was about to strike down the world.

The fog rushed forward to envelop us. My vision blurred, and for a moment I felt like I wasn't really there.

Jo swung.

Episode 10: Parasite

The world stretched————
————and snapped back into focus.

I stumbled forward, arms still locked on Jo's shoulders. She rocked gently on her heels, then slumped to her knees in the dirt. Dirt.

I looked down and found yellowing grass at my feet. To the left, tarmac. Above, a reassuringly blue sky. And there was Jo and me, and my trusty Ford Escort, and the corpse, and even the old busted tire lying on the verge as if it had every right in the world to be there.

A small, mad laugh escaped my throat.

How had I done that? *Had* I done that?

I looked behind me and saw the narrow stone bridge I'd first used to cross into the Nether. It was a picture of countryside serenity, except for a flicker of neon on the grassy verge. Remnants of police tape. I wondered how long we'd been gone. I suffered a compelling urge to find a local newspaper so I could check the date.

I didn't bring us here. I *know* I didn't.

Jo hadn't said a word. I stooped beside her and tried to gently pry the crowbar from her fingers.

'Ouch!' I snatched back my hand and sucked where it had burned. The iron was *hot*. And Jo's knuckles were white.

A strange thought trickled into my head.

Maybe there is more than one way to pass through a wall.

My way is sly and subtle, a gentle easing of the self through the partitions of reality. Maybe Jo had punched a hole right through. All you'd need is a big enough hammer, she'd said.

But that's absurd. No one could punch a hole *that* big, and on their first try, too! It takes years of practice to move anything besides yourself, let alone a two-ton car and a couple of adult bodies. And don't forget the coblyn.

Jo didn't know that, I realised. Maybe ignorance and sheer force of will can make for one big hammer. I looked at her with a mixture of fear and admiration. She stared back, with an eerie faraway gaze.

'Jo?' I said softly and touched the back of her hand. In contrast to the iron, her skin was cold. A new chill swept over me. I'd seen eyes like that before.

They had belonged to the girl who taught me how to unfocus, so many years ago. She had been a bit like Jo: a stubborn brick of a woman who would punch holes in your understanding of the world as easily as poking a finger through soggy bread. She was a natural, fluent in the language of the lost; an expert in navigating the dark pathways I now tread myself. Her eyes had always been golden and warm, and filled with delicious promises of forbidden knowledge and unruly adventure.

Then one day she punched too hard, took a wrong turn, and my golden world turned to grey mulch. Her eyes had gained that vacant gaze of a person lost, forever treading water in the darkness of their own head. I never found her again.

It shocked me, the surge of memory that hit like a tide. It had happened so long ago. They tell you pain dulls over time.

'Jo,' I said again, more firmly. *Shake it off,* I thought. I wasn't sure if I was referring to myself or her. 'Listen to me, Jo. You better snap out of this, otherwise I'm giving you up for dead, y'hear? I haven't got time for this. I'll stick you by that bush and ring for an ambulance, and then I'll be long gone.' Nothing, not a twitch. 'There isn't a doctor on earth who'll know how to pull you out of your head if you can't do it yourself. Are you hearing me? Do you want to be a cabbage for the rest of your life? Stuck in a wheelchair in some hospital, how does that sound? Maybe they'll put you down, like a lame dog. How about that, Jo? Or maybe they'll just leave you to stare at a white wall for the rest of your life. For *eternity,* even.'

She remained vacant. I grabbed her chin and forced her to face me. 'If they do, I'll know it's because you let them, Jo. Because you gave up, you quit. Because you left everyone who loves you, and you didn't bother coming back for them.' I knew my voice had started to break. 'Because you decided to stop fighting. Because you let yourself be bound to a chair and a room, and the inside of your own eyelids. I'll leave you here, I really will. Because I've done it before, you see. I can't save you on my own. I've never saved anyone. I'm not that guy, Jo. And I'll leave you if you quit. *You mustn't quit.'*

Her pupils flickered, and there was a downturn at the corners of her thin lips.

'What are you talking about, Hansard?' she murmured. Light filtered back into her eyes.

I tried to mask my overwhelming relief.

'You were gone with the fairies for a moment there,' I replied gruffly. 'Stupid thing you did, but at least it worked. You want to let go of the crowbar now?'

'What? Oh.' She released her grip and the iron thumped onto the grass. Four finger marks were scored into the metal.

'Huh,' I said.

Her gaze followed mine. 'What happened to that?'

'I think you hit reality with it.'

'I did?' Her brow furrowed further. 'I thought . . . it was almost like a dream. But it was all so clear . . .'

'Do you remember what you did?'

'There were those shadows, coming out of the fog. We were going to die.' Her eyes sparked. 'Dying's not an option.'

'It's certainly at the bottom of my list.'

She stared at her hands. 'There was this moment where it all made sense. Where I could feel, I don't know, *waves* of reality around us. Like currents in a vast, churning ocean. And I could just *see* which direction we needed to go in, we just needed, I don't know, a push, or–'

'A hammer.'

'Exactly!'

'Well, points for effort, but you've certainly got a lot of work to do in terms of finesse,' I said tersely. In truth I was intensely unnerved. It's never been that easy for *me*.

Jo seemed to take in her surroundings for the first time, the bridge, the tape, the comforting absence of police (well, it was comforting to *me*). She shook her head as if trying to rid it of cotton wool, and then climbed shakily to her feet. I thought I saw a shadow fall across her face for a split-second, but it was gone as soon as I'd noticed. There was still something odd about her, something in the way she moved, that I suddenly found very off-putting.

'Are you all right?' I asked her.

'Sure. Why?' she replied, leaning heavily on the car.

I studied her carefully. 'You seem sort of . . . fuzzy. Around the edges.'

She shifted uncomfortably. 'I'm fine, Hansard. Just a little woozy, that's all.' She motioned to Ang, bundled in the back seat. 'Now what are we doing about your friend?'

I blinked. 'We?'

'She needs help, doesn't she? Let's go!'

'Yes, but I could drop you off in the nearest village or . . .' I trailed off under her hard gaze. She pointed to the dishevelled corpse lying by the roadside.

'Hansard, if nothing else, you are explaining the whole of this matter to me. I'm not going to let you just walk away with a dead body in your possession. Even after what we've been through, I . . .' she faltered, and her eyes moved off into the distance. An unnerving calm settled over her features again.

'Jo,' I barked. 'Dead body, right?'

Her eyes snapped back to mine. 'Exactly. And maybe at the end of all this I'll arrest you, or maybe I won't, but I'm not letting you out of my sight until we've seen this to the end!' She marched over to the passenger door, yanked it open, and strapped herself in. She sat straight-backed, legs crossed, and arms folded sternly across her chest.

'I'll put the stiff back in the car by myself then, will I?' I muttered under my breath. Mallory was heavier than I remembered, or perhaps I was more tired. I threw a clean rag over his face once I'd forced it into the boot, and then placed a crate of unlucky charms over it for good measure.

I also took the opportunity, while Jo wasn't looking, to adjust my license plate. Amazing what you can achieve with some very precise black tape – an F becomes an E, the J is cunningly disguised as U, or a P suddenly turns into R. I've said it before, and I'll say it again: duct tape can do anything. Add a splatter of mud and you're good to go.

'All right, settle in,' I said, turning the key in the ignition.

'What were you faffing about with?'

'Just checking the new wheel is roadworthy.'

'Oh. Of course,' she said faintly. I suspect I was lucky that she was still too dazed to pick up on such an obvious lie. 'How long's the journey?'

'Less than an hour from here, I think.'

'You're not going to take us over any more bridges, are you?'

'No. Normal roads from now on.' I refrained from pointing out that it was her own intervention that had forced me off normal roads in the first place.

'Okay. No speeding.'

'I've learned my lesson.'

I eased us cautiously onto the main road, heading for the nearest village. A quick stop to refuel and we'd be breezing on up North. I kept an ear out for sirens and an eye for flashing blue lights, but neither materialised.

Jo had her notebook out again. 'Okay, Hansard. Tell me why you put the dead guy in your car.'

There was no point dancing around it any more. 'I thought he might be needed. Maybe we'll have to do an autopsy or something to figure out how to help Ang.'

'That makes sense, I suppose. You called it a . . . demon slug? I'd like to know what it did to him. What it's doing to your friend.'

'I can only tell you what I know.'

And so I filled her in, as best I could, on what I remembered of our ill-fated meeting with Mallory, though I skipped over some of the harder bits – like the Floating Harbour and the pooka and Mallory's strange glass meadow – which, in a way, didn't leave much left to tell.

She kept silent as my story sunk in, and stayed silent after I'd finished. We both stared at the empty road ahead, and for a long minute I felt my world consisted only of grey tarmac and Ang's raspy breathing.

'So where are you taking her?'

'Who?' I said muzzily.

'Ang. Who else?' Jo scrutinised me. 'Maybe we should stop for a bit, Hansard. You look awful.'

I bucked up and rubbed my eyes. 'Can't stop now.' *Need to stay awake. Need to get out of here. Keep talking.* 'I'm taking Ang to a witch.'

I saw the thought glide across her face as she pursed her lips. The expression said: 'So there are witches now?'

'The thing you've got to remember,' I continued, fighting the weight on my eyelids, 'is that the world is always stranger than you think.'

She threw down her pen. 'This is still ridiculous. How can things like coblyns and witches and demon slugs go unnoticed in this day and age?'

I gave her an incredulous look. 'Just because *you* don't know about them doesn't mean that everyone else is in the dark. Sure, maybe the things in '*my*' world have become harder to find, but only because the things in *your* world have pushed them further into the shadows. Take coblynau. It used to be common knowledge that they dwelt in the Welsh mines.'

She responded with exasperation. 'That's like saying it used to be common knowledge that pixies were real.'

'Exactly.'

'No. No, Hansard. I don't believe you're about to tell me that pixies are real.'

'Let's just say it's a bad idea to cross one, and leave it at that, eh? Anyway, did you know that the miners used to leave out food for coblyns to eat? Hell, some of the little buggers were even on the payroll! But then the mines closed down, people forgot, and the coblynau moved on to pastures new.'

Jo glanced at the quivering blanket again. 'But it's all just folklore, isn't it? Bedtime stories and odd local legends. That's what you're really talking about.'

'Wasn't folklore, once.'

'Oh, fine. Let's say I'm willing to accept there were all these weird creatures that were once as common as cats and dogs but have faded into history. Like an endangered species, I can get my head around that. But I'm not so sure about witches. Are we talking magic? Of the spells and potions and pentagrams variety?'

I pinched the bridge of my nose. 'You've happily travelled into the void between worlds, accepted the existence of mythical creatures, and believed my story about the evil red slug in Ang's throat, but 'magic' is a step too far for you?'

'Well?'

'*Yes*, spells and potions and pentagrams. And again, witches used to be a thing of common knowledge. Distinguished members of the community, even. Still are, if you move in the right circles.'

'And how does someone get into *your* circle? Is there some super-secret handshake I should know about?' she said resentfully.

'Oh, Google it, or something.'

'What?' She glared at me as though I were making fun of her.

'I'm serious. We're not as far removed from 'your' world as you think. You'd be amazed the curses you can buy on the internet these days. They've probably got an app for it now.'

'That's ridiculous,' she grumbled.

Jo flipped to a clean page in her notebook and became engrossed in her scribbling, though I got the impression she was putting on a show. There was a slight giddiness to her voice; I wondered if she was still dizzy.

I glanced at her from the corner of my eye. She was strangely pale. I had a momentary impression of a black cloud hanging over her head, but I blinked it away. The exhaustion was drumming on my skull.

The familiar scritching of her pen was oddly soothing, even if it didn't quite take my mind off the tension in the pit of my stomach. I couldn't remember when I had last relaxed. It was a long time before that last tin of soup with Ang. I hadn't eaten since then either, but my insides didn't feel up to the task anyway.

The roads remained calm, despite the churning in my gut, and we wound our way deep into the rolling hills of the Lake District with no more excitement than a stray sheep crossing the road. I caught Jo staring blankly once or twice, but if I gave a sharp word she would snap back into focus with a frown and then bend over her notebook again.

We rolled onto the witch's estate while the sun was still high in the sky. The goats, thankfully, looked rather livelier in their paddock than when I'd last visited.

Mark opened the door before I'd even knocked. He didn't look surprised to see us, which bothered me at once. I know I'd be extremely troubled if I opened the door to a disgruntled police officer with a corpse slung over one shoulder and a scruffy man in a long coat holding a small blanketed bundle which emitted sounds of whimpering.

The witch regarded us coolly.

'What's wrong with your friend?' he asked.

I took a step forwards, holding out the bundle. 'Long story. But there's this slug inside her and–'

'Not the coblyn. Her.' He pointed a slender finger at Jo. She stepped back warily, eyeing the accusatory digit as though it might explode.

'What do you mean?' I said, perplexed.

'She's not all there.'

'I'm fine,' said Jo, though there was a tremor to her voice I hadn't heard before.

Mark leaned in closer, peering at Jo's face with interest.

'Aren't you that copper who was kidnapped?' he said.

'I wouldn't say kidnapped–' I began. 'Wait. How on earth do you know about that?'

'Your face has been all over the local papers,' he told Jo. 'Weird circumstances. The reporters seem quite confused on the story. Some had it that you'd died in a car crash, others that you'd drowned in the river, and another that you'd simply disappeared off the face of the earth. That's the kind of story I pay attention to.'

'How long ago was this?' I asked. It felt like we'd only spent half a day travelling through the Nether. Don't tell me several days had passed outside.

'About a month,' said Mark, throwing me a lopsided glance. 'That's a shock to you, isn't it?' Jo and I nodded, dumbly. He sighed, like an experienced dog owner who knows to expect regular messes on the carpet. 'Have you been doing some exotic travelling? Never mind, I can see where you've been. I trust you enjoyed your stay in the Nether.'

'How does he know that?' Jo demanded, brimming with suspicion.

'Witch,' I said bluntly.

Mark pursed his lips. 'What were you doing in the Nether in the first place? I thought you'd know better, Hansard.'

'I was running from the police,' I muttered.

'I see that worked out wonderfully for you.'

I offered up Ang in my arms. 'It doesn't matter now. I just need you to help Ang.'

He glanced at the coblyn and then back at Jo. 'Of course. Come in,' he said, stepping aside with a wry smile.

I hurried in gratefully and placed Ang gently on the large wooden table that was the centrepiece to the witch's kitchen.

I spun on my heel when I heard Jo let out a painful yell behind me.

My eyes took in the sight of her held in the doorway, back arched and head thrown back, feet several inches above the ground. And then she was flung back out into the courtyard like a rag doll, gasping on the flagstones. A shadow followed her.

'Your friend can't, however,' Mark said placidly.

'*What have you done?*' I shouted, aghast.

'Calm down. I've done nothing. It's that shade wrapped around her you should be concerned about.'

It was still there, a coil of darkness around Jo's shoulders and torso.

I watched it dissipate into the air, yet I got the sense that it hadn't left at all.

Jo was trembling. Not with fear, I realised, but rage. 'What is it?' she hissed. 'What the hell is it now?' She leapt to her feet and shouted at the sky. 'I'm warning you! If you try anything with me, you'll regret it!' She glared at myself and Mark. 'Well?'

The witch answered. 'Shouting at the universe may not be the most effective option.'

'Is this funny to you?' I growled.

'It's very *interesting*,' he replied evenly. 'It's rare to see this sort of thing. Your friend seems to have gained a lodger, shall we say.'

'She's possessed?'

'Oh no, not at all. This thing from the Nether, this shade, has merely latched onto her. Like a parasite,' he added.

'I'm not playing host to some ethereal tapeworm,' said Jo through gritted teeth.

He gave a one-shouldered shrug. 'You don't have much choice. You're not entirely here, you see. You might say you left one foot standing in the Nether, and the shade is clinging onto it.'

A droning sound began to form on the edge of hearing. I swatted by my ear, expecting a fly, but it only grew louder.

I turned back to see Jo, eerily motionless outside the doorway. Mark was watching her with keen interest. He blocked me with an arm as I moved forward.

'Stay put,' he said.

The air was vibrating. It began to fill with the noise of buzzing, as if a hundred enraged hornets had exploded in our midst. Jo clapped both hands to her head and dropped to her knees.

'Jo!' I darted forward but Mark yanked me back by the collar.

'Nothing you can do about it,' he said.

The coiled shade was re-forming, rising like a black cloud over Jo's head. It hung over her reeling body, a faint suggestion of head, torso, limbs . . . claws. It didn't seem a solid shadow, more like a mass of tiny points of buzzing darkness tumbling over one another to create the illusion of a whole being.

I shoved back at the witch. 'Do something! Help her!'

'Nope.'

'Use your eldritch powers, man!'

He shrugged again. 'If I sever the connection she'll die.'

The shade reared and a slit opened, a gash of mouth spread in a grotesque, lipless grin. Crumpled underneath it, Jo's body convulsed in gut-wrenching spasms as she if she was trying to vomit up her insides.

The maw opened wider, big enough to swallow Jo's head. It leaned down.

'She's dead if she doesn't concentrate,' observed Mark. I looked at him like he was mad before comprehension hit.

I thrust past him and fell to my knees in front of Jo. Her hands still shook against her head.

'Jo, listen to me. You need to unfocus,' I said urgently. 'Remember everything I told you. Think yourself unsolid. That thing isn't really here, not all the way. You've got to put yourself on its level to fight it. Stop trying to be solid, Jo!'

She made a noise somewhere between a choke and gurgle. I bent closer to hear.

'What is it, Jo?'

'Hansard–' another strangled noise as she looked me in the eye, '–shut up.'

Then she was on her feet, fist curling round in a wide arc that connected with a resounding *crack* where the monster's nose would have been.

The thing pitched backwards, writhing without a sound. Jo

rebounded, shook her fist, and swung in with another punch. It landed like a crack of lightning.

'Good show,' said Mark.

'Shut up and *help*,' I yelled angrily.

I ran to the car, flung open the boot. Crowbar. Iron. It was good and heavy in my hand.

'That's a bad idea.'

I ignored him and lunged for the shadowy parasite. With satisfaction I watched the crowbar slice right through the black mass.

Jo screamed in agony. She clutched at her sides and then her head, as if she didn't know where the pain was coming from.

'Told you,' said Mark.

I reached for Jo's arm, but she snatched it back from me.

'*Get away,*' she snarled, except it sounded like wasps in her throat.

Shocked, I dropped the crowbar. Behind her the shadow seemed to gather and rise for a retaliatory strike.

'Jo, look out–!'

It struck like a cobra. Jo met it with a howl and an outstretched hand. It impacted and stuck, a rigid shape pinned in the air, balanced sideways against her palm.

The buzzing returned, but this time it seemed to come from Jo herself. The dark shade began to disintegrate, its bulk collapsing into a cloud of disjointed specks until it was only as thin as mist, and then like a cowed animal it slunk down onto Jo's shoulders and seemed to sink, until there was nothing left to see at all.

The wasp-like drone subsided, and Jo opened her eyes. Slowly, she lowered her arm. There was something clenched in her hand.

'Jo?' I said faintly. She looked at me, and her eyes were her own. She looked drained, tight exhaustion pulling at her features, but she offered me a weak smile before sagging to the ground.

Mark nodded, as if he would begrudgingly allow us to continue disrupting his day. 'Kettle's in the kitchen, Hansard. Your friend could probably use a cup.'

I shot a dark look at the witch. 'Can she come in the house now?'

'No.' He pointed to the iron horseshoe on the door. 'Keeps out unwanted spirits, like that one attached to her. So, I'm afraid she stays in the yard.'

I wanted to shove that horseshoe somewhere painful and decidedly unhorseshoe-shaped. But I chewed the inside of my cheek and resentfully dug through his cupboards. I found the tea – unnervingly housed next to the deadly nightshade – and brought a cup out to Jo.

'I don't like tea,' she said despondently.

'Suit yourself.'

We sat on the flagstones, watching the sun draw nearer the horizon. Pale pink already streaked the sky. The goats watched us with their curiously slit eyes, chewing cud in that slow, brainless kind of serenity that only livestock can achieve.

I held my mug close to my chest. There's something comforting about just having a warm cup of tea nearby. Jo's steamed on the ground next to her. Her arms were folded across her knees, but I could see she still clutched something tightly in her right hand.

Eventually, she said, 'I can still feel it on me, you know.'

'The shade?'

'It's like a . . . fog, sitting on my shoulders. Curled around my spine.'

I tried not to let her see the way I glanced over. Was that a shadow that fell across her face there, or my tired imagination?

I tried to push it from my mind. 'What happened back there? For a second I thought it had you.'

'No,' she said ferociously. 'I had *it.*'

I sipped my tea. It eased the tension in my muscles. 'What's your secret weapon?' I gestured to her closed hand.

She exhaled and uncurled her fingers. She was holding a black wallet, which she opened with a deft flick of a thumb. Inside was an ID and a metal badge.

'My warrant card,' she said. She tapped the badge, a seven-pointed star with a Tudor rose in the centre and the Queen's crown at the crest. The words 'Lancashire Constabulary' were emblazoned in a circle around the centre.

'It's important to you.'

'Makes me what I am.'

She tucked it into a pocket in her police vest and her gaze became distracted.

'Hansard.'

'Mm?'

'Has it really been a month?'

''Fraid so. Time can be as fluid as reality, so I hear. Very sci-fi. But look on the bright side: you're now technically one month younger, compared to everyone else.'

'I've always hated science fiction,' she said distantly. 'My family probably think I'm dead.'

'This'll be a nice surprise, then.'

'I don't know if I can go back to my life.'

I was expecting this. It's familiar ground. Once exposed to our world, it's very hard to leave. In my experience.

'Sure you can,' I said cheerfully. 'Think of all those people missing you.'

She poked the ground with a piece of straw, expression pinched and withdrawn. 'And what do I tell them when they ask where I've been for a whole month? What do I say when they ask about the man who pulled me into his car and drove into thin air?'

'Make it up. Make it good. Everyone loves a good story.'

'Speaking for the police force, we prefer true stories.' Then in a soft voice that I almost didn't hear, she said, 'Will this thing kill me?'

I considered making up something comforting. But ill-founded comfort is often unhelpful. 'I don't know. Bit out of my realm of experience, that. Might be that your body can't take the strain and slowly dies. Might be that it saps your mind away instead – that's what I'd put my money on.' Her expression hadn't changed. She'd guessed as much already. 'Or maybe it just sits there, occasionally making you itch. In any case, if I were you I'd seek help, tout suite.'

'Help from where? If your witch can't do anything–'

'There's a guy I know, specialises in possession. Or rather, exorcism. I reckon he's your man. I can give you a name, and a last known address.'

'Last known?'

'You might have to do a little detective work, but I reckon you're up to it.'

She passed me the notebook to jot down the details. I tore a page out to write on and she winced. 'Sorry, old habit,' I said apologetically.

I handed her the paper with a sincere hope that she would find what she was looking for. I realised I'd screwed up her life. All this because I decided to drive thirty miles over the speed limit down some quiet country road. I bet she wished she'd never pulled me over. She must wish she'd called in sick, swapped shifts, or any number of other alternatives that could've caused her to not be on the same road as me, on the day that I was ferrying a corpse and a sick coblyn towards a witch.

Jo stood up suddenly, with a new sense of determination about her. 'Think you could call me a taxi?' she said. 'I ought to get going. No sense waiting around, letting people think I'm dead.'

I nodded. Practical thinking. Matter-of-fact. She'd probably do all right.

As we waited for the cab to find its way to this slice of quiet nowhere, I left Jo with some parting advice. 'Carry iron,' I instructed. 'Reliable stuff. Hurts the things that aren't quite there – spirits, and the like. And if it's a physical entity you're up against, well, a bloody great bar of iron will hurt anybody if you swing it hard enough.'

'You think I'm going to be attacked?'

'Not as such. It's just good advice. In case you never quite find the way back to . . . 'your' world.'

I think she understood. We spent those final moments watching the sun dip below the crest of the hills, spilling rose gold rays across the valley. She left with hardly a word of good bye. Neither of us, I suspect, believe in ceremony.

The goats continued to give me the devil's eye through their fence. Their gaze seemed accusatory as I thumbed through Jo's little black notebook. Sleight of hand is something I feel I've perfected. The handwriting was very messy; I was surprised. Hasty scribbles on top of other scribbles, some doodles, and a lot of smudged bullet points. I picked out words about my character, my car, Ang, the Nether, unfocusing, and at the end a few notes on witches with many, many question marks. I'd burn the whole thing later.

I'd have to change the registration plates on my car again. Lay low, hope the police aren't still looking for me in a few weeks' time. Maybe Jo would find a way to smooth it all over.

Or, she might brand me a fugitive and have the whole country on red alert with a description of my face. I've never been a fugitive before. Might be fun. But something told me I was probably safe from that option.

'It's getting dark, Hansard. Come inside, or I'm locking you out.'

I shoved the little book inside my coat. 'How's Ang?'

Mark was stirring some unidentifiable brew in a tall mug. Could be a magical tonic; could be pretentious coffee. Hard to tell with a witch. He took a sip, which didn't narrow down the options. 'The coblyn should live. Tough job, though. Time-consuming, if you understand me.'

I didn't hide my exasperation. 'You really want me to pay for your help? After all this?'

He shrugged, a gesture so infuriatingly habitual that it verged on being a tick. 'Time is time, and work is work.'

'I'm broke, Mark. This time I really am broke. I'm asking you as a friend–'

'As a friend, you can do a small favour for me. That's all I want. A favour.'

'There's a catch.'

'Where would we be, without life's little surprises?'

I sighed gloomily. 'Surprises like demon slugs and parasitic shadows? I think I could do with less of those.'

He patted my shoulder and said, unsympathetically, 'So could I.' He disappeared back into the kitchen where Ang still lay on the table, though now covered with a duvet and a pillow under her head. An array of slim metal tools were lined up beside her, and bottles with contents I couldn't fathom.

I collapsed into a chair and rested my head in my hands.

'You're going to be all right, Ang,' I murmured. 'I'd say I'm sorry for all this, but you're as much to blame as I am. I guess we both got in too deep, huh?' My eyes drifted closed. 'I hate drowning, Ang.'

My head slipped down onto my forearm, nestled in the folds of my coat. Fatigue finally caught up with me and drew my conscious mind into darkness.

The witch's favour would have to wait.

Episode 11: Lament of the Lake

S quelch.
'Damn.'
Squelch. Squelch. Splash.
'*Damn!*'

I clambered to my feet, soggy and irritated, for the third time in one morning. With a groan and a sucking plop, I dragged one foot out of the mud and forged a step onwards.

Squelch. Squelch.

Damn that witch. Sending me out here on a fool's errand. 'It'll be in the shallows close to the bank,' he'd said. 'Expect to get your feet wet.'

Feet. *Ha.*

My trousers were caked with mud and I was dragging weeds around my knees. I'd sensibly removed my trench coat and carried it over one arm, but the first slip into the lake had it as sodden as the rest of me.

I climbed back up the bank and emerged out of a shady patch of trees into bright sunlight. In crisp contrast to my mood, the scene before me was practically glowing with tranquillity.

Autumn had left its calling card on the hills and valleys of the Lakes. A fine dust of gold and burnished copper on the trees glinted in the sunlight against a clear blue sky. All around me the gentle ripples of the Wastwater twinkled invitingly against a stark neighbouring peak. The eastern side of the lake butted up against a towering wall of steep scree slopes, a dramatic backdrop of natural architecture.

If I weren't cold, and wet, and tired, and wet, I groused, *I'd probably be enjoying this.*

I once thought that days like this were the reason I wanted to travel. I thought that the freedom of the open road would come hand in hand with the freedom to enjoy life's small pleasures, on my own terms.

Of course, once on the open road it quickly becomes apparent that life's small pleasures are less about enjoying the scenery, and more about knowing where your next meal is coming from. Whether that azure sky can be traded in for a solid roof over your head. Whether you're going to be able to dry out your clothes later. Romantic notions like smelling the flowers and soaking up the sun are far, far down the list.

I wondered if Ang would appreciate this vista. Though she was brought up in the hot dark of a mine, her beady eyes had swallowed up the outside world with an avaricious appetite that almost – almost – matched her appetite for cooked pastries.

Right now, she was in the care of Mark Demdike, the Witch of the Lakes. I've known the man for nearly a decade (and I swear he hasn't aged a day past twenty-five in that time) and as much as I despised him for sending me out to look for an aquatic weed, I was grateful for the treatment he'd given Ang.

He wouldn't let me watch at the time, but I got the impression he was performing the occult equivalent of a surgical procedure. Immediately after inspecting the creature he'd removed from Ang's stomach, he took me to one side.

'Who have you antagonised this time, Hansard?' he inquired gravely.

'No one of consequence. Why do you ask?'

He frowned. 'A little advice, Hansard. Whatever it is you're dealing in at the moment . . . don't. Someone, and by this I mean a very *formidable* someone, has gone to a lot of trouble to make a corpse of you.'

'Didn't go to enough trouble, by the looks of things.'

Mark shook his head. 'You see that worm I dug out of your friend?' He pointed to its oozing, blood-red remains in a tray by the sink. 'It is a thing not of our world.'

I waited for him to say more, but he didn't.

'A lot of things aren't,' I prompted.

His eyes narrowed. 'It's an anomalous entity, Hansard.'

'Yes.' I could tell he was starting to get wound up, and it was proving amusing.

Mark folded his arms, a sure sign he was about to unload something heavy. 'There are some things so dangerous, Hansard, so perilous a threat to the existence of our world that they have been *sealed off*. Locked away in their own hellish dimensions and banished to eternity. And this worm, as you call it, lives only in one of these forbidden dimensions. What does that tell us?'

'Someone has a key?'

'They would need a more than just a key. They would need resources to capture and contain a creature like this, and then the ability to unleash it onto its victim – *you.*'

'But it wasn't unleashed on me,' I protested. I jerked my thumb at the courtyard where, out in an old barn, Mallory's body was currently residing inside a large freezer. 'That poor sod out there was the target. We were just unlucky bystanders.'

'I doubt that very much. It's easy to kill one man. Why then, go to the trouble of using a creature that will endeavour to destroy the people around him, as well?'

I rubbed my chin thoughtfully. 'Do really think so? I didn't think they'd even noticed us, to be honest. But then again, if what Mallory knew was dangerous to them, and they knew someone might come sniffing around for information . . .' I let the pause hang, then dropped the name in casually, '. . . then I suppose Baines and Grayle might well try to dispose of anyone he came into contact with.'

There was only the slightest twitch on the witch's face.

'I'm almost flattered,' I went on. 'Mind you, I'm not the only person here they've tried to kill, am I?' I added brightly.

'You don't know what you're talking about.'

'You work for them?' I shot back.

He looked appalled. 'Of course not.' But he frowned again, thinking it over. 'You might say they sent me a business proposition, which I refused. So they sent me another kind of . . . message.'

'Looked more like a bloody great troll, to me.'

'Indeed.'

'Lucky I was around to save the day, eh?'

'Lucky I'm willing to help your friend. Eh.'

I took the point and left it there. No amount of pressing was going to make him open up about what he knew, if he knew anything at all. There was the slightest scent of fear about his refusal to discuss the subject, and fear on a witch is not something to be taken lightly.

I had only gotten so close to Baines and Grayle – at least, I hoped I was close – through a complex web of bribes and favours and whispered half-truths. Trouble is, a man will feed you information with one hand and alert your enemy with the other. That pooka, for example. It had helped us, sort of, but did it then go on to inform its masters about Ang and me? Were we now on a list, somewhere?

Mallory had worked for Baines and Grayle, and he knew something. More importantly, he knew something about what they were doing with the missing coblyns and knockers. From the tone of his voice, it wasn't good.

I wished I knew what Mallory had wanted to tell me, but I couldn't help feeling a little sorry that he'd become a casualty as a result of my poking around.

On the upside, this demonic slug, or worm, or whatever, it felt like another piece in the puzzle. At the very least it proved that Baines and Grayle were not just petty thieves of bluecaps: they were murderers too. Murderers with the power to open the gates of Hell, if Mark's explanation was anything to judge by.

I wondered, for the thousandth time, whether the quiet eyed thief was Baines or Grayle. Or whether she merely worked for them. Maybe there was a whole hierarchy above her, before you got to the names at the top.

Most people know better than to stick their nose deeper into things they know absolutely nothing about.

I hate not knowing things.

But at this very moment, I most hated not knowing where to find the bloody quillwort I'd been sent to retrieve from this lake.

'It looks like a kind of spiny grass,' Mark had said. *Lots* of things looked like spiny grass.

Eventually I thought I spied it, growing just a few feet from the edge of the bank. I gingerly placed a foot in the water, testing the depth. And then it seemed I slipped, or maybe an aquatic root tangled around my foot; whatever it was dragged me into the lake. Foetid water hit my throat before I could close my mouth. I thrashed blindly in what should have been two feet of water but felt like miles above my head.

Be still, murmured a voice by my ear.

I tried to comply, biting back against the watery fire in my lungs. Something slid free of my ankle, and suddenly I burst back into air and sunshine. I flung myself back onto dry land, spluttering.

Feeling wretched, and soggier than ever, I sat down heavily in the mud and stared out into the lake. I was only mildly surprised to see eyes staring back.

I took them for feminine immediately. Perhaps it was their graceful almond shape, or the suggestion of long eyelashes. They were framed by a ragged mane of hair, and rested just above the surface of the water, peering at me with curiosity.

'Go on then,' I said wearily. 'What are you, and what have I done to offend you?'

The eyes bobbed uncertainly on the waves, then rose slightly, revealing a nose and mouth underneath them. Besides the grey-green pallor of the skin, it was quite a handsome face.

'No offence,' it said, and the voice confirmed it as female. Her tone had a lyrical quality, but it contained a lilt of sadness as nuanced and beautiful as a minor chord in a major symphony.

'What are you?' I said again.

The eyes looked down towards the water. 'I am nothing.' Then they flashed upwards and speared me with a look of such soulful despair that I momentarily forgot my own misery. 'Help me,' she said simply.

I began wringing the water out of my coat. 'And why should I? Didn't you pull me under the water just now?'

'No!' The tone was so insistent, I almost believed it. 'You fell. I saved you.'

I considered this, and decided not to voice my doubt. 'You think I'm in your debt, lake lady? What favour are you about to ask of me?'

The eyes bobbed down again, and for a moment I thought she was about to disappear under the rippling surface. She looked as though she was afraid to speak. And when she did, I understood why.

'I was murdered,' she whispered.

'Ah,' was all I could think to say. So that's what we had here. Some drowned victim turned water ghost, an avenging spirit, maybe. Poor woman. 'What happened?' I asked, as delicately as I could.

'I was walking by the lake. A man attacked me. Dragged me under and held me down until the water swallowed me.' The water around her stirred, as if moved by her memory.

'That's very sad. And I sympathise, I really do. But if you're about to ask me to help you kill the guy responsible, well, I'm afraid vengeance isn't really my thing.' Technically a lie. I deal in vengeance all the time. But I draw the line at outright murder.

She shook her head wildly, flinging fine spray from her weed-ridden hair. It caught the light like a fine sand of diamonds. 'No killing,' she said, and it sounded like a plea. 'But let me speak to him. Ask him why. Ask him why all those children.'

'Children?' I wish it hadn't slipped out. I really wish it hadn't.

Around her, several small, dark shapes bobbed to the surface of the lake. Bodies. Small, small bodies.

'I don't think talking will do much good, love,' I said quietly.

'Please.'

I don't know why the 'please' got me. Maybe it was how simply she said it. Maybe it was the heartache in her eyes. I'll bet she was a mother, in life.

'Do you have a name?' I asked.

'My name was Lillian.'

'Lillian. I'm not sure I can be of much help. I've no way of finding this man, you see, not unless I've got something that belonged to him, or a name at the very least.'

Something shot out of the water and landed with a splat next to me on the bank.

'Will this do?'

I stared at the muddy – bloody – gift. Three severed fingers.

The lady phantom had the grace to look ashamed. 'I bit down hard when he first tried to choke me,' she said. 'I didn't die like a frightened squirrel.'

'I suppose that'd make him easy to identify,' I murmured, mostly to myself. *This isn't my business,* I thought. *I have my own troubles.*

She must have sensed my hesitance, as the next thing to land on the bank – startling me, with the thought that it might be another body part – was a large clump of quillwort.

'You were looking for this?' she said hopefully. 'Payment, maybe? A favour for a favour?'

I nodded slowly. That might do. After all, I was only going to find the guy and bring him to the lake. No actual harm involved. It's not like she was asking me to help her drown him.

The small bodies, still floating despondently in the water, caught my eye again.

Not that it would necessarily be a bad thing, if the man responsible happened to slip in the mud and sink under the still waters of the Wast, never to be seen again. Not a bad thing at all.

'All right, Miss Lillian. I think I can do you a favour,' I said.

She nodded gratefully and sank, along with the small bodies, back into the cool, watery dark.

* * *

There are many unconventional ways to find a person who doesn't want to be found. My favourite consists of a finely tuned quartz crystal – in this instance, with a severed finger attached to it with string – used to point at the target's location on a map.

I sat in my car with the heater full blast, futilely trying to steam the dampness out of my clothing, while the crystal homed in on the resonations of our lakeside murderer. Technically speaking, I couldn't have asked for a better item to tune the crystal with. Usually one would have to make do with a piece of clothing or jewellery which echoed its wearer's resonances, but only enough to help the quartz indicate a vague location. An actual body part should provide pinpoint accuracy down to just a few metres. The only downside was that it meant I had to handle a grotesquely wrinkled and slightly rotting digit.

Couldn't fault the accuracy though. Led me straight to the hospital in nearby Whitehaven. Which, in hindsight, was probably the most obvious place to search for a man who had recently had his fingers bitten off.

A & E seemed the most logical place to begin my search. I realised I hadn't asked the aquatic spirit when her untimely demise had taken place. Was it just this morning, and I should expect to find her killer waiting in the queue? Or was it several days ago, and he's been unceremoniously confined to a hospital bed to heal up? Or, as I rounded the corner, was he that man with the bandaged hand arguing loudly with the nurse about making a quick getaway?

I paused and leant casually against the wall. I unfocused a little, just letting myself drain away from the scene. Wouldn't want them to think I was intruding, would I?

'Sir, please calm down. We'd just like to wait for the doctor to give you a final evaluation–' The nurse, clearly harried and tired and trying her best, was cut off by the patient.

'Don't give me that shit. I heard you talking. 'Psych consult', right? You think I'm crazy? You want to keep me in here so I don't take my crazy onto the streets, is that right?'

'Not at all, sir,' she replied. 'But we *do* want to make sure your hand is in good condition before we discharge you–'

'*Does it look like it's in good condition to you?*'

'Please don't shout at me, sir. We really are just concerned for your own well-being.'

'You think I did this to myself, don't you? I didn't cut off my fingers for fun!'

'You did say it was self-inflicted, sir.'

'Yes, but not in the way that you think!' He seemed to catch himself, as if realising how crazy he really did sound. He tried a different tack. 'Please listen to me, I didn't do this to self-harm, and I promise I'm not suicidal. I don't need some kind of mental evaluation. I just want to go home.'

The nurse was a credit to the very concept of patience. 'I understand that, sir,' she said calmly. 'But I really would recommend that you stay with us for just a little while longer.'

The man threw up his hands in frustration. 'What's to stop me walking out of here right now?'

The nurse sighed. 'Nothing, sir. But I would ask that you sign a piece of paper for us, just to say that you've decided to discharge yourself.'

'Why?'

Her eyes flashed. 'So that if you drop dead as soon as you walk outside, you admit that it's your own fault.'

He seemed taken aback, but not enough to reconsider. 'Fair enough. Give me a pen.'

I trailed the man as he left the hospital, keeping a distance, and struggling to stay unfocused so that I could remain part of the background. I judged he had been in the ward overnight: he still had the hospital tag on his wrist, and the dishevelled appearance of someone forced to spend a night out of the comfort of their own home. His jeans and denim jacket were muddy and green with grass stains. Still damp around the cuffs.

It occurred to me that I hadn't given any thought at all as to how I was going to approach this man. This serial killer, in fact. Child murderer and woman slayer. Suddenly it seemed that walking up to him and proclaiming 'I know what you've done' wouldn't be the safest course of action.

I followed his determined march to the car park and watched as he stopped by a grey Volvo, stared at his bandaged hand, and suddenly broke into tears. He slid down the side of the car and collapsed onto the tarmac, sobbing into his disfigured fist.

'Danny,' he said softly. It sounded like the voice of a broken man. 'Daddy's coming. I'll bring you back. I'll bring you back.'

I was nonplussed. These were not, to my mind, the words of a cold-blooded killer. He continued to weep while I watched and considered my options.

I groped inside a pocket and my hand closed around car keys. I weighed them thoughtfully and brushed the jagged metal tip with my thumb. Not exactly the most ferocious weapon, but it gave me the nerve to make myself known.

'Hello,' I said, stepping forward. 'Need some help?'

'Leave me alone,' he answered, voice thick with tears.

I took a shot and sat cross-legged opposite him, taking care to keep his hands in view.

'I've lost someone,' I said.

'Shut up.'

'I know grief can make a person do crazy things . . .'

'*I didn't cut my fucking fingers off!*' he screamed in my face. Then he withdrew, huddled in on himself. 'I'm not crazy,' he wept. 'I just want my son back.'

Grief is a monster. It twists and turns in the mind, fuelling pain and guilt and anger. I wondered how it had twisted in this man's mind, corroding reason and poisoning his sanity.

'What happened?' I asked quietly. 'I'll listen.'

He looked at me with eyes as heart-rendingly pain-filled as the eyes of the drowned lake woman. There were depths of despair in those watery irises that were uncomfortably familiar.

'You'll listen, but you won't understand,' he said, sounding as world-weary as I felt. He began to dig in one of his pockets – I tensed and gripped my keys tightly – and he withdrew a wrinkled, wallet-sized photograph. Beaming up from the picture was a little boy wrapped in a red raincoat and blue bobble hat, who was proudly pointing a mossy stick at something off-camera. Behind him another two faces beamed over his shoulders. One was a woman with curly hair and deep, compassionate eyes; the other was recognisable as the face of the man in front of me, although the version in the photo seemed a whole, happier world away.

'That's him. That's my Danny,' he said. 'You want to know what happened? You want to hear about lake monsters and fairy kidnappers?' His gaze fell to the ground, and when he next spoke it was in a dull, lifeless tone. As if he'd said the words so many times before. 'I was out walking by the Wast with Danny. We said we'd walk round all the lakes and tarns this summer. Every one. We didn't though. There's never enough time.

'I only left him for a second. He wanted me to find some big sticks, so we could build a den. We left a den at Windermere, so he wanted it to be a tradition. Leave our stamp on the lakes we visit. Leave a den for when we come back.

'I turned around, arms full of branches, and I see Danny petting a horse right on the edge of the lake. Big horse, it was. Grey and glossy. And as I shout at Danny to be careful, I see his hand get stuck to the horse. Its glossy coat turns all to weeds, and the weeds seem to grow right around Danny's hand. I'm shouting and running towards him, and Danny's laughing like it's all a game. He thinks it's funny that there's this sticky gross weed coming off the horse.

'Before I can reach him, the horse bolts for the water. Drags Danny with it. Right underwater.' He paused, and his voice became a mumble, filled with exhaustion. 'I tried to save him. Swam for hours.'

He looked up at me – glared, really – as if challenging me to call him crazy. I was lost in my own train of thought, racing away down a track of dreadful possibility. It added up. The dead children, the shape changing, and in fact the aquatic horse was the biggest clue of all. There was only one beastie it could be . . .

'. . . A kelpie,' I muttered.

The man bolted upright, suddenly hanging on that word as if I'd just offered him a lifeline.

'Kelpie!' he exclaimed, nodding madly. Now he spoke very fast, full of vigour. 'Mum used to tell me stories. I grew up round here and you know what kids are like, always playing by the water's edge. She'd tell us that the kelpies would pull us into the water if we weren't careful. They were demon water horses, she said. Children's fairy tale, I thought. I thought, I thought . . . Danny . . .' He strangled another sob in his throat. 'So, she always said that the only way to kill a kelpie was to take its bridle off, right? Because then it'd turn into a normal horse, and you could kill it.

'So I went back down to Wastwater with a knife, so I could cut the monster's bridle off. I stood on the lakeside and screamed and cursed until it came out of the water. And when it did, I grabbed hold of its stinking mane . . . but there was no bridle. No nothing. And the weeds started to grow over my hand, and no matter how hard I pulled I couldn't get free. So I . . . I took my knife and I . . . I remembered stories where the children escaped by cutting their hands off . . .'

He went silent again, breathing, it seemed, for the first time. His eyes turned on me again, this time with a plea in them. *Please tell me I'm not insane.*

I felt he deserved some words of truth.

'I don't think you're crazy,' I said carefully. 'And I do think that a kelpie took your son. But I'm afraid your mum was only half-right, as you've learned for yourself. Kelpies don't wear bridles. They'd never bow to being ridden. But that's where its weakness lies – if you can force a bridle onto a kelpie, it becomes powerless.'

A ray of hope shone from his face. 'I could kill it?'

'Bingo.'

'And I'd get Danny back, alive?'

I thought of small bodies, floating on the water. I shook my head mutely.

'I'm going to get Danny back,' he insisted. He rose to his feet with newfound purpose.

'Hold on there, you're in no state to be monster-hunting!'

'Watch me.' He beat his chest with his bandaged hand. 'It won't get the better of me twice. I'm not scared of some fairy monster. It can hide in the deepest, dirtiest waters and I will hold my breath until I get to the bottom and drag it out by the weeds in its tail. I will make it *pay* for taking my son!'

It was a formidable war cry, and I found myself wanting to see the kelpie confronted by this flaming pillar of paternal wrath. However, I also felt a duty to keep this man from walking to his death. Because that's clearly what the kelpie had intended: to have me lure him to the lake so that she – it – could drag us both into the water, and eliminate all threat of discovery.

The very least I could do was make sure he was armed correctly.

I grabbed his shoulder before he could storm off. 'First thing's first, we're going to need to purchase a bridle. Two bridles, actually,' I said.

He turned around, brow furrowed. 'Right, of course. There's the big country store down the road. Who are you, anyway?'

'Jack Hansard. And you?'

'Toby Everest.' He raised an eyebrow. 'The local nutjob who thinks his son was abducted by a kelpie. Don't you read the papers?'

'Ah. No, not really.'

* * *

The sun was still golden warm when we reached Wastwater later that day. We approached the southern tip of the lake on foot, through the trees where it was less open, more secluded. I instructed Toby to hang back and stay out of sight. I'd do my best to draw the kelpie out. The bridle, made of surprisingly heavy leather, sat snugly in one of the large inner pockets in my coat. If all went well, Toby wouldn't need to be involved at all.

I strode to the edge of the lake as nonchalantly as I dared, keeping one eye trained on the ground for errant weeds that might suddenly and suspiciously betray my footing. The water's surface was still and serene. It didn't look like a mass grave.

'Lillian,' I called out. 'Lillian. I have some news for you.'

I waited patiently for a few minutes. Then, one by one, the ripples on the surface began to gather at a specific point in the water, and there rose the striking grey-green head of the kelpie.

'What news?' she quavered.

'Come closer, it's something I need to show you.'

She swayed back and forth, apprehension flowing clearly on her features. 'What is it?'

'I think I've found an image of your killer. I'd like to know if you recognise the face in this picture.' True to my word, I held up the small, wrinkled photograph that represented so much grief. I'd learned that Toby had carried this photo as a memorial to his wife – and now it would have to serve as one for his son as well.

'That's him,' said the kelpie, with hardly a glance.

'Are you sure? I've got a couple of other photos here, and I just want to be really, *really* sure that I'm looking for the right guy. Wouldn't want to go accusing the wrong man of murder now, would I? So could you come over and give it a proper look? You'd put my mind right at rest.'

The waves swirled around her for a moment, and then she drifted forward. I began to reach for the bridle. 'Let me just get these other pictures out for you to check over . . .'

I threw it out like a whip and part of the leather strapping caught around her neck. She shrieked and bellowed, and the water frothed up into a bubbling fountain. It cascaded down over the skeletal form of a horse, an equine corpse with weeds for tendons and pond scum for flesh. Mad black eyes stared out from deep, hungry sockets.

It tossed its head and the bridle slapped against the shore.

'Shit,' I said.

Something slimy wrapped around my ankle and yanked. I hit mud and pebbles and then freezing water. The rope around my waist tightened with a jolt, forcing the air out of my lungs.

Rope. That was the other thing we'd purchased at the country store. It'd seemed like a good back-up plan at the time. But now it felt like I was going to be torn in half, with the weight of a tree anchoring me on one end and the strength of a kelpie on the other.

Silt and water washed high over my head. Pain burned bright in my lungs, crawled its way up my throat. I tried to stay calm, knew that flailing like a fish would do no good except to wear me out quicker. But then I opened my mouth and gulped icy cold, and reflex took over and I thrashed and I flailed and I beat against the water as if it was a door I could open. The lake gripped me hard and churned, and in my head I drowned over and over and over.

And then I was on my back, shivering, being rolled onto my side, and spewing lake water from my lungs. Something slapped me hard on the back and I coughed up more pain and more water.

'Thought you were almost a goner there, mate,' said a voice by my ear. It sounded exhausted, but triumphant.

'Di' we win?' I mumbled to the earth.

Toby hauled me upright. 'Worked just like you said. It was so distracted by you, it didn't notice me until I jumped on its back. It tried to pull me under, too. But I wrestled it even under the water, and I forced my bridle over its damned evil head, and I tightened that sucker til not even a flea could get under it. And the kelpie– it just turned to foam in my hands.'

He pointed to a thin layer of froth now dissipating across the lake's mirror surface. One less beastie in the world.

'Good job,' I croaked, and coughed up more water.

'What are they?' said Toby, looking out towards the scree slopes.

One by one, small shapes bobbed to the surface of the lake. One of them, I noticed, wore a red raincoat. I saw realisation wash over Toby's face, and then horror, and then pure, unalloyed anguish.

'Danny,' he whispered.

I watched him dive into the Wast, swim like a man possessed, and heave one of the bodies to shore. I watched him caress it and speak to it and plead with it, and finally I watched him crumple into a broken heap over it, clutching the dead child to his chest as he lay in the dirt.

I called for an ambulance, and I left. I don't do aftermath.

But I drove back to the witch's house, and I thought of small bodies.

* * *

I didn't exactly storm into the witch's kitchen. A storm is a wild, lashing, emotional thing full of noise and energy and destruction. Whereas I walked into the witch's kitchen like the pressure before a storm. Straining under the weight of a fury yet to be released. Grey clouds gathered overhead.

I set the bridle down on the wooden table with a heavy thump.

Mark turned round from his place at the sink, where he was scrubbing his hands.

'You were a while,' he remarked airily. My jaw clenched.

'There were some complications.' I saw him glance at the bridle. 'But you knew that already, didn't you?'

'It was a kelpie then, was it?' he said in his usual, affable way, as if it was only of mild interest.

'It was killing children,' I said evenly.

'It's what they do. I presume it won't be killing any more?'

'*Why didn't you tell me to expect a kelpie?*'

'I thought you could handle it. I was right.'

I smacked the table with the palm of my hand and left it there, shaking with barely suppressed anger.

'Next time,' I hissed, 'deal with your own monsters.'

He nodded pleasantly, as if he hadn't noticed my outrage. 'You deal with my monsters, I deal with yours.'

'What?'

He calmly indicated a figure lying on the floor that my eyes had completely omitted from the scene. I recognised it as Mallory's corpse. Only, when I'd last seen it, the chest had been intact. Now there was a . . . cavity.

And it was at this point that my mind finally registered that Mark was cleaning blood from his hands. Lots of blood.

'What happened here?' I demanded, unwilling to let go of the anger still pumping in my veins.

Mark dropped the bloody towel in the sink. 'Parasites tend to do two things. One: they feed. Two: they lay eggs.'

A grotesque picture began to form in my mind. 'Eggs?'

'Many, many eggs. I wonder if Baines and Grayle knew what they were setting loose, when they hatched this thing in our world?'

'Did you . . . deal with it okay?'

'Fortunately, it's my job to deal with this sort of thing.'

''Twas a right mess though, wi' all them worms squirming all over the place,' sniffed a gravelly voice from the doorway.

'Ang!' I exclaimed, and the last of the anger drained away, washed off in a swell of relief. 'Feeling better?'

'Aye, *gwas.*' She stepped gingerly around the corpse and poked it with her toe. 'This'un dead fer good, now?'

'Dead for good,' assured Mark.

'Wasn't he dead before?' I said, puzzled.

Mark smiled grimly. 'Complications.'

''E got up an' walked, *gwas*,' Ang said darkly. 'But there was no life in 'im, I'll swear it. And all under his skin there was *wriggling* . . .'

My face screwed up in revulsion. 'You can spare me the details.'

'And then it started splittin' *open* . . .'

'No, really–'

'But witchy here got 'em trapped in some magic net, and spiked 'em all good wi' iron and silver. He's all right, for a *wrach*,' she concluded.

Mark flashed a sardonic smile. 'High praise.'

'Then I guess we're even,' I said uncertainly. I wondered if it was a fair trade, one kelpie in exchange for a diabolic pest removal. Judging by the blood splattered on the walls, I supposed it was.

Toby's grief-stricken face crossed my mind. Some things will never be fair.

I put thoughts of the kelpie behind me and tried to convince myself that I'd helped a distraught father find closure, even if the outcome was still too tragic to bear.

Ang, at least, was making a swift recovery. She showed me what looked like a purple scar on her abdomen from Mark's procedure, but it didn't seem like the flesh had been cut open. Occult surgery, indeed. He'd also given her a poultice of salt and sage to keep on it for a further twelve hours: some kind of protective ward, was my guess.

We stayed at the witch's house for one more night, savouring the walls and the roof, knowing we'd have neither come the following day. Life's small pleasures. I wrapped myself up in a thick fluffy duvet, relishing the bounce of the mattress, the aroma of fresh sheets, and the feel of real feather pillows cushioning my descent into the last comfortable night's sleep I would have in a long while.

And I dreamed of small bodies.

Episode 12: Memories

The air in the room was uncomfortably warm.

There were no windows, and the musty odour of rising damp was fighting with a pungent lilac incense over territory. Inky shadows spilled out of dark corners and advanced upon the small circle of candlelight held by a table in the middle of the room. In the centre of the table sat a smooth crystal ball of clear quartz. It glowed eerily under the flickering light.

'O, spirits of the nether realms. O, voiceless souls of the immortal void. O, forgotten ghosts and wandering wraiths,' I intoned. 'We beg you hear our cries through the ether, harken to our plight. Note ye our fervour, heed our misery and our desperation. Grant us but one audience with the lost spirit of . . . of . . .'

'Barry,' supplied my visitor, sitting across the table from me. She took a drag on her e-cigarette and blew cherry smoke in my face. It didn't mix well with the damp or the lilac.

I picked up my monologue with vigour. 'Barry!' I cried. 'If you can hear us through the darkness, if you can find your way to this circle of light, if you wish to make your presence known to us, then knock th–'

Three knocks sounded against the wooden tabletop.

'-ree times,' I finished impassively.

Again, smoke billowed into my face.

'Anyone can do that,' she pronounced. 'Tables are easy. You got a knocker and a pedal strapped to your foot under there?'

In response, three knocks resounded on the wall to the left. My client, a thin, fifty-something woman with a face like an owl, nodded to herself. 'That's good. You got hidden speakers rigged up? I bet you can do all sorts with technology these days.'

At the back of the room, nestled in darkness, a set of miniature Chinese temple bells began to ring discordantly.

'The spirit announces its presence,' I said authoritatively, hoping to regain the flow.

'Ooh, coo-ee,' she said, looking round. 'I was hoping you'd do poltergeist activity.'

One of the bells apparently unhooked itself from the stand and launched itself towards her head. It missed by a few inches. 'Lever operated?' she said, unfazed.

'Ah, t'hell wi' it, woman!' barked a voice from the shadows. 'Din't ye want t'speak with yer old man or no?'

'Barry?' she answered, eyes bulging. She leaned eagerly across the table and peered into the crystal ball. 'Is that you, Barry?'

I raised my palms solemnly in the air. 'We shouldn't place too much stress on the spirit. We should expect it to communicate *without* words–' I shot a dirty look into the shadows, '–lest we cause it to lose its conscious mind altogether.'

'What's it like on the other side, Barry? Is there a light? Is Aunt Rosie there? Does she mind that we buried her without her teeth?'

'Please, Ms Reynolds,' I implored. I thought I could hear a faint muttering behind me. 'The spirits are *silent*. We can ask them but one question at a time, and expect a simple answer–'

'What did ye do wi' her teeth, you mad bat?' exclaimed the spirit.

'They were only false teeth. They cost a lot of money.' Her brow wrinkled. 'You're not Barry.'

'Aye. I pities the man as had t'kiss your ugly beak. Must've had an iron stomach, breathin' in that filthy smoke all the time. I likes a pipe as much as anyone, but what kind of uncanny laggard wants t'smoke fruit?'

'What!'

It was an abrupt end to the séance. Ms Reynolds stomped out of our basement room and up the stairs to the bar above, angrily huffing on her cherry e-cig. Ang hopped up onto her vacant chair.

'Good riddance,' she said. 'Can we gets a beer now?'

I rubbed my eyes. It was still early in the evening. I had a lot more phony séances to wade through yet. 'For the last time, Ang, we can't afford it. Mr Chambers was good enough to give us a room in his pub, but the deal was that we provide our specialist brand of entertainment for a whole evening. Work first, drink later. And if you stopped aggravating customers, we might reach the drinking part a whole lot sooner.'

She sniffed. 'I dun't call this work. Knockin' on tables and making noises in the dark.'

I wondered if Ang understood the concept of irony. Coblynau are especially well known for the knocking noises they make in the deep, damp, dark of a mine – hell, why'd you think the Cornish ones are *called* knockers? I refrained from pointing it out.

'Just think of it as an easy meal,' I tried. 'It's simple for you to move in the dark and hide from sight. You've had lots of practice, after all. But let me do the talking, all right?'

'Right,' she grumbled.

'Let's see who the next customer is.'

'Gullible moron, ye mean.'

'That too.'

I'd worked this con so many times before that I felt I'd honed my understanding of exactly what clients are looking for in a séance – so much so, that I'm adverse to really calling it a con. You see, they don't actually *want* to contact their dead relatives, as I tried explaining to Ang. Such a thing would terrify and disturb them out of their wits. What they *want* is a bit of a show, some candles and mysterious occult symbols, and then for a nice friendly voice to reassure them that everything is fine beyond the veil, dying doesn't hurt, and yes, it's perfectly okay that you sold the house and blew all the inheritance on a big holiday.

Ang had narrowed her eyes at me and said, 'Them's lies.'

I'd shrugged. 'How do you know?'

She was reluctantly (and incompetently) playing a part in the show while we lay low for a while. Taking a breather, as it were, from our probably ill-conceived pursuit of Quiet Eyes and Baines and Grayle. And we were also, more importantly, taking the chance to refill our coffers, which were meagre even at the best of times.

Mr Chambers' pub was a gig that I could always fall back on when times were tough. He was the type of man who believed earnestly in the Spirits From Beyond, and would always welcome a travelling ghost hunter or psychic practitioner to liven up his premises.

Upstairs, by the door to our basement, a waiting line of chairs had been set out by Mr Chambers. Pinned to the stained walnut wood of the bar were posters that proudly announced the arrival of a mystic-psychic-medium-clairvoyant-soothsayer-fortune-teller for ONE NIGHT ONLY!!!

I convinced myself to be thankful that it stopped at three exclamation marks, and that Mr Chambers hadn't also tried to call me a wizard.

Only one chair in the line was occupied. There sat an elderly gent in a tweed jacket and tie, one hand resting on a walking stick at his side. He smelled faintly of mothballs. The air of loneliness that hung about him was almost tangible.

This would be an easy one, I decided.

I strode forward with a warm smile and outstretched hand. 'Good evening, sir. My name's Jack Hansard, professional channeler of spirits.'

'Frederick Lawson,' he replied. His voice had a weary edge to it.

'Right this way, Frederick. Easy, old boy, mind the steps there.'

He was far from steady on his feet; he shuffled more than walked. It was a relief to get him seated again. I didn't want to be faced with telling Mr Chambers one of his patrons had fallen and broken a hip.

'Now then, Fred – may I call you Fred?' I began. 'What do you desire? To know the future? To witness the arcane arts? Or to make contact, perhaps, with a lost loved one?'

He nodded his head, and the candlelight threw weird shadows across his wrinkled features. 'Maggie,' he said quietly.

'Your wife?'

He nodded again. Perfect. So long as Ang could keep her mouth shut, this should go off without a hitch. Appeasing lonely bereaved spouses is the mainstay of the séance racket.

'Will I see her?' Frederick asked, staring down at the tabletop. He hadn't looked me in the eyes at all, really.

I hesitated. 'No. The spirits cannot manifest themselves into any physical form. We will first try to summon the spirit of your wife, and then you will be able to ask her any questions you desire'

'Will I hear her voice?'

I bit my lip, feeling just a little wretched about the poor guy's misplaced desperation. 'The spirits cannot talk.'

'Then how will she answer?'

'We can use a number of communication methods. We will start by asking the spirit to knock against a surface . . .'

The old man sighed, and it looked as though his last breath was escaping his body. His features seemed to sag, his shoulders slumped, and the shadows grew larger under his eyes.

'You're a fake,' he said quietly. 'I don't want to hear some knocking. I want to see my Maggie.'

'I'm afraid that's not possible.'

He raised his head and looked me in the eye for the first time. In a near lifeless voice he said, 'I'd give you every penny I have, *everything* I have, just to see my Maggie again.'

Wheels turned in my head. There was a ring of truth to his words, which was rare in these circumstances. Possibly he really *was* looking for the genuine article, and not just some fleeting sense of comfort. His eyes said he'd pay any price.

I wondered how many pennies he had to his name. There might be a way I could fulfil the old boy's wish in a way that left us both happy. The hospitality of Mr Chambers was all very well, but I wasn't making a *lot* of money from this phony psychic gig. Now where had I put that thing . . .

'Mr Lawson. Fred. I can't bring Maggie back to life for you. Nor can I conjure her spirit in the flesh. But what if I could reunite you with her, as she once was, as you remember her to be?'

His expression remained downcast. I was offering him the impossible, and he knew it. But impossibility, to my mind, is subjective.

'Listen, Fred, wait right here. I'll be back in a jiffy, and I'll show you something that'll blow your mind to kingdom come. Just wait here.'

I took the stairs three at a time, racing outside to my car. Not that I was worried I'd lose the guy – if Fred decided to leave, I'm quite certain I'd be back before his tottering knees could get him up the second step. I riffled through the goods in my boot, flinging aside out of date potions and cheap talismans. I emerged with my prize, held it joyously to my chest. Up until this moment I'd had no idea how I was going to sell the bloody thing. Potions and curses are easy. This required more finesse.

I was only slightly out of breath when I re-entered the basement and reclaimed my seat in the circle of candlelight. I set down a box, two bowls, and a bottle of water on the table. Frederick looked at me with interest.

'I've been speaking with your associate,' he said.

'My what?'

'The dwarf, you know.'

'*Ang?*'

She emerged from the shadows, holding a bag of crisps. 'Din't know how long ye were gonna be, *gwas*. And the gent needed a glass o' water.'

'I've been persuaded to hear you out,' said Frederick. He sounded drained, like he was running on empty. 'I don't know if I honestly believe in ghosts. I don't even know if I believe that Maggie's spirit still exists, anywhere. But I know that I want to see her again, and I'll do anything, believe anything, if you can make it so.'

'I think I can.' With a ceremonious flourish, I removed the cap from the water bottle and poured its contents into the two bowls. Then I opened the lacquered box and lifted out two small teardrop vials, each only as big as my thumb. One shimmered like liquid mercury; the other like molten gold.

'I need you to open your mind a little, Fred, and allow yourself to believe what I'm about to tell you.' I held forth the silver vial. 'This is called Mnemosyne. Pure, liquid memory.' Then I held aloft the gold vial. 'This is Lethe. Blissful ignorance, bottled.'

Frederick seemed to chortle. 'I expect you got them out of Hades yourself, eh?'

'Can't say I've ever visited,' I replied, masking my confusion. 'Why do you ask?'

'I've studied Greek mythology, lad.' He closed his eyes and spoke as if reading an old book on the back of his eyelids. 'Departed souls may drink from two rivers in the afterlife. Drink from Lethe and lose all recollection so you may be reborn. Drink from Mnemosyne and remember everything that ever was and will be. The rivers are also twinned with the goddesses of oblivion and memory, if you care to know.' He gave me a pointed look. 'Perhaps you had an audience with a deity instead?'

'He got 'em off a man in a pub,' supplied Ang.

Frederick cracked a smile.

'Rest assured, *someone* embarked on a perilous journey to obtain these precious liquids,' I interjected. 'And they do exactly what it says on the tin. With Mnemosyne, you can walk clear-eyed through your memories. You'll remember things in such detail it will feel like you're really there, all over again. Like I said before, I can't bring Maggie back to life – but I *can* bring you to your memory of her. You can relive your time together, and it will feel as real as it did the first time round.'

Fred's hands began to tremble where they rested on the table. There was a tightness in his jaw and pained uncertainty in his eyes. 'How?' he said hoarsely.

I tipped the silver vial into one bowl of water, and then the gold into the second. They glittered. The fluids seemed to break apart and spread over the surface, until a sheet of rippling silver and a pane of placid gold shone upwards. Frederick stared at them hungrily. Whatever doubts he had were quickly being pushed aside by hope.

'Before we continue,' I said tactfully, 'I must broach the subject of financial reparations. I am of course willing to let you try before you buy, as it were, but I must request some token of commitment from you first . . .'

With a shaky hand, Frederick pulled out his wallet and pushed it across the table. 'I have more,' he said. 'If that's not enough.'

A sly peek told me roughly two hundred pounds in notes were stuffed into the neat leather holder. I love old people. They always carry cash, and so much of it!

I cleared my throat delicately. 'That will certainly do for a deposit. Now, here's how it works. You will place your right hand in the silver bowl. Think of Maggie as you do. Think of the best time you ever had together. You will enjoy, let's say ten minutes, in her company. I'll give you a tap, and then you'll place your left hand in the golden bowl. It will bring you out of it, back to the present. Is that clear?'

'Perfectly.'

I pushed the bowls forward, had him rest his hands next to each one. 'When you're ready,' I said.

After a moment's hesitation, he lifted his right hand and dipped it into the silvery liquid. It crept up over his skin like a glove. His eyes drifted closed and his breathing slowed.

'He sleepin'?' asked Ang.

'In a sense.'

His eyelids flickered rapidly, as though he was dreaming. I pulled a watch out of my coat and made a note of the time. Ten minutes. Seemed fair for a taster session. I wondered how much of his pension he'd be willing to part with if I got the pitch right. This was exactly the big sell we'd been waiting for.

I ticked off the things I would spend the money on. I would start with a few nights of luxury in a hotel with proper beds and a breakfast of something other than tinned spaghetti – then I could get my car fixed so that it didn't rattle my teeth over forty miles an hour – then I'd take my money to market and find the biggest, rarest, *shiniest* mythical artefact I could afford and I'd figure out the best way to turn it into a pyramid scheme.

And for this small price, dear old Fred could enjoy Mnemosyne and Lethe for the rest of his life.

Ang climbed up on the table and peered closely at Fred. 'He really relivin' his memories, *gwas?*'

'As if it were happening for real,' I affirmed.

'No trick?'

'Nope.'

'No catch?'

'No catch.'

'That's a first, *gwas*.'

The minutes ticked by, until they were up. I nodded to myself and tapped Frederick firmly on the shoulder.

'Time's up, old boy. Put your left hand in the bowl now.'

We waited. He didn't move.

'Don't think he heard you, *gwas*.'

'No matter.' I lifted Fred's hand into the golden bowl myself. The surface shimmered and sparkled, but Frederick remained still.

I snapped by fingers by his ear, pinched the thin skin of his wrists.

'He's not wakin' up,' panicked Ang. 'Why's he not wakin' up?'

'I don't know,' I muttered. I grabbed his right hand and lifted it out of the silver Mnemosyne. 'Hand me some tissue, Ang. I'm going to try cleaning it off.'

'Will this do?'

Someone handed me a wire brush.

I blinked the light out of my eyes and stared at the brush in my hands. 'That'll do fine,' I heard myself say.

I turned back to the old iron fence and continued to scrub away the rust and flaking paint. I'd have it good as new by the end of the week, and then I'd see to Mrs Palmer's chipped window frames. Some sandpaper would do the job nicely.

'Mother says you're to come in for dinner in an hour,' said the same voice who had handed me the brush. I looked up into the slightly pudgy face of a twelve-year-old girl.

'Thanks Maggie,' I said.

* * *

Life in the country wasn't so bad. I'd seen other kids crying on the train over here, missing their parents already. Not me. I was ready for an adventure, and if I was too young to go off and be a fighter pilot like my Pa, then I'd guard Britain from a farm in Norfolk instead. Let's see Fritz try and take our shores while I'm on duty.

'What are you doing, Fred?'

I whirled round, a sharpened stick aimed level with the face of the intruder. Maggie regarded it sceptically. 'Hunting for Nazis again?' she inquired.

'Hush! You'll give away our position.'

'There aren't any Nazis in the woods, Fred.'

I crossed my arms and sat grumpily on a tree stump. 'How d'you know? They could've snuck in under cover of darkness. Travelled down the river, maybe.'

'They wouldn't invade here though, would they.'

'Could be.' I nodded wisely. 'Could be they know we wouldn't expect them to attack here. Could be that's precisely why they *would*.'

She sniffed haughtily. As if knowing how to milk a cow gave her more authority than me. 'Stop being silly, Fred.'

'S'not silly. It's *prepared*.'

She sighed and flicked her amber hair. 'Father needs help bringing in the hay bales. Come and be useful, will you?'

I grumbled but rose to my feet anyway. I'd already learned that uselessness was a quick road to meeting the back of Mr Palmer's hand. And the front of it too, if he'd had a drink.

* * *

The fields were a rolling, rippling sheet of gold under the setting sun. It made me think of a river, for some reason. For a moment I wanted to dive into it, into a golden oblivion.

Maggie rested her head on my shoulder.

'Thanks for what you did,' she said.

''Tweren't nothing,' I replied. 'That slob should've known better than to foul-mouth a lady.'

'I did call him a pig's arse first, though.'

'S'not a crime to tell the truth.'

She giggled softly and leant into my side. Shyly, she slipped her hand in mine. Her skin was rough and weather-worn, but still felt fragile to me. I felt the heat rising in my cheeks. And other places.

'Maggie,' I began, but felt the words stifled in my throat.

'What is it?' She squeezed my hand and gazed up at me. Her eyes were a dull hazel colour, but they seemed to shine in the light of the golden fields. I mustered my courage to speak.

'There's talk of my going home, back to my Ma in Manchester. They say it's a lot safer now.'

'Stay,' she said simply. 'There's a job for you here. Father needs you on the farm. You'll always have a place at our table.'

I avoided her golden gaze. 'Ma needs me. Four years on her own self, and working at that factory, too. This past year her letters have been . . . Well, with Pa gone, she needs a man in the house. She needs me home, Maggie.'

She pulled away and stared off into the distance. 'Will you come back?' she asked quietly.

'If you'll let me.'

She drifted in her own thoughts awhile, then suddenly threw her arms around me. 'You better swear it, Fred,' she whispered in my ear.

'I swear it,' I murmured. I kissed her, for the first time, and it seemed the very fields stood still to watch. In the background, I thought I heard someone shouting.

* * *

The train juddered to a halt at the platform. My palms were sweaty with anticipation. This was the moment. How would it go? Would she run down the platform and fold me into a loving embrace? Would I pick her off the floor and swing her round, like in the flicks? Would she kiss me first? Should I kiss her first? What if none of those things happened, and there was only silence between us?

I turned over the tin of Farrah's Harrogate toffee in my hands. Her favourite. Would she like it as much at twenty as she did at sixteen?

I squared my shoulders and stepped proudly onto the platform. My heart burbled in my chest. I couldn't see her. Surely she was waiting nearby.

I started forward but was stopped by a strange, dishevelled man in a trench coat. He gripped my shoulder and tried to say something. His voice sounded as though it was underwater; I couldn't make out any of the words. Something about his intense expression scared me, the way his eyes flared and his mouth strained.

And then Maggie appeared. The man was brushed to the side, and, with tears running down her cheeks, Maggie hugged me tight. I kissed her hair and savoured her smell. I was home.

Together we forged through the crowd of alighted passengers, smiling the dopey smiles of reunited lovers.

Behind us, the man continued to shout on the platform.

* * *

The wedding was a grand affair. Everyone in the village was in attendance in some unofficial capacity. Children had already scaled the walls of the churchyard just for a peek of our party. I'd saved pennies we would throw to them later.

I beamed at Maggie in her mother's high-collared wedding dress. She was speaking with my mother, currently the proudest woman in all of England.

Mr Palmer – Nathan – came up to shake me firmly by the hand. His expression, as always, was stern, but this time I thought I saw a hint of pride. He gave a gruff, 'Congratulations, son,' and marched off to speak with the vicar.

Another well-wisher grabbed me roughly by the elbow.

'Steady there!' I said jovially. 'Had too much to drink already, eh?'

I peered closely at the newcomer, trying to place his face. I know I knew it, but I couldn't figure out from where. It was an unassuming face, dark scruffy hair, light stubble, and grey rings under the eyes which I felt made him look older than he should. But it was the long coat which jogged my memory.

'Hey now!' I cried. 'You're that fellow from the train station!' I knew it was a ludicrous thing to say, but I couldn't help it. The stranger planted his hands on both my shoulders, brought his face level to mine, and in a firm but strained voice he said:

'Cora Tomaras.'

* * *

It felt like something snapped at the back of my head. Like an elastic band pinged at me from afar. I rubbed the spot distractedly. Cora was still laughing at me.

'I don't see what's so funny,' I said peevishly.

'It's the face you make,' she snickered. 'You look constipated. You're meant to be fading away, not taking a shit.'

'I'm concentrating,' I huffed.

'Then you're trying too hard. Come on, Jack. Follow me.'

She stepped back into the shadow of the alley and faded from sight. It was like the alley had swallowed her.

'I know you're there,' I said uncertainly.

'Follow me, then,' demanded a disembodied voice.

I closed my eyes and exhaled. Just let go. Imagine you're looking at yourself through a camera lens, and change the focus. Blur the image so that the background is sharper and the foreground is all fuzz. Or is it the other way round? I screwed my eyes tighter – I could hear her giggling – and imagined myself melting into the brickwork, into the air, spreading my molecules thin and wide and stepping out of the picture . . .

I opened my eyes, slowly. The world had turned to a fuzzy grey, with strange shadows shifting in and out of view at the very edges of my vision. But there was Cora, sharp as a knife in the middle of it all.

'Looks like you did it, shithead. Well done. This way.'

She turned and ran down the length of the alley, disappearing round the corner.

'Wait!' I struggled to keep up. But I was elated. Look at me, slipping in and out of reality as I pleased. Look at me, following this crazy girl into some upside-down version of the world. She was like a colossal icebreaker slowly demolishing every idea of normal and facet of common sense I had taken for granted, and I couldn't break out of her wake even if I wanted to.

I caught up with her, where the darkness gathered into a pit at our feet.

She grinned at me, and it was that beautiful, evil grin.

'Do you want to see some monsters?' she said.

* * *

There were monsters gathered about her in the ward. They were always there, just on the edge of vision, whenever I visited. I got the distinct impression they were there for her. Feeding, maybe.

I fished a pendant out of my trench coat. The same coat she'd stolen off Greenwich market, to show me how easy it was if you knew how to fade away. I placed the talisman round her neck, the latest in a series of protective ornaments I'd dredged up. I hoped it was doing some good.

'Another trinket for you,' I murmured. 'I know how much you like shiny things.' I glared at the shadows shrinking against the ceiling. 'Shoo,' I said viciously.

I sat next to her in silence. I thought about telling her of my latest adventures, about how I'd met this witch up north and managed to barter for spells, and about my narrow escape when he discovered I'd purloined a few extras as well. I could tell her about my new car, and what it was like living on the road. I could tell her how much I missed her, and I wished she'd laugh at me again.

Instead, I brushed her hair back from her olive-gold skin and kissed her lightly on the cheek.

'I'll be back soon, Maggie,' I said, then furrowed my brows and shook my head. 'Maggie,' I repeated, tasting the name. It wasn't right. This was Cora, in front of me. Cora, here, but not really. Stuck somewhere inside her own head, where only monsters and shadows can see.

I caught sight of my reflection in the window. I was shouting at myself.

To a normal person, this would be brushed off as the workings of a tired mind. Not to me. In my world, if your reflection tries to talk to you, you probably ought to listen.

I turned to face myself, but I couldn't hear what the words were. I decided to unfocus, letting myself drift into the space between spaces. My reflection sharpened, became more solid in the glass. And then it changed shape, became an unfamiliar face. A young, handsome man with cropped blonde hair and neatly trimmed whiskers. He looked confused.

'Hello,' I said amiably. 'What are you doing in my reflection?'

'Where's Maggie?' he said. Then he leaned forward, squinting at me. 'I know you,' he said at last. 'That Hansard fellow. The mystic.'

'Yes. I'm afraid I can't introduce you in the same way.'

'Fred Lawson. We met in The Clam and Cockle. I was with Maggie until you– You took her away from me! Let me go back to her, please!'

The world tried to rush back and envelop me, but I resisted. I planted my feet and firmly faded. As the world melted away, memories began to drop back into my head, in the correct order.

'Mnemosyne,' I said grimly. I remembered grabbing the old man's hand. Had I touched some of the silver gunk? From the patchwork of jumbled events I could recall, it seemed like I'd been drawn into Fred's memories. I'd experienced them first hand. For a time, I *was* him.

I took a deep breath. 'It's time to go back, Fred. We can't stay here.'

Like a petulant teenager, he stamped his foot. Suddenly we were under blue sky and church bells were ringing. Fred wore his wedding suit.

'You will not take me away from this!' he said. He looked over at his wife, still chatting pleasantly with the other Mrs Lawson. His eyes misted over. 'My Maggie.'

'Frederick. Fred. I know this is hard. But she's gone. It's not really her.'

He glared. 'Wouldn't you do anything to have your Cora back?' he said harshly.

I let it slide over me, like a breeze. 'She was never mine to keep.' I spread my hands imploringly. 'In any case, I wouldn't want this, to be kept in some loop with her til the end of time. Reliving the same adventures over and over again. *She* wouldn't want that.' *She'd call me a shithead, and mean it.* 'Don't you think Maggie would want you to go on with your life?'

'What life? What's left for me to live?' Fred's gaze dropped, and for a second I saw a shadow of the old, tired man underneath. 'We never had children. I regret that now. I'm just waiting for the end to take me.'

Here the recollected Maggie, in her white wedding dress, wandered over.

'Who's your friend, Fred?' she chimed, with a bright smile.

He beseeched me with his sad eyes. 'Let me stay,' he said simply. 'Let me have my oblivion.'

Christ, I'm a soft touch. There was nothing more I could say. He'd made his choice. How do you pull someone out of their own mind? I tried for years with Cora and never found a way.

I regarded the happy couple, how Maggie's face shone, and how she hung on Fred's arm like an anchor to its ship. How Fred looked like a drowned man who had finally found port in his storm.

'Congratulations,' I said.

* * *

I awoke to Ang fanning my face with an empty crisp packet. Cheese and onion wafted up my nostrils.

'Ye awake, *gwas?*'

I nodded groggily. 'Where's Fred?'

She pointed to him, slumped over the table, one hand still in each shining bowl.

'Why's it not working for him?' quaked Ang. 'When ye went out cold I put yer other hand in the gold bowl, like ye said. And here y'are, awake as day. Why's he still sleepin', *gwas?*'

'He decided to stay.' I looked down at my hands and saw the remnants of gold and silver. It trickled over my skin into the air, and into nothing.

Beside me came an eerie rustling noise. Ang looked first, and shrieked.

Where Frederick's hand draped over the silver Mnemosyne, the mercury-like liquid was slithering in veins up his wrist and around his arm with a sound like paper.

'Don't touch it!' I shouted.

In seconds it enveloped Fred in a silver net. It spread over his skin, his clothes, encasing him like a silver statue. Then Fred's gleaming form melted, shrank, and disappeared into nothing except a silver pool in the bowl.

After a few moments, Ang remembered to close her gaping mouth. 'What was *that?*'

'I suppose old Fred faded into his memories for good,' I pondered. 'Faded all the way.'

'We should get rid of it,' said Ang, glaring suspiciously at the bowls.

'Not necessarily. Could still turn a tidy profit in the future.'

'Put it away.'

'All right, keep your cap on.'

I fished out the vials and held them over the bowls. Mnemosyne and Lethe flowed back into them, sucked in like a vacuum. Ang eyed the bottles warily.

'Is the ol' man in there now?'

'He's in his memories. Different time, different place.'

'So long as it's far away from here.'

'It is.'

She tapped her chin. 'Ye said somethin', *gwas*. While ye were out.'

'Oh? What was it?'

'Dunno. Sounded like 'Cora-T'mariss', or somesuch.'

I stiffened. 'Did I say anything else?'

'If ye did, I din't hear it.'

'Oh. Good.'

She looked at me curiously. 'S'it a spell, *gwas?*'

'No-o,' I said uncomfortably. 'Well, maybe. I suppose in a sense, it was.' I avoided her shrewd gaze.

'Ye ain't gonna tell me what it means, are ye?'

'No,' I said flatly.

Trust Cora, to still be saving me even now.

I placed the glass vials back into their ornate box and produced a key for the lock. I'd never actually felt a need to lock it, until now. I'd throw the key in the river in the morning.

Or maybe I'd throw it away tonight, just to be safe.

Maybe I should throw the whole box away, like Ang said. Remove the temptation entirely. I can't deny it was there, gnawing on a dark place in my head. I should put the box in a sack with stones and let it sink to the bottom of the riverbed.

But I couldn't. I couldn't do it, knowing that somewhere, inside that box, was Cora.

Episode 13: Proposition

I don't have very many friends.

Contacts, yes. You need them, in my line of work. Old mates, chums in the trade, people who owe me favours, that kind of thing.

But in terms of genuine friends – people I might bother to put myself out for and who might do the same for me, people whose company I might enjoy just for the sake of good company – I realistically have very few.

It's hard work keeping up any kind of relationship with other human beings when your job takes you all over the country at a moment's notice (especially when that notice is the fact that someone is out to kill you). I'd been avoiding London for a while in particular. When I was last there, I crossed a man named Scallet and narrowly escaped with my life.

But this meant I had also been avoiding one of my oldest and dearest friends. A visit was long overdue and, on balance, I'd rather risk the wrath of a cheated businessman than the ire of a friend who holds a wealth of potential blackmail material on me.

So, perhaps unwisely, I found myself back in London on a sunny Tuesday in October, standing under Waterloo Bridge with Peggy. Shopping.

Like a lot of women, Peggy loves to shop.

'Oh, look! A first edition *Compendium of Blood Rituals of the Basilisk!*' Unlike a lot of women, Peggy loves to shop for extremely rare books of a macabre and supernatural nature. She specialises.

'Are you going to buy it, or just fawn over it?' I said.

'Hang on. I need to check whether the teeth are in good condition.'

I tried to show willing. 'Is that a technical term for part of the–' I stopped and stared as she produced two sets of heavy pliers from her handbag. She grabbed both covers of the book and then, with no small amount of effort, levered the pages open.

'Oh,' I said. 'Those are some big teeth.'

'Healthy, too,' Peggy replied cheerfully. The book began to growl. I edged behind Peggy. 'I think it likes us. Who's a good boy, den?' she cooed.

'How do you know it's a boy?'

She released the pliers and the book snapped shut.

'Don't be silly, Jack. Books aren't gendered. They don't mate.' A thoughtful look passed over her face. 'Well, except for–'

'I don't need to know,' I said quickly. I didn't want to learn about literary mating rituals, and I definitely didn't want to know what parts qualified as the genitalia. But I knew I was going to spend the rest of the day wondering about it, so she had won anyway. I watched her haggle with the vendor.

The Southbank Centre Book Market is one of those locations where a regular marketplace overlaps with the Black Market. On the surface, it's just an open-air, second-hand book market. A good stomping ground for readers and collectors to come and riffle through heaps and heaps of literature to their heart's content. But if you want access to the rare stuff, you need to know what you're looking for, and who to talk to.

There's usually the friendly and energetic dealer at the front. He's the salesman: the one who asks if you need any help, if perhaps he can recommend you a title, if you're having a good day, and my, what uncharacteristically nice weather it is today, we take cash and credit cards, would you like a bag for that?

Ignore him. The man you want will be sitting near the back, slouched in a cane chair, usually wearing a cardigan and a grumpy expression, with his eyes closed. If you speak to him, he'll be rude and pretend to go back to sleep. But if you persist and quietly indicate that you are looking for goods of a darker nature, he may grudgingly rise from his rickety chair and lead you to a table set aside from all the others.

This table wasn't there a moment ago, mind. It's here now, and only for you.

Peggy is well known to all the unconventional book dealers in the city. Most of those tiny, musty old antique bookshops tucked into peculiar corners tend to run a Black Market operation alongside their normal book selling (or book-hoarding, as the case has often seemed to me). The shop owners are hard-nosed, ruthless collectors who would sell you the same rare volume of prose for several hundred of your finest pounds but refuse to buy it off you for more than a fiver.

Peggy, with her bright blue hair and slightly dumpy features, was no exception.

A cloud of defeat settled over the prickly vendor. She'd beaten him down to a half price deal on her *Compendium*. Peggy claims to hate confrontation but will haggle like a tiger. If she picks up a book, it's hers.

'Pleased with yourself?' I said, eyeing the tome now being wrapped in tissue and a thin silver chain.

'I'm sure Larry doubles the price for me just because he knows I'll get it for less, one way or the other,' she said, a little petulantly. She tossed her head – I think she still forgets she cut her hair short – and her nose stud glinted in the light. It was shaped like an elephant today.

I wondered vaguely why anyone would want to decorate their nose with a large land mammal.

'The man has to make a living,' I remarked.

'Well, I deserve a discount, all the books I buy from him,' she replied irritably. I felt a spark of sympathy for Larry, having Peggy as a regular customer.

'How about that drink now?' I suggested.

'Sure. I know just the place. It's right up your street.'

I frowned at that. 'Right up my street' didn't sound like a very good thing. 'My street' is usually more of a dark alley full of broken glass and weird shapes lurking in the shadows. I would be deeply suspicious of anything claiming to be right up my street.

I was right to be.

Now, I enjoy pubs as much as the next man. There's nothing quite like the companionable atmosphere of a respectable drinking establishment. Even the less respectable ones have a certain charm to them (even if actual charm is lacking in their patrons).

But then you have the downright seedy dives, the ilk of which would consider dirt to be a step *up*. The kind of place where shady dealings occur so frequently that criminals need to wear name tags to make sure they don't end up in the wrong meeting. The kind of place where the things you find on the bottom of your shoe look more appealing than the menu – and, indeed, the clientele. The kind of place, in fact, where you couldn't catch a moment's peace without a shifty character in an oversized trench coat sidling up and asking in an urgent whisper whether you want to buy a watch.

'Peggy,' I said carefully, while taking in our surroundings. The bar staff had fists for faces, and I could already feel the tell-tale squelch underfoot. And there was, of course, a man in a trench coat now hurrying furtively towards us. (I do wear a trench coat myself. But mine is stylish and not shady whatsoever. Although it does have a lot of pockets. But I have never sold watches from it. Except maybe once.)

'This is a lovely place to drink, Jack. I've been here before.'

'Peggy, this isn't lovely. This place is so far from lovely it lives in the opposite end of the dictionary. No, we don't want to buy any watches, thank you.'

This was to the trench-coated man, who froze halfway through his sidling.

'Not just any old watches though, guv,' he implored. 'Time-catchers. Special, see? They catch time and store it. Stay ageless, hold off those wrinkles, miss.'

Peggy's expression turned to ice.

'Wrinkles?' she enunciated with glacial precision.

'We all get 'em, miss,' he continued, blissfully unaware of the mountain of frosty rage building before him. 'Look see, you take your watch, you set it to 'store' and–'

I stepped in between Peggy and the hapless tradesman. 'Look, mate. I've run this con before and I know those watches absorb about as much time as the Pope swigs sambuca. I think you should sally off before you lose a limb, okay?'

He shot me a bitter glare, but at least had the decency to leave.

Peggy scowled after him. But despite herself, she asked me, 'What do his watches do, then, if you know all about it?'

'They don't catch time,' I explained. 'They do catch wrinkles, though. Thing is, they take them from one part of your body, your face, for example – but not your face, I didn't mean *your* face! – and deposit them all elsewhere.'

'Like, on your feet?'

'Potentially.'

'Doesn't sound too bad.'

'Say that after you've seen fifty years' worth of wrinkles compacted into one foot. Not much use for walking, I can tell you that.'

'Huh. Like voluntary elephantiasis. Gruesome. C'mon, let's get a drink.'

I followed her to the bar despite my feeling of unease. I couldn't help looking over my shoulder even as she asked me what I wanted.

'Will you stop doing that?' she insisted. 'Just because it looks a little bit . . . down-market, doesn't mean it's a dangerous place. They have good beers on tap.'

I tried to keep my scepticism to myself. 'Sorry. I'm just a bit on edge, I suppose. It's been a rough couple of months.'

'Still slumming it?'

'I'll have you know my car is far from a slum. But yes, I am still enjoying mobile living. We had a brief span camped out in a pub basement telling people's fortunes and what-not, but you know me. Can't stay put for long.'

We forged our way to a clean-ish table wedged in a corner. I grimaced as I sat. Even the chairs felt sticky.

Peggy was unfazed. 'Tell me more about this coblyn friend of yours. She sounds like a character.'

I unstuck my glass from its coaster. 'Ang, well. She likes pasties and tea and beer, and once you know that you've pretty much got her sussed.' Ang had opted to stay and snooze in the car rather than join me on this trip. Books, she had made it quite clear, were not her cup of tea.

'Isn't it weird that she's travelling with you?' said Peggy. 'I thought knockers – and presumably coblyns – preferred to stay close to home.'

'I think her home stopped feeling like one.' I mulled it over. 'She says she misses the people, misses the work, and misses . . . Well, misses having meaning.'

'I suppose it's horrible to feel you've been forgotten.'

'She's not the only one, either. Some of her friends left home and now she's looking for them.'

Peggy's eyebrows shot up. 'And you're helping her?'

'It's business. She paid. I don't work for free.' I hid my expression with a quick swig. To my surprise, the taste was acceptable.

'Must have been a big fee.'

'Mm.' The hairs were prickling on the back of my neck. My feelings of unease remained extremely present. 'Speaking of business, how's your shop? Going well?'

'As well as I like. Got a big consignment of spell books in. You know, the 'cycles of the moon' and 'crystal healing' junk you like so much.'

'They sell well.'

'There's also a grimoire on demon-summons I think you'd be interested in. We should swing by later so you can have a look.'

I smirked and shook my head. 'I always seem to come off the poorer one, whenever I do business with you.'

'It's not my fault you haggle like a dithering grandmother.'

'I'll take that as a compliment. I'll have you know my gran is a fine haggler. Once saw her beat a man down from fifty to ten pounds on a pair of orthopaedic slippers. And she made him throw in a pair of socks as compensation for the trouble.'

Peggy chortled pleasantly. She had a good laugh, one that could start as a warm rumble in the throat and graduate into a full *hyuk hyuk* of belly laughter if provoked. I'd have followed up with another joke about the ruthlessness of OAPs, if I wasn't already preoccupied with trying to surreptitiously peer round the room again over the rim of my glass.

That was when I noticed the two grim-faced men staring at us from a dark corner. Not a good sign.

They locked eyes with me.

'Actually, Peggy,' I said urgently, leaning over the table. 'I am interested in picking up a few books off you. We could head to your shop now?'

'Nonsense, Jack. We've only just got here. Have one more drink, at least.'

I took her arm and pulled her from her seat. The men rose from their corner.

'Peg, there may be some bad men here who want to kill me. We have to leave.'

She gave me a concerned look, but it was quickly surpassed by anger. 'You bloody fool. What have you done this time?'

'No time!'

We were nearly out the door when I felt a steely hand clamp down on my shoulder.

'Mr Hansard?' came a voice like a death toll.

I spun, fist flung out for a punch.

I'm not a good fighter, and I don't *look* like a good fighter either. I've learned to use this to my advantage: if you look incapable of swinging a good punch, no one expects you to throw the first one.

The first man staggered back, shocked more than anything. His friend's boot caught me in the stomach, and a swift blow to my jaw had me winded and dizzy. I grabbed a glass from the nearest table and hurled it at his face. The glass missed, but the beer didn't.

The other one grabbed a fistful of my hair and wrenched me backwards.

'Let go of him, you bastards!' Peggy, somewhere to my left.

'Run!' I tried to shout, but it was muffled by a mouthful of fabric as one of the goons twisted my trench coat around my head. I flailed blindly for a moment, and suddenly there was a piercing scream.

I escaped from my coat to see one of the men – the screaming one, to be precise – stumbling around with a . . . a book, firmly clamped around his head. It had teeth.

I was so stunned by the sight I couldn't move. Evidently, so was the other assailant. And most of the pub's patrons, for that matter. We all stood motionless for a good two, three seconds watching the guy get chomped on by a vicious piece of literature.

A hand closed round mine and pulled me out of the gloom and into the street.

'Where now?' said Peggy, wide-eyed.

'Anywhere,' I said. 'So long as we get there fast.'

We took off, twisting and turning through the crowds, who took no notice. Funny how easy it is to not be seen when there are so many people around.

We came to a stop a few streets away. Peggy was clearly struggling.

'You all right?' I asked, sidestepping the thought that she had just saved both of us when that really should have been my job.

I patted her shoulder as she caught her breath. And then I realised she was crying. I stepped back in astonishment.

'There, there,' I said uncertainly. 'We're safe now.' I'm not particularly good at being comforting, but I'd give it a shot for Peggy.

She mumbled something through the tears.

'What was that?'

'. . . bloody book . . .' she sniffled.

'What?'

'I really wanted that book, Jack!'

I stared at her, nonplussed.

'You're upset about the book,' I said flatly.

'It was one of a kind.'

'*We're* one of a kind. We're lucky we got out of there.' *Not that you should have been drawn into that in the first place,* I mentally added. 'I almost feel sorry for the guy. That *Compendium* looked brutal.'

Peggy sniffed and dried her eyes. 'You should see my Jane Austin collection. Bloodthirsty.'

'I don't doubt it.'

'Who were those men, Jack?'

'Can't say for sure. Best guess is they work for a guy I sold some inspiration to, last time I was here. But that was all months ago. Long story.'

She gave me a doubtful frown. 'Just how many people are you hiding from in this city?'

'If I counted, it would ruin the surprise.' I offered her my arm. 'I'll walk you home, and then I think I'll get out of the city as fast as I can.'

'In a hurry to get into more trouble elsewhere?'

'It's a living.' I grinned.

We turned a corner and found ourselves on Oxford Street, thronged with traffic and shoppers and noise and chaos. I breathed in the fumes and felt at home.

Together we pushed our way through the crowds, jostling shoulders with strangers and banging knees on wayward shopping bags. I enjoy crowds. You need to always be on your toes, constantly watching for that errant elbow that might catch your face or sly fingers groping for undefended wallets. But more importantly, a crowd means lots and lots of witnesses, which significantly lowers the chances of impending death.

'Why would they be after you for selling inspiration?' asked Peggy after a while. 'Those men, I mean?'

I shrugged. 'Usual shtick. The inspiration might have not been perfectly up to scratch, per se. I get the impression this may have slightly vexed the fellow who bought it, because he threw me off a bridge.'

'Oh. Was he a bad guy?'

'He threw me off a bridge!'

'Well, I never know with you, Jack. Sometimes I think you're asking to be thrown off a bridge. You never know when to leave well enough alone.'

245

'I don't always deserve it. Occasionally I'm even honest.' I noticed her face still seemed tight with worry. 'Look, I'm sorry our catch-up was interrupted so rudely. It's my own fault, I know. But I promise I'll try and keep out of trouble, at least for a little while.'

'That's like a fish promising to give land a shot.'

'Well, the catfish did all right.'

She smiled but it faltered, and her gaze was torn across the street.

'What's wrong?' I said?

'Do you think they could have followed us?'

'Nope. No chance.'

'You're sure, are you?'

'Certain.' Suspicion dawned. 'Why do you ask?'

'I just feel like we're being watched. Like that man over there, he keeps looking at us. And outside that shop, that guy in the red hat is— Oh.'

We stopped. We had no choice. As if from nowhere three men in slick grey suits had stepped apart from the crowd and encircled us. Ambush.

'Mr Hansard?' said one of them.

'I'm popular today,' I observed to the world in general.

'We'd like you to come with us, Mr Hansard.'

Peggy stepped closer to me. 'I don't have any more *Compendiums*, Jack,' she whispered.

I beamed at the most heavy-set of the three. Young lad, dark hair; bright, intelligent face. Shame he'd found such immoral employment. 'We aren't going anywhere. And these gentlemen aren't going to do anything,' I said firmly. 'Lots of people here. Lots of people to remember faces. And faces usually lead back to names. I don't think Mr Scallet would like that.'

I stared down the one in front of me, fixing my smile in place. I felt Peggy's hand close around mine.

'Jack,' she said softly.

My ears began to register what they weren't hearing. The noise. The bustle. The hum of activity, the roaring of buses and the drone of hundreds of people all talking, laughing, shouting at once. It was all gone.

I risked a glance up the road.

All the people. All those busy, busy people. Gone.

Oxford Street. Empty.

I was impressed.

And, for the first time in a long while – well, for the first time in at least a couple of weeks – terrified.

The dark-haired youth gave me a cool smile.

'I think you should come with us, Mr Hansard.'

* * *

We were blindfolded and bundled into a car. After a swift, quiet journey there were hands to guide us upwards and forwards, into a building and down a steep staircase. We came to a halt in what I guessed to be a cellar.

Our hosts hadn't taken kindly to my commentary on the way over. I had merely pointed out that their kidnapping ideas left a lot to be desired in originality.

'I don't think disappearing a whole street of people can be called unoriginal,' Peggy muttered by my side.

'But blindfolds? And did you see that black car that picked us up? Blacked out windows and everything. No imagination at all.'

'No, Jack. Because I was *blindfolded*.'

'I was peeking.'

Our blindfolds were removed, and we found ourselves in a room far more lavish than I'd pictured. Good carpet on the floor, walls painted an inoffensive shade of teal. It didn't look like an interrogation room or a prison.

We were facing our three captors. The tallest of them, whose grey hair matched his suit, locked the door.

His voice was surprisingly genteel when he turned to us and spoke. 'It was thought best for your arrival to be as discreet as possible.' He gestured to the one with the muscles and the intelligent face. 'My young associate here has quite the talent for–'

'–showing off?' I supplied.

'What did he do to all those people?' demanded Peggy.

The young man in question, perhaps too young to be called a man just yet (I wouldn't put him past the age of twenty) languorously detached himself from the wall, moving his shoulders with an infuriatingly smug shrugging motion. The smirk on his face was one of the most punchable I've ever seen.

'I didn't do anything to the people,' he declared, in a predictably condescending tone. 'I did something to *you.*'

I wouldn't give him the satisfaction. I cut in and explained it to Peggy as if he wasn't there. 'He means he unfocused himself to occupy a small gap in reality, and he pulled us in with him. Very dramatic and all, but not nearly as impressive as he'd like you to think. I use a similar technique when I want to blend in somewhere.'

The smirk twisted into a scowl at having been robbed of his thunder. Take that, you little twerp.

I was impressed, though. Unfocusing is a talent anyone can learn if they try, and I myself am very at home with the trick of fading into the background. It's a simple matter of finding the spaces where people don't look so hard. You become sort of fuzzy. And the world becomes fuzzy to you.

If someone is specifically looking for you, this trick is not much help – searching eyes tend to snap you back into focus. But if you just want to be quietly unobtrusive, just lurking on the edge of peripheral vision, it's highly effective.

Takes a bit of effort though. I've never seen someone snap into it so quickly as the lad in front of me. And to unfocus so fully that a whole street full of people couldn't see you *even if they tried?*

It's the only way I can explain the disappearance of all those people. We, in fact, were the ones who had disappeared.

The fact he had done this to Peggy and myself against our will is an even more worrisome thing that I was trying not to dwell on. The one time I'd tried a trick like that, I stranded myself and my ill-fated companions in the void between worlds . . .

'Vincent is our protégé,' said the tall, soft-spoken guy. 'He is our greatest aide to subtlety.'

'I wouldn't call this subtle,' snorted Peggy. 'Why'd you have those guys assault us in the pub? I was enjoying my drink!' She adopted a hard expression to match that of the gang leader. He seemed a little taken aback.

'It wasn't our intention to start a fight. Our man tells us you swung the first punch. We'd have preferred you to come quietly.'

'*Why?*'

He nodded his head at something behind us.

'I hear you've been looking for me,' said a voice that made my ears tingle.

Have you ever had someone whisper in your ear when you're not expecting it, and felt an ethereal tickle in your brain? It was that kind of tingle. It ran from my ears down my spine and into my toes.

I turned to face the owner of the voice, heart pounding against my rib cage like a lump hammer. Somehow, I knew who I'd find on the other end.

'Hello, Mr Hansard,' said Quiet Eyes. She was sat against the wall in a large, comfy armchair of deep crimson chenille.

Now, the chair I could describe to you in intimate detail. It was clearly well-cared for, though the colour was a little faded with age. The plush crimson bulk perched on four round wooden castors, and a fringe of braided silk dangled from the bottom edge to provide a shield of modesty against anyone who would take unorthodox pleasure in leering at the unders of an armchair. But the woman who sat in this tasteful arrangement of not-quite-velvet cushions? I drew blanks, even as I tried to catalogue her face right then.

'It won't matter how hard you try,' she said, and my ears registered a faint Parisian cadence that lilted on each word. 'You'll never see me. Never know me.' She smiled, and though I couldn't give you the details, I felt that it was in a coy sort of way.

'I know your eyes,' I muttered back.

'Yes,' she said softly. *'Where is the woman with the quiet eyes?'* These are the words that keep drifting back to me out of the shadows. Why do you want to know me, Mr Hansard?'

'You stole something of mine,' I said evenly. 'Bluecaps.'

'Oh? This sounds like something I would do.' It was impossible to read her expression. It was as if the image of her entered my retinas but skipped the optic nerve and passed right through the back of my head.

I tried to keep my voice level. 'You sold them onto another trader. Edric Mercer. Remember him?' I don't know if I was masking anger or excitement to be finally speaking to her face to face.

She tilted her head. 'Mercer, yes. Interesting you should mention him. He has been useful at times. But he is irrelevant to your being here, Mr Hansard.'

'Why *are* we here?'

She spread her hands guilelessly. 'We are here to discuss what you want from me. Why have you been trying to hunt me down, Mr Hansard? For revenge? Were your bluecaps worth that much? Are you going to kill me?' The last was delivered with a giggle. I unconsciously squared my shoulders and thrust my chin forward.

'I'm not the vengeful type. But I do like to look a person in the eye when they've wronged me.'

'Then go ahead and look.'

She let an uncomfortable silence draw out as we remained in place, eyes locked. In my peripheral I was aware of the widening smirk on Vincent's face, while by my side Peggy had mustered a glare that should rightfully have set fire to the crimson armchair.

'Who are Baines and Grayle?' I said finally. The words sounded feebler in the silence than I'd intended.

Quiet Eyes leaned back in her chair. 'Looked long enough, have you?'

'Are we here at your behest, or theirs?'

'That is quite irrelevant.'

'I disagree. I like to know who I'm working for, before I accept a job offer.'

I wish I knew for certain whether she had a good poker face, or if it was just her unique invisibility that kept her expression impenetrable. Whatever the case, it didn't extend to her lackeys – I saw Vincent's stupid eyes widen. His associates were equally bad at bluffing ignorance.

'Who said anything about you working for anybody, Mr Hansard?' said Quiet Eyes.

I crossed my arms in front of me. 'You didn't go through all the theatrics just to get me here for a chat. Perhaps you're concerned that I've been asking too many questions, so you want me out of the picture. I've already seen how you handle that kind of situation, though. You sent that demonic parasite to kill Mallory, and maybe me for talking to him, but I sidestepped it easily enough. Seems a very round-about way to assassinate someone, by the way. Why not just use a gun?' I caught sight of Peggy's face. She looked horrified. '*Anyway,* if you wanted to kill me today, you'd have done it already. So this has nothing to do with what I want from you. It's what *you* want from *me.*'

Quiet Eyes smiled in that indefinable way of hers. 'My employers are overly concerned with image. I advised them against using the worm. As you have learned, it is not entirely reliable and the aftermath can cause complications. But my employers prefer not to leave *conventional* traces of their activities.'

'And your employers are Baines and Grayle.'

There was a metallic click as Quiet Eyes withdrew a pistol and coolly held it level with my face. I heard Peggy gasp.

I've never looked down the barrel of a gun before. My insides went cold.

'Unlike my employers, I have no aversion to guns,' said Quiet Eyes. 'As you can imagine, conventional traces do not worry me.'

'I can imagine,' I murmured, painfully aware that my ghost would be able to draw you a picture of my own murder weapon, but nothing more than a blurry shadow of the woman wielding it. In a flash, I wondered how many other people had looked down this same barrel and thought the same thing. 'I notice you haven't pulled the trigger,' I said, against my better judgement.

Again, that intangible smile. 'You have proven tenacious, Mr Hansard. Tenacious people are . . . useful, to my employers.' With a delicacy more befitting a piece of ornate glass than heavy metal, she set the gun down on a tall side-table next to her. 'I may not always agree with their methods, but I am happy to clean up the odd mistake made by my employers.'

'So don't become a mistake, is that right?'

'You catch on fast.'

Peggy, who until this moment had kept her tongue still and her thoughts silent, suddenly lanced our conversation. 'Why don't you get to the point? All this posturing, you're as bad as the show-offs back there – *both* of you, Jack. You,' she pointed an accusatory finger at Quiet Eyes. 'Was all this necessary? Why make a whole street full of people disappear, or make us disappear, or whatever, and go to the trouble of kidnapping us? If you really want to offer Jack a job, couldn't you have just *asked* him?'

'This is what I am doing,' laughed Quiet Eyes. Her eyes lit up; I think she was genuinely tickled. She brought a hand to her mouth and contained her laughter. 'I like her, Hansard. A plucky one. Would you like to work for us as well?'

'*No*,' said Peggy fiercely.

'We pay well.'

'I already have a job. You're keeping me from it.'

Quiet Eyes nodded sagely. 'Yes. You sell books. I apologise for disrupting your recent acquisition. Don't look so surprised. We do our homework. And we have done business with you before.'

'No you haven't. I think I'd remember someone pointing a gun in my face. Or stealing from me. Or kidnapping me and bringing me to some basement.'

'Sometimes business is legitimate,' said Quiet Eyes sweetly.

'But not this kind,' I interjected. 'Are you offering me a job or not?'

'Why don't you sit down, Mr Hansard?'

Vincent placed a chair behind me. I remained standing.

'You can tell me who Baines and Grayle are, first.'

I swear she tried to stifle another laugh as she replied. 'Oh, Hansard, you are stubborn. Or perhaps stupid.'

'Tell me, or I walk away.'

'How?' She gestured to the locked door and three guards, though I felt they were more for decoration than anything else. Quiet Eyes could handle herself.

She fingered the gun in a playful kind of way. 'You're not going anywhere, and not just because we will stop you. And you will accept our generous offer, and not just because the money is good.'

'Why?'

She leaned forward and crossed her long legs. 'Because I am going to offer you a score so big it will make men like Edric Mercer green with envy. I am offering you bragging rights of the highest order. The actual acquisition is just icing on the cake.'

I hesitated, but I knew she'd caught me, hook, line, and sinker. Judging by the way Peggy was looking at me as though I were a drowning carp, she knew it too.

'I'm listening,' I said.

Quiet Eyes smiled. 'Sit down, Mr Hansard.'

* * *

'And ye just let the flamin' *ast* walk away?' Ang screeched at me.

'Technically, she let us walk away,' I replied calmly.

'That stinkin', thievin'– and ye took a *deal* off her? Are ye thicker in the head than I thought, *gwas*? I knew ye were a bit touched an' all . . .'

'It does seem rather dumb, even for him,' agreed Peggy. 'But I can't say they gave us much choice. Anyone for tea?'

She set down three steaming mugs on the table, though there was barely room for them. Like every other surface in her shop, it was covered in books.

We were seated in the back room – *every* bookshop has a back room – away from the prying eyes of customers. Not that there would be any customers. In the tradition of all truly independent bookshops, Peggy kept erratic hours and closed the shop when it pleased her.

The shop was also (in the spirit of tradition, Peggy duly assured me) an utter mess. Sure, the shelves had some loose organisation – there were labels professing to categories as narrow as *Miniature Zen*

Gardening and as broad as *Science* – but whether the books you actually wanted lay on the labelled shelf or wedged in one of the many stacks that took up floor space, well, your guess is as good as mine.

Ang grumbled into her tea. 'An' ye never even got her name.'

'*Wrong*,' I said. 'I asked. Her name is Rien.'

Peggy slumped onto the ratty sofa next to me. 'She was pulling your leg, Jack.'

'What?'

'Didn't you notice her accent?'

'Yes,' I said proudly, and turned to Ang. 'She's French!'

Peggy shook her head. 'Jack, 'Rien' is French for 'nothing'. She literally told you nothing about herself.'

There was a beat, and then Ang's guffaws filled the room.

'Well, at least we know she's probably French,' I muttered.

'Sure, that narrows it down. If she wasn't putting it on.' Peggy rolled her eyes, then grew thoughtful. 'How does she do that trick? Of not being remembered, I mean?'

'I've got some ideas,' I fibbed. 'Maybe she's permanently unfocused, so our eyes can't see anything but the blurred image.'

I knew that wasn't right, though. If you're unfocused, the sheer act of someone looking at you should be enough to bring your appearance back into sharp relief. If you're skilled enough to remain unfocused even under a person's direct gaze, then the alternative is that you shouldn't be seen at all – that had been Vincent's trick.

It wasn't just normal invisibility, either. I've sold spells and potions that make you disappear (for a short while the market was flooded with invisibility cloaks, after those books about the magic kid with the scar got popular), but the point is that they make you *disappear*. Not what Quiet Eyes does, to be there and not there at the same time. How can she be hidden while in plain view? I couldn't figure it out.

'What do you think of the job, Ang?' Peggy asked brightly. 'I know it's come from an unpleasant source, but it does sound exciting.'

Ang sniffed haughtily and drew herself up in her seat (she sat on the table rather than in a chair – fed up with being looked down on, she said). 'Don't see what's so int'restin' about some bird. What's so special about eggs this feenix lays, then? Good omelettes?'

Peggy's face lit up. I don't think she gets enough opportunity to show off all that knowledge she absorbs from being around books all day. *'Well,* the phoenix is a mythical regenerating bird that's said to live forever. Or rather, it begets a new phoenix from the remains of the old, so it's either asexually reproducing or rising from the dead. Most people think it dies in a burst of flame and is then reborn in the ashes. There are phoenix stories from all over the world and all throughout history.'

She paused for a fleeting breath. 'The Greek historian Herodotus says the phoenix is native to Arabia but flies to Egypt to be reborn. Pliny the Elder claims to have seen a live phoenix specimen sent to the Roman Emperor Claudius – but that one's probably a fake. It crops up in all sorts of medieval bestiaries, and of course it's in lots of religious imagery and symbolism, you know how popular the idea of rebirth is–'

'Myffical, ye said,' Ang pointed out flatly.

'Well–'

'That's the interesting part,' I inserted tactfully. 'Despite all the stories, nearly everyone agrees that the thing doesn't exist. You'd think it'd have turned up on the Black Market by now, if it did.'

'Hasn't anyone tried to find out?' said Peggy curiously.

'Of course. Every so often some smug layabout like Edric Mercer will announce he's off to capture the fabled such-and-such, on a grand adventure to Egypt or India or some other exotic, mosquito-ridden place. And then we never hear of them again. Unless they're Edric Mercer.'

'Did Mercer go looking for it?'

'Yes. He made a big palaver about phoenixes some years ago. Came back empty-handed I presume, seeing as he quietly forgot all about it a year later.'

Peggy gave me a sidelong glance. 'So it's not worth asking him how far he got?'

'Not even if you paid me,' I said.

Ang scrunched her mouth into a frown. 'So does this bird lay eggs, or what?'

'Rien– I mean, Quiet Eyes seems to think so. That's the job: find a phoenix egg. Are you certain she was joking about her name?'

'Certain,' said Peggy bluntly. 'C'mon Hansard, don't be *that* guy. She's not going to be your femme fatale.'

'*Excuse me?* Are you suggesting I've got a thing for her? I don't even know what she looks like!'

From the table I could feel Ang's scrutinising glare. 'Ye do seem awful willin' t'do her dirty work, *gwas,*' she said.

'Because it's *our* dirty work!' I said defensively. 'The Black Market is all about taking shady deals from people you openly distrust. It's my entire *living.*'

'An' what about my kin?' said Ang, eyes narrowing. 'Did ye forget about them? Why're we workin' for the same people as might've had some dark hand in the vanishing of knockers an' coblynau? Did ye ask her about *that* in all yer cosyin' up? *Bradwr.*'

I've picked up a bit of Welsh (particularly the swear words) having suffered Ang's company for so long, but I didn't know what that last word meant. Ang's crossed arms and dark, suspicious silence told me it was probably something like 'traitor'.

Peggy delicately cleared her throat. 'Ang, you should hear what Jack asked for as payment.'

The coblyn squinted at me. 'Out wi' it.'

I steepled my fingers – classic mastermind pose – and grinned. I like to think I'd be good at chess, if I ever bothered to learn how to play.

'Our end goal is Baines and Grayle. Quiet Eyes is our way to get to them. What we need is her *trust* . . . and a way in.' I leaned forward. 'We do this job, Ang, and it proves we're worth her trust. In payment, I've asked for *more jobs* . . . a contract, if you will.' I held up a hand to silence her objection. 'And a meeting with our new, mutual employer. Baines and Grayle.'

'I ain't never workin' for them!'

My shoulders slumped. 'You're missing the point, Ang. It's just a lie to get close to them.'

'You're all about lies,' Ang muttered. She relaxed her arms. 'But I s'pose this'un's worth it.'

'Good. Glad we're finally on the same page,' I said. 'Now we just need to catch a phoenix and steal its eggs.'

'*Just*, 'e says.'

Peggy rolled her shoulders, stretched her arms, and cracked her knuckles. '*Right.* Time for some heavy-duty research then.'

I grinned. 'Knew I could count on you, Peg.'

'I'll just get the laptop.'

'What?' I looked at her blankly. 'You're not going to use the *internet*, are you?'

'Whassat?' said Ang.

Peggy raised an eyebrow. 'It's a lot quicker this way.'

'But this is a *bookshop!*' I spluttered. 'This is what it's *for*. You're meant to haul down some big, leather-bound book and dramatically blow the dust off the cover–'

'My books aren't dusty,' said Peggy, with a chilly calm that skimmed over my head.

'–and then spend hours poring over the cracked pages–'

'They're in good condition, too.'

'–going 'ohh' and 'ahh', and making notes in the margins–'

She aggressively removed my mug of tea and replaced it with a slightly battered laptop. She snapped it open and shoved a wireless mouse under my hand.

'Welcome to the twenty-first century, Jack. Today, you're going to learn how to use Google.' She brought her mouth level with my ear. 'And if you ever make a single mark in any of my books, *I will cut you.*'

Episode 14: Phoenix

The night passed in a glare of pixels and eye strain. The next morning, I awoke on Peggy's sofa to find her standing over me in full battle gear.

She was dressed in greyscale instead of the usual rainbow: a no-nonsense stud in her nose in place of the silver elephant and a distinct lack of chunky beads and dangly earrings. Her plain jeans were topped with a dull t-shirt that nevertheless loudly declared her affinity with the works of Tolkien. (At least, she assured me that's what 'I Last Longer Than Boromir' meant.) It was all very militant, by Peggy's standards. Even her hair was gelled to attention.

'Tea, Jack?' she said briskly.

'Please.' I rubbed my eyes, stared at the clock, and groaned. 'It's seven A.M.' I complained. 'Why are you up so early?' I rolled over and buried my head in the cushions.

She whipped away my blankets. 'Don't be a baby. We've got work to do.'

'Aye,' said Ang, rising from the armchair. 'Coblynau be up two hours b'fore dawn to work in the pit, *gwas*. This ain't nuthin'.' She tried to stifle a yawn. Too long on the road with me had eroded her early-bird tendencies.

Tea and bacon sandwiches fixed our moods, and before long we were discussing our game plan for the day. Peggy solemnly handed us each a notebook and pen, as if she were handing out rifles.

Ang wrinkled her nose. 'What's this fer?'

'We're not going to interrogate the phoenix,' I remarked.

Peggy straightened her notes. 'Honestly, Jack, you're never prepared. You never know when you might need something as simple as pen and paper.'

'I'm prepared in different ways,' I said, patting the protective paper charms in my pockets.

'Jack, when have your charms ever actually worked?'

'They *all* work!' I said indignantly.

This, at least, was true. I don't often lie to my customers (*That's a lie,* part of me pointed out), it's just that I sometimes omit important information. I will give a lifetime guarantee, on my word and my honour as a tradesman, that every one of my protective *omamori* amulets are in fine working order. What I can't guarantee, however, is what they protect you *against*.

I've learned over time, and through an array of consumer complaints, that my stock of oriental paper charms can variously protect you against finding moles in the garden, slight breezes, rains of fish, tripping over on a Sunday, burning your tongue on hot tea, sneezing in alleyways, and success – one charm so counter-intuitive that I could've sold it as a revenge curse if only I'd known what it did at the time.

I can't read Japanese, you see. I just had to hope that one of the *omamori* about my person deflected sharp things or guarded against bad luck. But it was a Sunday, so I'd settle for not tripping over anything if the opportunity arose.

'Them charms'd be better used as firelighters,' said Ang, sucking up the rest of her tea. She nudged Peggy. 'But it makes 'im feel useful, don't it.'

'You can lose that tone,' I said. 'Are you ready to go, or not?'

We all have our own ways of squaring up to danger. We conjure a thin veneer of defence that gives us the confidence to go into the dark unknown. For me it's a trench coat full of unreliable charms and cheap tricks. For Peggy it's a severe change of wardrobe. And for Ang it's the way she straightens her shirt, buttons her waistcoat, and glares witheringly at the world.

The coblyn tied her bluecap lantern to her belt so her hands were free, and the blue flame dimmed as if it sensed our collective forbidding mood.

We exchanged nods. We were ready, and we set off.

We were going to visit a museum.

The British Museum.

* * *

The one thing we knew for certain was that the phoenix was somewhere in London. This was the only solid piece of information Quiet Eyes had divulged on the matter. She was tight-lipped on virtually everything else I asked. What does the phoenix look like? Why is it here? Is it dangerous?

She'd dismissed my questions with wry amusement and the contention that if I was as good as I claimed to be, then I should be able to find the answers for myself. I began to suspect that maybe she didn't *know* the answers.

'Why me?' I'd asked. 'Why can't you obtain the thing yourself?'

She'd giggled and called me obtuse. 'Think of this as a test, Hansard. We want to see your skills in action. Prove to us you are worth employing.'

'All right. I'll play the game. So you want us to find this bird, catch it, and deliver it you you?'

Her calm eyes sparked with fire. 'No. When you find the phoenix, you can keep it. Or kill it. Whatever you wish. Just bring me an egg.

One, solitary egg. Do whatever you want with the bird. Think of all the stories they will tell about you.'

It was horribly, tantalisingly exciting.

No one's *ever* caught a phoenix before. And based on our long night of research, it seemed few people had ever seen the thing, either.

Descriptions of it were schizophrenic, at best. The bird has gold and red feathers, said some ancient texts. Or maybe it's kind of purple, said others. No, actually, orange is more accurate. No, no, no, gold and purple, with a blue tail. The phoenix looks exactly like a peacock. But it's also an eagle. And maybe definitely a heron.

Part of me began to doubt it was even a bird at all.

It lived in Egypt, according to some 'experts'. But also Arabia. Or India. Hell, take the whole of Asia. And it also liked to go on holiday around the world sometimes.

How many phoenixes are there? Only one, in the whole wide world. Except when there are two.

Or more than two.

By some accounts, the younger phoenix sets out to rebirth its parent in an endless cycle. By others, the bloody thing apparently created itself. Maybe it dies in a burst of flame, or maybe it doesn't ever die. And the earliest stories, Peggy pointed out, don't mention fire at all.

In short, we got nowhere fast with this line of enquiry.

Instead we'd latched onto the fact that the phoenix was in our immediate vicinity. How did it get to London? Did it fly here? Or was it already in someone's possession, seized and removed from its native lands?

Google, I will begrudgingly admit, captured my heart with how quickly it returned an answer:

Temporary Exhibition: Faith in Flames; the Phoenix and the Egyptian Sun-Cult, Sep 14th–Nov 14th.

Peggy had grabbed me by the arm. 'I know about this!' she exclaimed, ignoring my exasperation. 'It was on the news. They've found the remains of a temple in Cairo – Temple of the Sun, I think they called it – and they're touring some of the artefacts around the world. I've been meaning to go and see it. How cool!'

Ang and I were less impressed by the historical importance of the event, but after hours of fruitless research we could acknowledge that it was the closest thing we had to a clue. As a starting point – and a place for further research, Peggy eagerly pointed out – it couldn't hurt to begin at the exhibition.

It was an idea that I came to regret very quickly.

'These are some interesting lumps of rock,' I noted sourly. I stared into a glass case filled with segments of stone which, the sign dutifully assured me, were fine and significant examples of ancient architecture. 'Sure glad I paid a whole ten pounds on the tube to come and look at it.'

'S'good stone, though,' offered Ang, with her tradesman's eye. Her presence was happily innocuous to the other visitors – she could be easily mistaken for a child in fancy dress, especially with one of Peggy's pink bobble hats pulled down over her ears.

Peggy was busily scribbling down notes as she read the information panels. 'It's not a waste of money, Jack. Look, there's all sorts of stories about the phoenix here.'

'Yes, I remember reading most them online last night,' I replied with irritation. I felt the museum staff had read the same bloody Wikipedia articles we'd pored over.

The gist was this: the legend of the fiery phoenix might have grown out of even older stories about some sacred Egyptian heron called the bennu. This bennu thing was the soul of their sun-god Ra, or whatever, and he was worshipped at the imaginatively named Temple of the Sun, which is where these lumps of rock had been dug up from. The rest of it covered the rise and fall of some city called Heliopolis and the nutty cult of sun-worshippers who lived there.

I kicked my heels and leaned against a wall. 'We're not learning anything here, Peg. We should put our time to better use elsewhere.'

She fixed me with a stern gaze that reminded me of blackboards and chalk dust. 'Were you like this in school, Jack? I don't know how your teachers made you sit still long enough to learn anything.'

'They didn't, mostly,' I said. 'How much longer do we need to be here?'

'At least until we've seen the benben stone. It's the prize gem of the exhibition.'

'I'll bet it's not a gem. I'll bet it's a lump of rock.'

The exhibit was designed so that you were funnelled around it in one direction, following a corridor winding into a spiral. The idea, I presume, was to present you with ever-more outlandish information the deeper you explored. At the centre we encountered a space with dramatically low lighting and a bright spotlight shining down on a tall plinth.

On top gleamed a large section of black diorite shaped like a pyramid. Gold inlay shimmered like liquid on its surface, picking out in fine detail the form of a heron backed by rays of the sun.

'What's so special about this one, then?' sniffed Ang, oblivious to the value of the precious metal and workmanship that must have gone into it. Gold was pretty useless, in her eyes.

'This,' breathed Peggy, with what I felt was a very bookish enthusiasm, 'this is the actual benben stone from the Temple of the Sun. They say it's where the phoenix came to roost every five hundred years.' The light in her eyes diffused as I failed to show the same excitement. 'I thought you were interested in this sort of thing, Jack,' she said with unconcealed disappointment.

I shrugged. 'It's just a stone to me, Peg. It'd make a nice sale for sure, but I doubt my car would take the weight of it. It's got a nice story, but ultimately it's just a bit of building.' I could see she didn't understand. 'I mean it's just ordinary, Peg.'

I felt an innocuous buzzing at the edge of my senses and turned round, momentarily distracted.

'It's ordinary?' Peggy said in clipped tones. 'Jack, sometimes I– . . . Sometimes I think you walk around with your eyes closed. You're so bent on finding the absurd that you miss the extraordinary right in front of your eyes! Are you listening to me?'

'Hmm? Oh, yes. But I've *seen* extraordinary Peg. It's hard to top the wonders of the otherworldly, don't you think?'

'You think you've seen it all, do you? The marvels of humanity are too boring for you?'

'You collect supernatural books,' I pointed out.

'*I collect normal ones too!*' she countered, throwing up her hands. 'You like to act like you're not part of this world, Jack, but you are, whether you like it or not. How can you sell dreams and magic and not care about their mundane influences? Right in front of you is a stone from a temple, an ancient temple, built by real people, from thousands of years ago, to worship the phoenix. This *ordinary* thing meant a lot to those people, and you've no right to dismiss it as 'just a bit of building'!'

I waited until she calmed down. There was an apprehensive twist to her frown that gave me pause for thought. 'What's bothering you, Peg? You know I've always looked at museums like a shopping catalogue. I'll pinch whatever bits of mythos are useful and find a way to forge the relics that take my fancy.'

'I was just thinking about people,' she said quietly. 'And about consequences. And how people are connected by consequences.' She nodded at the benben stone. 'Right now, we're connected to the people who built a temple for a phoenix – we're seeking the same thing they were. And we're here *because* they built that temple. And I can't help but wonder why the phoenix is so valuable, and what the consequences will be, and for which people.'

'Getting a little abstract on me there, Peg.'

'Jack,' she sighed. 'When you're running around with your head in the clouds, you seem to forget that there are people out there with guns who are very much living in the real world, and they have real tempers and real bullets and *real consequences.* What happens after you find the phoenix? Have you even wondered why Baines and Grayle want an egg in the first place? What if they try to breed them? What if they're doing something cruel?' She looked at me sadly. 'Have you *ever* thought about what happens to the things you sell? Whether people might get hurt?'

I swallowed the lump in my throat. Ang was observing me closely, her steely eyes daring me to say what was on my mind.

'As it happens,' I began. Yes, I wanted to say, of course people get hurt. That's the entire point of at least half my stock. Vengeance hexes are my best-sellers. They are *designed* to hurt. But I'm just a supplier. What happens after money has changed hands is none of my business whatsoever. That's just how business works.

You did choose *this business,* pointed out a treacherously guilty voice in my head.

'As it happens,' I said instead, 'I think we're close to finding the phoenix right now.'

Peggy's brow wrinkled and she took a step back, derailed and deflated. 'What?'

'You hear that buzzing?'

'No.'

'I hears it,' murmured Ang. She nodded towards the benben stone. 'Coming from that thing.'

Baffled, Peggy watched me move past her to inspect the stone. As I honed in on the buzzing, I realised it wasn't so much the glinting gold inlay that gave the stone its shimmering effect. More accurately, the whole benben stone seemed to shimmer in and out of focus.

'What are you staring at?' whispered Peggy. Right now, we were the only ones in this quiet space.

I let her see my grin. 'Do you know how to unfocus, Peg?'

'The trick that nasty twerp Vincent pulled? No. Why?'

I mulled it over. I've done this sort of thing before. Once. I'm sure I could do it again. I exhaled, pushed back my anticipation.

'You know about the folds in reality, right? How there are pockets of *other* reality you can reach, if you know how?'

'You've told me,' she said warily.

'This stone, here,' I couldn't help waving my hand over it, gleefully stopping short of making contact, 'it's a *bridge,* Peg. A weak point. An easy way across.'

'Across to what?'

'*To wherever the phoenix is!*'

Ang had figured out my line of thought by now. 'Y'think it locked itself away, *gwas?* Took itself out o' this world, like us coblynau?'

'Or maybe someone else locked it away,' I pondered. 'In any case, I think we've cracked it!'

Peggy grabbed my arm. 'Wait. This is exactly what I mean, Jack. If it's locked away then, well, *why?* Maybe someone put it there for a good reason. Maybe it put *itself* there for a good reason!'

'Then we're going to find out why,' I answered cheerfully. But she wasn't buying. 'All right, Peg, how about this. What if the phoenix is harmless, right? What if some ancient Egyptian or someone found a way to *imprison* the poor bird this way. They worshipped it, right? Seems like it would be mighty handy for a priest to be able to conjure his sacred bird at will – right? Then their civilisation crumbles and the phoenix is lost to the sand, trapped for eternity. What if freeing it is the *right* thing to do, eh?'

I could tell she knew that my heart wasn't in that argument at all. But the way she bit her lip told me it had struck a chord anyway.

'Okay,' she said at last. 'What do we do now?'

I reached out an arm. 'Both of you, just touch my hand. Try not to concentrate. I'll do the rest.'

I breathed slowly, tried to not let exhilaration get the better of me. *I'm going to be the first to find the phoenix,* I thought.

I let my edges blur, then let them expand to encompass Peggy and Ang. We aren't here, I told myself. We're insubstantial, part of the background, inconsequential. Fog seemed to slither forth from the benben stone.

I leaned over the rope and dreamily placed my hand on the stone's cool surface, fingers splayed across the glimmering gold on black. The whole world glimmered, became golden mist, and then settled. The world came back into focus. It was dark, and silent.

Next to me, Ang and Peggy swayed dizzily as they adjusted. I pulled away my hand and doubled over, wheezing. *Damn. That really took it out of me.*

'You all right, Jack?' asked Peggy, laying a hand on my shoulder.

'Nngh. Fine.'

'You look pale.' She stopped and went pale herself. Her eyes fastened on something over my shoulder. My eyes fastened on something over hers. Turning in a circle, I discovered it went all the way around the horizon.

The sky, if that's what you could call it, was a sheet of obsidian stretching over our heads and to the edges of vision. At the horizon it met with what at first appeared to be an unending pane of black glass, until tell-tale ripples proved it to be liquid.

There was no source of light that I could see, though clearly there was some kind of light to see by. It felt thin, as if the light itself was filtered and weak. So was the air, for that matter. The whole place felt thin, of little substance. Even the rock we stood on seemed eerily delicate.

Ang crouched down and stared at it impassively. 'No rock I recognise,' she muttered to herself. 'Looks like granite here, limestone there. Could be both at once.'

'What is this place?' said Peggy. 'Are we on an island?'

It was an island: grey and rocky, rising out of an infinite, inky sea. We squinted into the distance, where the land grew into a craggy peak. I took a few steps forward, testing the solidity of the ground.

'Seems stable enough,' I said. 'Definitely looks like a prison, doesn't it? I mean, if I was going to capture an immortal fire-bird I'd probably buy a cage like this.'

'It's very bleak. I'd hate to be trapped here.'

'Then let's not be.' I scanned our surroundings. There were two landmarks I could make out. The first was next to us, a shoulder-high pillar topped with a duplicate of the benben stone – though of course I knew it wasn't really a duplicate. It was the same stone, existing in two places at once.

As for the second point of reference, it was the high crest of rock which the whole landscape rose to meet.

'Looks like the only way is up,' I said.

We started to climb, cautiously. It was hill all the way, in some places deceptively smooth and slippery, in others jagged and unsubtle.

Ang surged past us, unfazed by the difficult terrain or the weak light. Her bluecap lantern lit her footsteps and I got the impression, by the way it strained against the glass, that it guided her towards the safest path over the craggy ground. Peggy and I followed as best we could. Our eyes struggled against the light, fighting to pick out the edges of one rock from another.

We mounted a ridge and rested. It was Peggy who shook me by the shoulder to point out what lay ahead.

'That looks like a nest, Jack!'

'A big'un, too,' said Ang.

I grinned. 'Jackpot.'

The nest sat on the peak of the island. I guessed it to be less than half a mile away, though the slope made it seem further. We'd be there before we knew it. Who'd have guessed finding a phoenix could be so easy? I could practically taste my victory.

I leant against a boulder and caught my breath.

Ang wrinkled her nose. 'Now this mightn't be stone I recognise, but I knows fer certain that no rock nor clay ought t'smell like that.'

My own nose caught it, a pungent, perfumed sort of smell. It seemed to be coming from the boulder I was leaning on.

'Smells like myrrh,' said Peggy, puzzled. 'And it does have a kind of orange hue, don't you think? Stands out against all the grey. So smooth, too.'

I gave the fragrant boulder an experimental tap. With surprise, I caught the echo that told me it was hollow. 'Fancy that. Reckon it's a geode or something?'

Ang looked at me with disdain. 'Ye know nuthin' of geology, *twpsyn*.'

'I'm surprised you know the word 'geology'.'

A tapping emanated from inside the boulder.

We stared at it.

'Did you hear that?' said Peggy, aghast.

'Do you reckon . . . Do you reckon it's an egg?' I ventured.

'Don't be daft!' said Ang. 'What bird lays an egg big as that? *Pentwp*.'

'Actually,' said Peggy thoughtfully. 'I think I remember reading something about the phoenix making eggs out of myrrh . . .'

'Daft!' Ang said again.

I began to cast around for something useful.

The knocking came again, more insistent. It was followed by a muffled cry.

'That sounded human,' gasped Peggy.

I found what I was looking for. A big, sharp rock. 'Stand back,' I said.

I hefted it with both hands, then swung as hard as I could against the myrrh boulder. It cracked. Another swing, another crack. Third time lucky, the crack split down the middle and one half of the egg slid away, throwing perfumed dust into the air.

Inside was a human figure, curled into a foetal position. It unfolded itself, stretched painfully, revealing a red leather duster and broad-brimmed hat with a bedraggled feather stuck in it.

The occupant of the coat and hat looked up into my eyes and swayed. 'Hansard?' he said blearily.

'*Mercer?*'

* * *

Mercer.

Edric Mercer?

Edric Mercer, here. Already. Before me.

His gaze wavered as he took in my companions: a grizzled coblyn under a pink bobble hat and a buxom woman with blue hair who could apparently last longer than Boromir. Quite tame in the grand scheme of things, but I imagine it's a sight that becomes outrageous in such a barren, unearthly setting.

Ang's face split into a grin. She stepped forward and socked Mercer in the jaw.

'That's fer me bluecaps, ye rotten *coc oen!*' she said gleefully.

The dishevelled figure toppled backwards and groaned.

'This is Mercer?' said Peggy sceptically. 'The guy you don't like because he's better than you?'

'I never said he was better than me!'

'Well, you sound jealous when you talk about him.'

'I'm not jealous. Who could be jealous of *that?*'

'That' was groggily rubbing his face with both hands as he lay ungracefully flopped like a ragdoll in one half of the broken myrrh shell. The feather in his hat drooped sadly over one eye.

Peggy bent down to him and said kindly, 'Hello? Mr Mercer? Are you all right?'

'Dear lady,' he mumbled through his hands, 'what part of being imprisoned in a rock cocoon could possibly allow one to be feeling 'all right'?'

She straightened up. 'Sod you, then. And it's a myrrh cocoon, *actually.*'

'What are you doing here, Mercer?' I said, suppressing my rising bile. I suspected I already knew the answer, and I felt wholly cheated.

He pulled himself to his feet, joints cracking as he stretched. He dusted down his stupid red overcoat and straightened his foppish hat. He even sported matching leather boots with some kind of knot-work pattern on them. Every bit the dandy cowboy. The only thing missing was his trademark smirk. Instead, crow's feet and a tight, tired frown made for a disconcertingly out of place expression on his features.

He ignored my question. 'Do you have any water?'

'Only if you've got an answer,' I shot back. 'I'm on the job here, and you're an unwelcome distraction.'

He eyed me wearily. 'Miss No-Face got to you too, did she?'

Drat. Suspicions confirmed.

'Whassat?' said Ang. 'He meanin' the quiet-eyed *ast?*'

'It doesn't matter.' I tried to mask the bitterness in my voice. 'Let's just go do the thing, we're wasting time here. Mercer can see himself home.' I waved vaguely in the direction of the benben stone. 'It's over there somewhere.'

Mercer flashed a wry smile. 'You don't stand a chance on your own,

Hansard.'

'You can clearly see I'm not on my own. We can handle ourselves.'

He eyed us up. 'Oh yes, quite an elite company you have there. I expect the knocker can help dig your grave, at the very least.'

'*Coblyn,*' Ang and I snapped at the same time.

'Same thing. Little dirt goblin. Far from your hole, aren't you?'

Ang flexed her hands like claws. With the way her scowl bared her teeth, she did look horribly goblinesque in the grey half-light. '*Not. Goblin,*' she hissed.

At her waist the bluecap flared brightly in its lantern. Ang's eyes drew to it, then widened.

'Settle down, little one,' Mercer continued to drawl. 'You can at least be grateful you aren't related to the gnomish folk . . .'

Ang grabbed my hand and Peggy's and at speed pulled us back down the slope we had just climbed. With a deft flick of her wrist she released the latch on her lantern and the bluecap whizzed off ahead. 'Follow it!' she ordered. 'Safe way down!'

We tripped and stumbled over the jagged stone until we passed a rocky overhang and found ourselves slipping and sliding over scree instead. We slithered into a dip in the ground and were pulled to the floor by Ang. She gestured for us to stay low. The bluecap flitted anxiously in front of our noses. Ang reached out and cupped the flame gently, drawing it back to the lantern.

I opened my mouth to speak, but Ang caught my eye and shook her head. The bluecap still danced erratically inside the glass. Obviously it had sensed some kind of danger, but what? And where was Mercer? Had he tried to follow us, or was he still pontificating at thin air?

I raised my head to peer over the edge of our hollow. It was a dead landscape, silent and still.

It was pierced, very suddenly, by a shrill cry and a streak of red arcing high through the air, followed by a bone-shattering thud as it hit the ground. A red hat with a feather drifted down after it.

We shared a pained wince. That's not the kind of fall you get back up from.

As I stared at the forlorn body on the rocks, a small, hunched figure shuffled into view. It was probably male, based on the lack of visible lady parts. It was naked from the waist up, sandalled at the feet, and its modesty assured by a wrap of white linen. Quite human, aside from the bird's head that rested on its shoulders – something long and narrow with an S-shaped neck, like a heron.

It advanced on Mercer's prone body, head bobbing backwards and forwards like a pigeon. It stopped and stared, flicking its head side to side in that juddery way shared by all avian creatures. The head dipped and the beak snapped at Mercer's red coat.

'What's it doing?' whispered Peggy. It seemed cautious, poking with its sharp beak as if prodding for movement. Apparently satisfied, it grabbed two handfuls of coat and began to drag the body back up the hill.

Peggy made as if to jump up – Ang and I both yanked her back down. 'We can't let it take him!' she exclaimed.

I held her in place. 'Yes, we can. He's probably dead.'

'No, look! He's moving!'

I looked up and saw that Mercer's corpse was squirming. It startled the bird-creature as much as me. It let go of the struggling cadaver and hopped back a few paces. Mercer sat up, coat wrapped over his head and arms flailing blindly. The bird-beastie bent double, then hopped forwards again, edging around towards Mercer's back. I realised it had picked up a rock.

There was a sudden void beside me.

'*Gwas,* look–!'

'*Peg, no!*' I leapt up and after her, briefly scrambling on all fours til I found my footing.

Peggy raced ahead, screaming a war cry that any berserker would be proud of. The heron-man dropped its rock and looked at Peggy open-beaked. I don't think it knew whether to run or attack. But then it spotted me, charging along behind. I like to think that my coat billowed heroically behind me.

Our valiant charge spooked the hell out of it. It jumped backwards, bent its knees, then unfurled the most ginormous wings I've ever seen. That hunched profile was all down to the feathered mass gathered on its back – and now, silvery wings outstretched, at least three metres from wingtip to wingtip, the creature looked huge.

With one massive downbeat it flapped its wings and took off in a graceful motion, spiralling upwards on a pillar of non-existent thermals. It became a silver speck against the obsidian sky, then veered off towards the distant crag where we had spied the nest.

Ang marched over to Mercer and ripped the coat off his head. He seemed quite dazed underneath. I would be too, if I'd just been thrown fifty feet in the air.

She stuck her nose in his face and demanded, 'Why ain't you dead?'

'Thank you for your concern,' he grunted.

'But seriously, why aren't you?' I asked, watching him stagger to his feet.

He straightened the leather coat and delved into one of the pockets. He pulled out an ornately decorated *omamori* charm constructed of green silk and gold thread. It was gently sizzling.

The embroidered kanji script glowed fiery red, gradually burning away the silk before our eyes. Within moments, only the smouldering characters were left hanging in the air, and then they too dissipated into nothing.

'That was my last one,' said Mercer grimly. 'Highly advanced amulets. Complete protection against physical harm. I travelled personally to the shrine in Itsukushima to have them prepared to my own unique specifications.'

'Huh,' said Peggy, sending me a pointed look. 'So, some charms *are* useful.'

'Mine are useful,' I muttered. *In highly specific circumstances.*

'Well, if I need any luck in passing an exam or avoiding strong winds, I'll let you know,' she replied sweetly. I heard Ang snigger.

Mercer regarded me dubiously. 'I suppose you do have some items of use about your person? I must say I've eaten through all my resources.'

The three of us exchanged uneasy glances.

'My charms are a decent calibre. Just a bit . . . specialised . . .'

'I got me bluecap.'

'. . . I brought a notepad and pen?'

It was a little funny, watching the expression of sublime stupefaction dawn on Mercer's face. Or, it would have been, were it not a sign of how abysmally unprepared we were. He picked his hat off the floor and ran one hand through his hair, staring into the distance.

'Do you realise,' he said slowly, 'I have been attempting to complete my task on this island for . . . about four days now. That does not include the extensive planning beforehand. It took three months to discover the location of the phoenix and track it to London . . . a further fortnight to plan the operation and ensure I had taken all the necessary precautions. Of course, I had to think of food provisions and other practicalities, alongside offensive and defensive measures . . . And you tell me that you all just . . . hopped in without a care?' He shook his head. 'I took you for a fool, Hansard, but I see I've underestimated the depths of your folly.'

Peggy bristled. 'And just what is your task here, Mr Mercer? Whatever it is, you're obviously not doing it very well.'

''E's stealing feenix eggs,' said Ang bluntly. 'Quiet Eyes offer you the job b'fore us, *pen pigyn?*'

'Months ago, by the sounds of it,' I said. 'I'm guessing you missed your rendezvous? I suppose Quiet Eyes figured you must've gotten into trouble, couldn't handle the job after all. Lucky we were in town, so she could send us to . . . save . . . you . . .'

I trailed off, smugness suddenly displaced by resentment as the full realisation sunk in. It descended like a cloud. We weren't here to steal phoenix eggs. We were here to find out what had happened to the previous schmuck. Mercer.

He gave me a look of pity. 'Surely it must have occurred to you that you wouldn't be the first choice for *any* task like this? Now, I'm no fool, Hansard. Once I located the benben stone, I did *not* divulge this information to little Miss No-Face – or Quiet Eyes, as you call her. I have ways of making sure she couldn't follow me, either. Until now my location, and by extension, the phoenix, has remained a mystery to her.'

'What do you mean, 'until now'?' said Peggy suspiciously.

'Call it a hunch, my dear, but I suspect you took no measures to cover your tracks. I'm right, aren't I?'

The three of us shared a sheepish look and Mercer pinched the bridge of his nose. He looked as if he was fighting the mother of all headaches. 'As we speak, that woman is probably assembling a reception party for us back at the museum. Stupid. Did you really think she was going to pay you, Hansard? Come to that, did you really think she expected you to get your hands on a phoenix egg? I imagine she expected you to find my corpse, maybe a clue as to my cause of death, and then for you to ram your tail between your legs and go squealing back to her with the information. For this you are, might I say, the perfect choice. Your propensity for running away is well-documented.'

My lip curled.

I struck out, snatched the stupid hat from his stupid head and threw it on the floor and stamped it down until it was flat and the feather was barely a feather any more, then I picked it up and rammed it down on Mercer's smug, scheming, soul-sickeningly self-satisfied skull so hard that he sank right into the rock, and then I stamped him down until there was nothing left but that hat sticking up out of the stone like a sorry crimson weed.

Well, that's what I did in the privacy of my head, at any rate.

Instead, I held my ground. 'That's where you're wrong,' I told him. 'You and Quiet Eyes. You can go running home if you want, go and get some more personalised charms, for all I care. I'm going to get my hands on a phoenix egg, and I'm going to find a *different* buyer.'

I suppose I was expecting derogatory laughter, but Mercer's resigned sigh took me rather by surprise. 'You can't, and you won't,' he said flatly. 'Trust me, I've used nearly every trick I know, and I am out of juice. The phoenix is powerful.'

'The phoenix being the bird-man we saw a moment ago?' said Peggy.

'Of *course*, dear lady. What *else?* There simply are no other creatures inhabiting this waste of rock.'

'No need to be sarcastic. And I'm nobody's 'dear lady', thank you.'

'It don't exactly match any of the descriptions, does it,' said Ang, scratching her nose. 'Seems t'me it could be anyone wi' a bird head pretendin' to be the feenix.' She shrugged unapologetically under our combined gaze. 'People says I look goblin – even though ye ain't never seen me eating babes. But if ye put me next to a goblin, ye'd know the difference straight away.'

'To be fair, I don't think I've ever seen you mining coal, either . . . Not-that-I-don't-think-you're-a-coblyn,' I added quickly.

'Allow me to enlighten you,' Mercer interjected. 'I know this creature is the same phoenix I have been seeking for it displays the key, unifying characteristic of that mythic bird. That is to say: immortality.'

'How could you possibly know it's immortal?' I said.

'I've killed it at least three times already.'

'Ah . . . Oh.'

Mercer paced while he spoke, punctuating his account with sweeping gesticulations. 'On each attempt the beast appears to pull itself back together. I have tried crushing it – it merely gets back up and fills out the flesh as good as new. I've tried burning it – but it walked through the flames until it was burnt to a crisp, and then kept on walking. I cut off one of its limbs, and discovered it was still attached by a thin thread which drew it back onto the body. I considered cutting it into pieces and locking each segment in a box, but I fear dismemberment would be impossible, for I've found no way of cutting that thread. I've never managed to disable the creature for more than a few minutes at a time . . .'

'O-kay,' I reflected. 'And how strong is it?'

'Very strong. I fear that we may be dealing with a creature of deific proportions.'

There was a weighty silence as we all tried to get our heads around this statement.

'It does look rather like an Egyptian god,' ventured Peggy. 'What with the animal head on a human body. Jack, do you remember reading that the bennu bird was the soul of the sun-god Ra?' Her eyes lit up and she turned back to Mercer. 'Are you telling us that we're dealing with an actual Egyptian deity?'

I frowned. That didn't sound good at all. Myths and monsters are one thing – but gods are a whole other can of celestial worms that I've never wanted to sample.

Mercer, on the other hand, was willing to eat his fill.

'Are you aware of the rich body of Egyptian creation myth?' he said to Peggy.

'Some of it,' she replied hesitantly. Then with vigour, 'Actually, it did occur to me, what with the link to the bennu bird, that this island might represent the primeval mound rising out of the ancient waters of chaos.'

Mercer was taken aback. 'Indeed. Then you understand how I made the connection.'

'How's about ye explains it fer the likes of us simple folk,' said Ang, squinting at them both. 'The bird be either a myff or it ain't. Now we know it ain't – else it couldn't've tossed you sky high – so what've myffs got to do wi' anything, any more?'

'It might help us understand what we've gotten ourselves into,' said Peggy. 'Do we even know where we are? What *is* this place?'

'Ye think it's this primeval whatsit, do ye?'

Mercer took over. 'Let's start at the beginning, with how the ancient Egyptians thought the world was brought into being. I'll even use small words so you can understand.'

Peggy shot me a warning look as I began to angrily open my mouth.

Mercer adopted his haughtiest pedagogical tone.

'In the beginning, there was nothing but the black waters of Nu. There was one god who existed in this realm of nothing, and he is variously named Amun, Atum, and Ptah. This god created . . . everything. But he started with the primeval mound, and the nine gods of the Ennead. These would be Geb, embodiment of the ground. Nut, the sky. Shu, the air. Tefnut, water. Osiris, rebirth. Isis, magic. Set, chaos. And Nephthys, death.'

Above us and around us, the sable sky and still waters remained conspicuously god-less.

'What does this have to do with the phoenix?' I said impatiently.

'In one version, it's a phoenix's cry that kick-starts creation,' explained Peggy. 'Which suggests the phoenix was around at the same time as the almighty creator-god.'

'Indeed,' said Mercer. 'Let's not forget that the bennu bird is intertwined with the identity of the god Ra, who is in turn bound up with the names of Atum and Amun.' That pompous smirk was back on his face, like it had never left. The man thought he was preaching a sermon, I thought.

'Hold up,' I said. 'You're not actually suggesting that we've just met the god of creation, are you? That this island is the starting point of the universe?'

Now I received the derisive laughter I had been waiting for. Mercer had the gall to sneer at me. 'My dear Hansard, that is truly preposterous. Quite frankly one would expect a creation-deity to be somewhat more *impressive*.' He said this with the aggravating tone of someone inferring that *they* should know, because *they* have the experience in this domain.

Mercer stroked his chin. 'However, all myths must spring from somewhere. It is my postulation that this dark island is the native homeland of our phoenix creature, and that at some time in the distant past it found its way into our world and thus into Egyptian culture, inspiring a rich body of lore that endured over millennia. But a true god? It's not nearly strong enough. Maybe a demi-god, at best.'

'That makes all the difference,' I said sarcastically.

'Indeed. I battled it for hours on end and it was able to throw me large distances with little effort. It has also attacked me with fire – issued from the hands, which I find interesting – and most recently I have discovered its ability to encase a particularly persistent enemy in a cocoon made of myrrh. Admittedly, it had knocked me unconscious first. I presume it had given up on trying to kill me or scare me off, so imprisonment was the next best thing.'

'You haven't made it to the nest, then.'

He waved a hand dismissively. 'Getting there is not the problem. It's a mere matter of putting one foot in front of the other. But the phoenix guards the nest and has knocked me back every time. I feel we can take no other course of action but to turn back.'

Peggy chewed her lip, looking pensive. I put a hand on her shoulder.

'You should head home,' I said. 'You've done more than enough for me already and you certainly didn't ask to be in this mess. I'll see you later.' I gave her a friendly pat and then turned and started up the slope.

'What?' she said, startled. 'What are you *doing*, Jack?'

Ang sighed. 'Puttin' one foot in front of t'other.' She checked the lantern at her waist and straightened her waistcoat. 'Someone's gotta pick up the pieces if he gets hisself killed.'

'You're going *with* him?' I heard Mercer say in astonishment.

'Wait for me!' yelled Peggy.

'Fools,' muttered Mercer. Then, grudgingly, 'Hold on. I'm coming too.'

One foot in front of the other, I told myself. How hard can it be?

Episode 15: She Who Holds A Thousand Souls

I don't know why I needed to prove myself so badly. *This isn't me,* I thought as I clambered up the ridge. This can't be me, climbing head first into danger just for the sake of my pride.

I don't consider myself a coward, but cowardice has its merits. When you know a client is about to be furiously dissatisfied, scarpering is only common sense.

I've been in plenty of risky situations before. I'm hardly a stranger to peril. But I usually enter it unwittingly, and my first thought is always towards my exit strategy. A healthy sense of self-preservation doesn't make a man a coward.

I suppose the key thing, the really key thing, is that I've only ever done small peril. Brief doses of danger and bite-sized chunks of calamity. Talks big, acts small . . . that's me, when you get right down to the bottom of the rusty barrel of my personality. It's the fundamental difference between Mercer and me.

Mercer does *big*.

Mercer came here prepared to kill a god. I came prepared to try and half-inch a piece of poultry.

I've done my fair share of otherworldly sight-seeing. But although I've traversed some peculiar corners of reality – and occasionally unreality – I can't profess to have visited Hades, or Nirvana, or Limbo, or countless other dimensions which are apparently a walk in the park for men like Mercer. I've one-upped a few beasties in my time, but never done battle with demons. I'm a tupenny merchant of curiosities; he an agent of incredibilities. If this were a film, he would undoubtedly be the main character. I probably wouldn't even get a walk-on part.

Little fish, Mercer had once called me.

It occurred to me, as I stubbed my toe on another black rock, that maybe I was tired of being treated like a bit player. I'd like to be a different character for a change – one with a speaking part and a place in the credits. Someone owed a little respect.

And this, *this,* is why the business with Baines and Grayle and Quiet Eyes had really gotten under my skin. Because friends, enemies, and acquaintances alike had all tried to fob me off in the same manner you warn a child not to touch the oven. That's grown up stuff. Leave it to the big boys. The bigger fish.

Quiet Eyes thinks I'm a joke. Mercer's her real lapdog, her first-choice pedigree – I'm the convenient mongrel who just happens to have a working nose. It dawned on me, with a twinned cloud of anger and gloom, that I could have been *any* Black Marketeer in the immediate vicinity when Quiet Eyes decided she needed some intelligence gathered on Mercer's fate. Hell, she probably has a bunch of others on the job, too. Who's to say I'm the only one?

At least I got here first, I reflected. *Or at least, I hope so. Could be we just haven't found the corpses yet.*

'Jack,' said Peggy softly, touching my arm. She pointed ahead to where a large nest of woven reeds rested on a rocky outcrop. The nest was easily twice as big as a man. You could comfortably sleep in it, and from the well-worn impressions it looked like someone did, regularly.

In the centre were a clutch of eggs. Each was fist-sized and a dull amber hue, the colour of myrrh.

'Jack,' said Peggy again, tearing my gaze away. 'We need to talk about this.'

'About what?'

'Why is the phoenix guarding these eggs in the first place? Shouldn't we try to find out?'

I waved a dismissive hand. 'Don't all birds protect their young? It's bound to be a bit pissed off. It'll get over it – we're only going to steal *one* egg.' *Unless I can carry more,* I added silently.

'Depends on what the offspring is,' breathed Mercer, on my other side. 'Some of those ancient creation stories . . . some say it was the phoenix alone who created the whole world. Hatched it, in fact, from an egg.'

We stared anew at the clutch of eggs. Mercer's eyes were hungry. 'I've never stolen a whole world,' he murmured.

Ang tugged me down to her level and showed me the lantern. The bluecap was going haywire inside. It threw itself against the glass in every direction.

'It really don't want to be here, *gwas,*' she said reproachfully. 'Hope you got a plan.'

'Sort of.'

'I knows that look, *gwas.* Means you're about to wing it 'n' hope for the best.'

'. . . Sort of.'

'Ye ever think about the danger ye put others in?'

'You all followed me. I didn't ask you to come.'

She arched an eyebrow. 'Ye gunna do your best t'keep us all alive, then?'

'Of course!'

'Good. 'Cuz the feenix is gettin' up, *gwas.*'

A large grey lump, which we had all taken for just another oddly-textured boulder, began to uncurl. Wings the colour of silver and slate spread wide, and a beady heron eye glared at us first from one side of the slender head, then the other.

'Quick Peg, give me your notebook,' I said.

'This isn't the time to be taking notes, Hansard,' Mercer hissed as I hastily scribbled.

The phoenix regarded us warily. Maybe it was waiting for us to make the first move. If it had been fighting Mercer for four days straight, it made sense for it to be extra wary of more human-shaped creatures joining in.

I wondered how Mercer would approach it. I bet he'd square up to it, stare it down, face off for a good few minutes like a respectful adversary. So what the phoenix would be least expecting us to do . . . was probably something like this.

I sprinted forward, covering the ground in five strides. The phoenix flinched and raised its hands. I didn't hesitate – I slapped a paper *omamori* charm to its crested forehead and rammed the notebook and pen in its hands. Channelling every ounce of focus I had I bellowed into its baffled face, '*Good luck with passing your exam!*'

Then I left it staring bewildered at the words on the paper in front of it and ducked under a wing. The feathers were soft. I dashed to the nest, vaguely aware of motion and noise behind me. I seized the closest amber egg – *I've got one!* – and stashed it in a pocket. Mercer was beside me, shouting in my ear. 'You bloody *fool!*'

There was a rushing, crackling sound. Mercer grabbed me by the scruff of my coat and hauled me into the nest. Flames screamed over our heads.

There was no time to think. Instinct, in any case, had quite fully taken over all thought processes. As soon as the fire ceased gushing, we darted up and over the lip of reeds and ran, ran, ran.

Peg and Ang joined us at our heels. An almighty cry sounded behind us: it lashed through the air and quaked the ground at our feet. I threw out my arms and came to an abrupt halt as the rocks tore and tumbled away before me. The others barrelled into my back.

Rocky hillside became cliff edge just inches from my toes – great chunks of rock crumbled and smashed into the black water below. The phoenix cried again and a crack shot through the stone like lightning. It began to split apart in a jagged circle around us.

'We need to jump!' yelled Mercer over the shriek of tortured stone.

I wobbled on my feet as the ground shuddered and groaned. I took a running leap across the widening gap – cleared it. Mercer and Ang thudded either side of me.

'Jack!' I heard from behind. I turned and there was Peggy, on her knees and clutching the slowly receding ground. Her face was white with terror.

'*Jump, Peg!*' I screamed.

'I can't make it,' she cried. Her pleading eyes locked onto mine.

I looked at the gap and it was wide, very wide, and growing inexorably wider with every second. I panicked. It was too far. I'd never make that jump. Definitely.

Probably, hissed the little honest voice in my head.

My muscles tensed. I flew across the gap, caught the edge with one foot and threw all my weight forward. I landed face-down on the rock.

'I'm sorry, Jack,' gasped Peggy, pulling me up. She sounded like she could hardly breathe. 'I'm sorry, I'm sorry I froze, it's so stupid, I'm sorry.' I caught hold of her as the island shook.

'Take this.' I thrust a crumpled *omamori* into her hands. 'This one prevents falling, Peg. You can't *not* make the jump now!' I pulled her back from the edge. 'We run at it together, right?' She nodded mutely.

We ran, hit the edge, we jumped. And I knew, I knew then, I could *see* that it was too far. My outstretched fingers brushed the stone on the other side, and I continued to fall.

Something *cold* seized my hand. Enveloped it, in fact, in a white-ish blue light. I stopped falling with a jolt – and then another jolt as Peggy grabbed the tail of my coat.

We hung, shell-shocked and overwhelmingly grateful, in mid-air. Then I heard Ang's voice overhead, and we were hauled upwards, back to solid ground.

Ang gave us both a few anxious slaps as we were deposited at her feet. 'No time t'be senseless, *gwas,* the world's fallin' apart! Hurry, hurry!'

'Where's Mercer?'

'He ran! We gots to run too, *gwas!*'

We staggered upright. Peggy threw the paper charm at me. 'I *knew* you were lying, Jack!'

'*No time!*' cried Ang. 'Bluecap will show us a safe way. Follow it down, *hurry!*'

The bluecap detached from my hand and sped off. The ground quaked violently and every other step some part of it collapsed right next to us. Great spikes of stone burst forth when we rounded a corner – the bluecap whizzed sideways and we slid after it through a narrow gap between two rock walls as they closed in behind us.

The bluecap kept changing direction, sending us back the way we'd come – and we'd see over our shoulders that the rock had heaved, thrust upwards or sunk into rubble. I thought I spied silver wings in the sky above us, and the enraged phoenix cry followed as we tumbled over ourselves and ran as fast as our legs could carry. A final drop onto a plateau and our goal was in sight. The benben stone shimmered in the air just yards away.

A dull, feathered *thump* from behind had us sprinting. I thought I could hear the roar of flames and heat at my back, but we were at the benben stone, we *made it,* and now I just had to unfocus *shit I had to unfocus . . .*

We touched the stone together, I forced myself to think straight. The world seemed to get very *hot* . . .

And there was the fog, soft and cooling, embracing, and there were the shadows, climbing out of the dark pit inside the mist. Formless claws snaked towards us . . .

Focus.

The light came rushing back, hit me square in the forehead. I dropped to the floor, dazed. The world was suddenly silent.

'You made it,' said Mercer. He was still panting. Probably only seconds ahead of us.

'No thanks to you,' mumbled Peggy, sinking against a wall.

The blinding glare resolved itself into a spotlight over my head, illuminating the benben stone in the centre of a dark, peaceful room. There were smooth tiles underneath me. I closed my eyes and sighed. I've never felt so happy to be inside a museum.

'How did you get out of there?' said Mercer. 'I was sure you'd be dead.'

'We gots our ways,' huffed Ang. The bluecap hovered at her side. She ushered it back into the lantern.

Mercer crossed his arms. 'I suppose I am a little impressed. If only because I didn't think you had it in you, Hansard. Tell me, I must know. How did you stall the phoenix long enough to get to the nest?'

'Hmm?' I replied, not altogether yet.

'The charm you used, what was it?'

'Oh, that.' I began to pull myself upright, thought better of it, and sat cross-legged on the floor instead. My coat was singed and my head was pounding. I leaned back against the benben's pedestal. 'If you *must* know, it was a simple good luck charm. For students. Taking exams. You know.'

Mercer's brow crinkled. 'Are you saying you tried to command it to successfully complete an examination? You compelled it to answer a question on the paper before it could move?'

I shrugged. 'Something like that.' *Mostly, I just hoped I would confuse the hell out of it.*

'What was the question you wrote?' asked Peggy curiously.

'It's a good one.'

'Go on.'

'What . . . is the air-speed velocity of an unladen swallow?'

There was a ringing silence.

'I can't believe you are alive,' said Mercer icily.

'I dun't get it,' said Ang. 'Why'd you need to know about swallows? Why you laughin' *gwas*, what's the joke?'

'I have a better joke,' said a sly voice. A familiar, but very unwelcome voice. The gloom began to coalesce, and out of it stepped Quiet Eyes. Two other bodies followed her. I recognised the smug countenance of Vincent, but not the other suited goon. How long had they been standing in the dark, waiting for us?

Quiet Eyes smiled. 'This is the punch line.'

* * *

I certainly felt like a joke. But I sure as hell wasn't laughing about it.

'This is your fault,' Mercer said flatly. 'I told you she'd have followed you.'

I couldn't argue. It was depressingly predictable.

Quiet Eyes sauntered forward, pistol dangling casually from her hand. She saw me glance at it.

'Oh, Jack,' she said sweetly. 'You don't think I'd *use* this do you? There's no reason to be uncivilised. Unless you give me a reason.'

Vincent and the other henchman cracked their knuckles behind her. I wondered if she really needed them.

Quiet Eyes gestured vaguely with her gun-hand. 'You know what I want.'

Mercer, to my surprise, gave up his egg first. I knew the slick-fingered weasel would have snatched at least one. He rolled it from his prone position across the floor. Quiet Eyes stopped it with the toe of her boot and motioned for Vincent to retrieve it.

'Now yours, Hansard,' she said to me.

Peggy was shifting anxiously by my side, looking in all directions. Her gaze locked on Vincent as he bent at Quiet Eyes' feet. 'You've done it again, haven't you?' she said. 'Taken all the people away. It's so quiet. You wouldn't dare do this otherwise.'

Vincent gave a violent burst of laughter. Quiet Eyes was classier, and merely smiled.

'The museum is closed, darling. All the people left hours ago.' She fingered the barrel of the gun. 'We really are so terribly alone.'

I felt in my pocket and my fingers closed around the myrrh egg. I felt the weight of it in my hand.

'Hey, Rien,' I said. 'Think fast.'

The egg arced through the air. All eyes fixed on it. Vincent made a dive. I grabbed Peggy and Ang and ran.

Behind us there was a loud *crunch*, the kind of sound I imagined a rock would make when cracked open. Then there was a shockwave, a tremor that shook the whole building, and a blinding light that burned glowing after-images onto my retinas.

I fell against the wall, smacked my head on a display of carved scarabs. I half-turned and painfully opened my eyes. Through the spots I could see Quiet Eyes and her boys on the floor, rubbing their heads and groping for their scattered weapons. Mercer too, on the other side of the room.

But in the centre. Just in front of the benben stone and hovering a few inches above the shattered remnants of a myrrh shell, the form of a naked woman hung, sublimely suspended in the air.

But I use the word 'woman' loosely. Her skin, or the surface where you would expect skin to be, was a fold of midnight blue, a blue so deep it was almost black.

And within that blue – and 'within' really is the best word, because there was a definite sense of *depth* and *distance* – tiny stars glittered, from the very tips of her outstretched fingers to the host of suns in her hair. Nebulae dusted the smooth curve of her thigh.

I found I couldn't move. I was transfixed.

The apparition opened its mouth and issued a booming series of alien sounds that rattled my eardrums.

It fell silent and surveyed us expectantly. Its eyes were twin voids.

I brought a hand to my throbbing ear and groaned. 'Did anyone catch that?'

The eyes narrowed.

The mouth opened once more.

'HEAR ME, MORTALS.'

The sound left a high-pitched ringing noise in its absence.

Quiet Eyes struggled to her feet. Although she wobbled, she still exuded an air of self-assuredness that the rest of us had long since dropped.

'We hear you loud and clear, great one,' she said evenly. 'We beg to know your name, that we might do your bidding.'

'Are you nuts?' I hissed. 'We don't want to do its bidding!'

'I AM SHE WHO HOLDS A THOUSAND SOULS. I AM SHE WHO BORE THE GODS. I AM MISTRESS OF ALL.'

Quiet Eyes, as far as I could tell, kept a perfectly straight face. 'We might need something a little shorter than that, great one.'

The dark form drew itself further up, arms raised and palms outwards as if to display its full magnificence.

'I AM NUT, COVERER OF THE SKY, SHE WHO PROTECTS.'

'She say she's a newt?' I heard Ang mutter.

'*NUT.*'

'*Noot* then, fine, ye daft sky woman.'

Quiet Eyes quickly stepped forward again. 'How may we serve you, great Nut?'

'TAKE ME TO MY TEMPLE, THAT I MAY ADDRESS MY FOLLOWERS. I AM RETURNED.'

There was silence as we all exchanged glances.

'You've left it a bit late for that,' I said. The black eyes centred on me. The stars flared.

'WHAT IS YOUR MEANING.'

A crowd of thoughts jostled for attention in my head. First among them was: how do you break it to a god that they're no longer all that? How do you sum up several thousand years of human fickleness?

One century golden cows are all the rage, next thing you know there's a pantheon of gods drinking and fighting like hooligans as if it's going out of fashion (which I suppose, in a manner of speaking, it inevitably was) and then suddenly it's all about big beards and solemn men in serious dresses staring solemnly at solemn books. How do you explain to a god that their religion just isn't trendy any more?

Still, a god's a god – so you've got to be polite.

'My meaning, uh, great one, is that there is no temple, and there are no followers. They all died some thousands of years ago.'

'What he *means,*' Quiet Eyes interrupted, shooting me an exasperated look, 'is that we are your only remaining followers.'

The eyes turned on her. For a daft moment I had the notion that the two of them were reflections of each other, twin voids of space that my mind couldn't fathom. Two sets of unreadable eyes staring each other down.

'TAKE ME TO MY TEMPLE.'

'This is your temple, Holy One,' said Quiet Eyes. 'This is where we worship you.'

'Ah, yes, we keep your treasures here,' I said, catching on. I scanned the museum display quickly. 'We revere you with all manner of ancient monuments and amulets and . . . and . . . paintings. See, your picture's on the wall there.'

'All with holy texts to remind us of their worth, and your magnificence,' suggested Quiet Eyes. Suddenly everyone was pitching in.

'People make pilgrimages here every day,' Peggy chimed in.

'They comes in droves,' said Ang, nodding vigorously.

'Everyone makes an offering at the door,' tried Vincent.

'No price is too high,' agreed Mercer.

'YOU SAID YOU WERE MY LAST FOLLOWERS.'

Everyone paused. There was a feeling of teetering on the edge of a precipice.

'Ye-es,' I said cautiously. 'We're your last, uh, priests . . . ?'

'Enough. It is time to be direct,' said Quiet Eyes. Her tone went from awed to abrupt in an instant. 'Nut. Your name has faded to little more than a whisper in this world. Your once hallowed halls have fallen to ruin. Aeons have passed since you last walked this earth and the people know you no more.'

'THIS CANNOT BE. I AM SHE WHO HOLDS A THOUSAND SOULS. I AM THE COVERER OF THE SKY, MISTRESS OF–'

'Yes,' said Quiet Eyes. 'And it is unthinkable that you should remain unknown to these unworthy mortals. We are here to change that. I am here, great Goddess Nut, to make you an offer. I beg that you come with me, and I shall make you great again.'

'I AM ALREADY GREAT.'

The suns flared. A galaxy of stars spiralled around the goddess' head like a crown. Heat radiated from her countenance.

'With respect, Great Nut, the world has changed,' said Quiet Eyes patiently. 'Its people have changed. They are no longer impressed by simple acts of splendour. They are sceptical, challenging, and they are confronted by marvels daily in the normal course of their pitiful, mundane lives. Take this.' She brandished her pistol. It glowed in the blazing starlight.

She pointed it at the suited goon next to Vincent, and in a breath pulled the trigger.

We watched the body slump to the floor. A burbling sound rose briefly from its slack mouth. With a vacant look of horror, Vincent slowly lifted a hand to wipe blood spatter from his cheek.

Quiet Eyes cradled the weapon. 'I hold death in my hand and think nothing of it. Look at this, a man-made miracle. Mere steel and imaginatively applied physics. Only a flex of a finger to steal life away. This is what you are up against, Goddess Nut. Inventive, critical, cunning humans. They no longer see miracles, only a trick as yet unexposed. The world is ruled by science and men of logic now. Gods of all kinds have lost their place here.'

There was no expression on that barren vacuum of a face, but I got the feeling that the deity was uncertain, shaken maybe. Or perhaps that was just my own nerves talking. I tried to not think that I had just watched a man shot dead. Peggy's face was buried in her hands. The furrows around Ang's eyes had deepened; her expression looked like a storm.

'Let me make you great again,' said Quiet Eyes with her snake-tongue.

The suns dimmed and the great goddess Nut bowed her head.

'I WILL CONSIDER.'

Quiet Eyes nodded. 'Allow me to take you to my employers. They have much to discuss with you.'

I stared. 'What do Baines and Grayle want with a *god?*'

'Hansard, dear. Don't be obtuse.'

Movement caught my eye and Quiet Eyes followed my gaze. She raised the pistol to point at Mercer, crawling to the wall on the other side of the room.

'Where are you off to?' she said.

My ears picked up the low buzzing noise, growing louder and louder–

I tackled Ang and Peggy to the ground. With nose to the floor I noticed the creeping fog, followed by roaring noise and intense heat at our backs. Unable to resist, I turned on my side to see the pillar of flame rise in the middle of the room, searing through the floor and ceiling and licking at the walls. Inside, the benben stone was a glowing, molten mass.

A winged shadow stepped forward, a silhouette against the flames. Nut screamed. It was a bubbling cry of rage.

The column of fire subsided, though persistent flames crept into the corners. Nut and the phoenix faced off, two gods staring each other down for a duel. The humans in the room were suddenly inconsequential, and prone to become toast.

'We needs to leave!' shrieked Ang.

The air became thick with black smoke. The fire was spreading fast. Smouldering plaster fell from the ceiling and smashed in front of my nose. The whole place would come down on our heads.

Ang flipped the catch on her lantern and out sprang the bluecap. It whizzed ahead, lighting the way.

'Come on!' I shouted. I could see Mercer's shadow through the smoke already scurrying towards the exit. We followed on all fours, ducking under the broiling blanket of smoke. On the edge of vision were flashes of lightning and bursts of flame, punctuated by ethereal screeches that rocked the ground from under us.

We poured out into the foyer along with the smoke, spluttering and blinking soot from our eyes. I was dimly aware that I was soaking – a sprinkler system had kicked in – and an alarm was blaring overhead.

I caught hold of Mercer's red sleeve and struggled to blink him into focus.

'Get off, Hansard!' We grappled for a moment until he shoved me off, winding me with a blow to the stomach. He staggered to his feet and lurched towards the glass doors, the way out.

Peggy pulled me up and slung my arm over her shoulder.

'C'mon Jack, let's go.'

'Hah. Hahahah,' I croaked.

'What could *possibly* be funny right now?'

'Look what Mercer had in his pocket.'

I raised my hand in a fist and uncurled my fingers. An amber egg of myrrh fit snugly in my palm.

Peggy gasped. 'He had a *second* one?'

Somehow, over the sound of the rolling smoke and gushing sprinklers, our clever hindbrains re-wired themselves directly into our ears in order to take note of the simple *click* of a pistol cocking.

'Give me the egg, Hansard.'

Quiet Eyes plucked it from my grasp.

'Some miracle you've got there,' I said hoarsely.

'It grants my every wish.'

Vincent emerged from the smoke, coughing into his sleeve. Quiet Eyes motioned him to her side, keeping the gun level with my head.

'Don't look so sad, Jack,' she said. 'It's not over. Why don't you pull some hope out of your pocket for me? It's been a long day.'

And then she was gone, swallowed once more by the smoke and the sprinklers.

Ang tugged urgently on my coat. The bluecap blazed behind her.

'Forget 'er, *gwas*. We gots to go *now*.'

All of that, for nothing. All of that, and it ends with a gun in my face. That's how it ended.

'Jack?' said Peggy. 'I think I hear sirens.'

I shook myself out of it. 'Yeah,' I said. 'Sure.' I felt dazed. Not enough oxygen. Too much heat.

That was when the phoenix and the sky-god burst through the wall. Sizzling fragments of plasterboard rained down on us, hissing as they hit the water.

Deity and birdman wrestled in a coil of white fire and amber stone. The amber crept up the legs of the tortured Nut while her spines of fire lanced like chains across the phoenix's wings.

They both bellowed, a sound beyond sound that left me with nothing but a bell in my ears. The phoenix reared, stretched open its burning wings, with charred feathers and tendons tearing. The white fire blazed orange and red and consumed its whole figure until it was nothing but a bird-like shape made of flame. Nut screamed and writhed beneath it. And then the phoenix folded its wings around the form of the goddess, pulling her into a tight, inescapable embrace.

Though I could no longer hear anything, the world roared around me. The very air was vibrating, juddering against the growing ball of fire.

Then, in a heartbeat, the air quietened, and the flames dwindled down to nothing.

Nothing but a blackened crater of tiles.

Ears still ringing, I stepped gingerly up to the edge. Nothing. Not even an egg. Or a feather.

Hands pulled at me and I found I had no choice but to yield. I was faced by an alien figure in a gas mask. It wore black with day-glo yellow stripes. I couldn't fathom it, and allowed the alien to lead me through the smoke and out into the open, cool night air.

* * *

'We shoulda stayed with the amb'lance a bit longer,' grumbled Ang.

I passed her a cup of tea and sank onto Peggy's couch. 'No chance.

They were already asking questions.'

'They gave me biscuits.'

'They thought you were a child. Besides, the police were on their way. Once you start looking like you're feeling better their questions become really *pressing*, if you know what I mean.'

'You mean like: why were you trespassing in the British Museum in the middle of the night?' said Peggy.

'Yes, exactly.'

'And: what were you hoping to achieve with this stupid, dangerous endeavour in the first place?'

'Uh-huh.'

'How about: was it really worth all the risk, just to be outwitted at the end by a woman you should never have trusted in the first place?'

'All *right*. I'm sorry, okay? I'm not happy about it either.'

What an understatement. I was fuming. I'd had it in my hand. An actual phoenix egg in my actual hand. *Twice.*

I'm used to failure. I make a *living* out of failure. But I've only ever failed small.

This time I failed big, big, big.

'You're right,' I muttered. Self-loathing rose in me like bile. 'I'm an idiot. A small-time loser. I'm fucking pointless.'

Peggy opened her mouth to speak, then closed it again. We sat in silence, a scorched, bedraggled party of misfits staring into our ordinary cups of tea.

'I tell people I sell miracles,' I said bleakly. 'The stuff of dreams and fantasy. I don't do any of that. I sell . . . vague inclinations and petty malevolence. Vengeance past its sell by date. Quiet Eyes is right, with her awful miracle. Little, efficient weapon. Doesn't go rotten if you store it next to the potions. Death in the palm of your hand. Grants wishes. She got that right.'

'*Ast,*' said Ang wearily. 'She ain't creative, *gwas*. Ain't worth the space she takes up. Not like the likes of you an' me.'

'The likes of you and me, Ang, belong in the gutter.'

She fixed me with a hard stare, then set her tea to the side with a poignant *clink*. She slid off the couch and walked to the pile of books where her bluecap lantern rested.

'That was a poor thing to say,' Peggy murmured to me.

Ang laid a palm on the glass and the bluecap flared in greeting. She unhooked the catch.

'It's the truth, is what it is,' I said. 'I'm a little fish, swimming in the gutters. I don't know how to get out of them. Fins are crap for climbing.'

'Self-pity don't suit you, *gwas*,' said Ang. She stuck her hand into the floating blue flame. It looked more solid than I remembered. When she withdrew her hand, it was curled into a fist, and a crooked smirk bent her mouth. 'I'll give ye one good reason why we ain't gutter-*ysbwriel*.'

She opened her hand.

'Oh my god,' said Peggy.

'That's right,' said Ang gleefully. 'Ye think there's a god in this'un, too?'

We stared at the little amber egg in her palm, although in Ang's small hands it looked as big as an apple. It glowed gently with some soft internal light.

'Hatching gods,' Peggy breathed, a little unsteadily. 'So this is how they're born?'

'No,' I said quietly. 'I think it's how they're trapped.' Ang set it on the coffee table, carefully nestled in a heap of Peggy's un-filed shop receipts. 'You got your bluecap to steal it? When?'

'Right after she put that dirty peashooter in yer face. 'Tis a crime against metal, a thing like that. Ain't what the ore is for. An' she so in love wi' watchin' it gleam, she din't even notice a little thing like a bluecap zippin' through her pockets.'

I felt the inexorable, lunatic grin spread across my face. All of a sudden I was back. Restored, revved and ready. *We won!*

And it was a *colossal* win.

'You're right, Ang!' I proclaimed. I threw an arm round her skinny shoulders and caught Peggy with the other. 'Quiet Eyes isn't creative. She's lazy. She relies on her invisibility and her hired muscle. Us, we rely on our wits. We don't need guns because we have guile . . . and *real* miracles!'

'I ain't sure that mouldy jar o' hexes in the boot can be called a miracle, *gwas*.'

'It will be to *someone*.'

'The real miracle'll be if ye can get anyone to buy it off yer.'

'Those count too.'

'Guys,' said Peggy. 'There's a phoenix egg in my living room. Could we talk about that, please?'

I tried to settle down. Every part of me itched. 'What's to talk about, Peg? We've *got* it!'

'And now what?'

'Hmm?'

'What are you going to do with it?' She saw my expression and held up a hand. '*Don't* just say you're going to sell it.'

'Why not?'

'Jack!' She threw up her hands in exasperation. 'I've known you for so long, yet I still don't understand you. You are one of only two people in the *world* who possesses one of these eggs. Don't you want to know more about it, before you auction it off like another piece of bric-a-brac?'

'I ain't sellin' it,' said Ang flatly. 'Been too much trouble to get hold of in the first place. And it's mine to do with as I likes.' She snatched it back off the table and beckoned the bluecap.

'Hang on a minute!' I cried, watching the flame fold round the egg like a mantle. 'Aren't we partners, Ang?'

'Are we?' she said, without malice. 'Ye was meant to be findin' missing coblynau for me, *gwas*. No coblynau been turned up so far, and none ahead that I can see.'

'Hey now, what about Baines and Grayle? We *know* they're part of it – surely you want to keep following this lead!'

She smiled thinly. 'An' what if it's still a long road to findin' 'em, *gwas*? How long does my payment keep you detectiving for?'

'Well.' I hesitated. Peggy watched us both, tensely. 'As I recall, I never agreed to a fixed term of service. I suppose it's up to you to terminate our agreement when it suits you. Whenever you reach your stop, as it were.'

'Mebbe this is my stop.'

Silence expanded between us for a moment. Ang was eyeing me carefully.

Being a little fish, I reflected, wasn't half so bad when you have good company in the pond.

'Maybe I'd like to offer you a position,' I said. 'Official business partner, of sorts.'

'Oh, aye?'

'Not like it's been up to now, mind. A proper partner does more than scoff pies under the table while I do all the hard work. It'd mean thinking like a salesman and finding new angles. And it means putting your bluecap to better use. It's done more for us in the past twenty-four hours than I ever knew it could.'

She appeared to mull it over. But I suspect her mind was already made up.

'Throw in a pork pie,' she said.

I grinned. 'Sure.'

'A big 'un. Not one o' them piddly pocket-sized ones. One o' them that's as big as your head. And at least half as thick, too.'

'It's a deal,' I said, ignoring the jibe. 'May I put the egg somewhere safe?'

She snapped the catch on the lantern, locking the bluecap inside. 'Nowhere safer, *gwas*.' She raised an eyebrow, and I decided to let it go. It probably was the safest place for it. And it occurred to me, in a moment of startling revelation, that the little coblyn had become a trusted friend. Another solid point, a fixed co-ordinate in an ever-changing sea of lies and loyalties. And next to Peggy, I was grateful to pin down Ang on my mental map.

'More tea?' said Peg.

'Please.'

'Aye.'

She re-boiled the kettle and dug out fresh teabags. We followed her into the kitchen. It was a small flat, but it felt light and roomy compared to our usual living quarters. Car seats aren't the comfiest. I was already longing to sleep on her sofa again.

Peggy ran a hand through her hair and grimaced at the soot it pulled out. 'What a day,' she said to herself. 'What do you suppose that woman is going to do with her egg?'

'Sell it to Baines and Grayle, I imagine.'

'You really don't know who they are?'

'I wish I could tell you.'

'Baines and Grayle,' she repeated, as if she was tasting the words. 'It sounds familiar, I think. Maybe. I can't place it.'

I brightened. 'Did you come across it in a book?'

'No. I don't think so. But whoever they are, they sound like bad news.'

'That's about the only thing we know for certain,' I said. 'It's not the first time they've tried to give me an early retirement.' I glanced at Ang's lantern. 'They'll come after us for this.'

'Then why you grinnin', *gwas?*'

I leant back with my elbows on the counter, staring contemplatively at the cracks in Peggy's ceiling. 'I was just thinking . . . we've got an angle, here. Let them come after us. Let them send Quiet Eyes, their little lapdog. We won't be strung along so easily next time. That egg there is our leverage. If they want it so bad, they're going to have to *work* for it.'

And inwardly I thought, *This little fish is going to learn how to bite.*

'What if they open their egg, Jack?' said Peggy. 'What if there's another god inside?'

I shrugged. 'Maybe there's one in ours.'

'Are you going to open it?'

Neither Ang nor I answered.

'When the time is right,' I decided.

'Which is when?'

'Whenever it is.'

'Huh.'

Ang pulled herself up onto one of the kitchen chairs. She sat cross-legged on it. 'Ye think the bird-man an' the newt-god destroyed each other?' she said.

'That's what it looked like,' replied Peggy.

Which, I thought, is the problem. If there's one fundamental thing you learn in this game, it's that nothing is ever what it looks like.

Take Peggy, with her blue hair and her big beads and elephant fixation. She doesn't look like someone who regularly wrestles with ferocious literature, but to use a tired expression, you shouldn't judge her – and you definitely shouldn't judge her books – by the cover.

And there's Ang, the naturally grimy little dwarf of a creature with the stone-cold stare. You wouldn't believe she could fit a heart so big inside her scrawny ribcage. And that she can pack one hell of a punch to back it up.

And me, I suppose, with my unkempt hair and my day-old stubble and my trench coat which, all right, maybe you can say the trench coat is a dead giveaway for my lack of credentials, but I bet you'd never look at me and see a man who defied a god, crossed dimensions and stole a phoenix egg, if only for a very brief moment.

That's what the little fish are all about. We blend into the background – Ang and I stick to the shadows, Peggy pays her taxes – and ultimately steal the sharks' dinner out from under them. Leave the bigger fish like Mercer (he's one of those fancy angel fish with all the rainbow colours and the frills) to go head to head with the sharks out in the open. I like my shadows. I'll keep to them.

And as for the future, well, it looks kind of grey and like it's about to rain outside. But I'd bet you whatever you've got in your wallet that it'll be one hell of a storm, and if I've got anything to do with it, it'll be packed with uncanny mystery and dark miracles in the clouds.

For now, the real story behind the phoenix egg, the real deal with Baines and Grayle, and the real face of Quiet Eyes all lay somewhere in that future. And for now, I was content to let them stay there. For now, while I drank tea and laughed with my friends and felt glad to be alive.

And tomorrow, I'll sink back into the shadows.

Acknowledgements

There are a number of people to whom I owe great thanks for helping me bring *The Jack Hansard Series* to fruition. First and foremost is my husband, who has patiently read – and in many cases re-read – every word of every episode, catching typos, testing my ideas, and pointing out plot holes before I could embarrass myself in front of an audience.

Next, despite the fact that she often gets exasperated with me singing her praises, I really couldn't have done this without my friend and cover artist Dominique Lane, who was creating art for the series long before I even had plans to publish it properly. As is so often the case, she quite effortlessly managed to capture the perfect visuals to match the weird goings-on in my head.

Likewise, I wish to embarrass my fellow author friend Cierra Goldstein-McGee, who began as an incredibly supportive reader and became a reliable sounding board for discussing all things indie publishing. She has yet to defriend me for forgetting to answer messages for weeks at a time.

I'm eternally grateful to my very first beta readers who read the *The Jack Hansard Series* in its original first draft form and spurred me to keep going. Special thanks in particular to the inimitable Dr Watson and the delightful Miss Parkinson who both provided a wealth of in-depth and valuable feedback on every episode.

Similarly, I wish to thank the wonderful and enthusiastic readers over at Wattpad, who rekindled my passion for the project and who still continually remind me why I am writing in the first place.

As to why I am writing at all, it is possible that the dream might have fizzled out if it weren't for the continued support and patient readership of friends and family over the years. My older sister helped cultivate my love of writing from a young age; my younger sister tolerated me spouting incomprehensible plot ideas at her; and my parents, though no longer with us, would no doubt have been proud with the result.

I would also be remiss not to include my high school form tutor, Mr Udall: a teacher who worked hard to find the best in all his students and to help them recognise it in themselves – even if this was often done with the aid of Sheffield Utd football idioms. His words of encouragement stuck with me, and I am pleased to finally make good on an old promise.

Thank you all, and see you next time.

About the Author

Georgina Jeffery lives in Shropshire with her husband and daughter. She writes in frenetic sprints during her daughter's naptimes, or very late into the night.

Her fiction often blends elements of fantasy, humour, and horror, and tends to reflect her penchant for mythology and folklore.

Her work can also be found in the urban fantasy anthology *The San Cicaro Experience* from Thunderbird Studios, which features her short story 'The Hub'.

You can connect with me on:
🌐 https://georginajeffery.com
📘 https://www.facebook.com/GJefferyAuthor

Subscribe to my newsletter:
✉ https://www.subscribepage.com/georginajeffery

Also by Georgina Jeffery

This short story is available as a free gift to subscribers of my newsletter.

Deus Ex Machina

When souvenir shopping, be sure not to accidentally purchase a powerful occult object. And always check whether the magic is past its sell-by-date.

This standalone story features our favourite occult merchant and is told from the viewpoint of one of his unwitting customers.

Lightning Source UK Ltd.
Milton Keynes UK
UKHW010635011020
370850UK00002B/354